LAST ONE TO LIE

JACK STAINTON

ALSO BY JACK STAINTON

A Guest To Die For

You're Family Now

Mother

An imprint of Windmill Streams *Publishers*

Last One To Lie

For Nia, Paul, Manon & Cari

AUTHOR'S NOTE

Thank you for reading 'Last One To Lie'

This is part three of 'The Family' Trilogy - three novels based around the central character, Matthew Walker.

They can either be read as individual stand-alone books, or in chronological order.

Either way, I hope you enjoy!

1

LISA

The day I'd been dreading finally arrived. The day he departed, rendered me disconsolate and afraid. Was it because I would miss him or more the fact I would be alone with George? Any unexpected noise or movement still made me jolt. Endless sleepless nights followed by skittish days protecting my beautiful baby boy from the evils of the world. But at least I'd found help, somehow able to cope, albeit on a day-to-day basis. It was the prescribed medication which allowed Matt to leave us that day. Ironic really, given it was my idea to move away from Scotland. Not that Matt took much persuasion, but that's an entirely different matter.

Fighting back tears, realising it would set George off too, the prospect of Matt getting on the train and travelling miles away threatened to tip me over the edge. This was the first time we would be apart, ever since…

Oh, that cabin. It was never far from the forefront of

my mind. That filthy, damp, blood-curdling cabin. Deep in the woods, where life is suffocated by the dark and deafening silence. And the doll they placed in the corner of the room, staring and tormenting. As soon as I realised they would take my baby away, they deliberately stuck that thing there, mocking me; the closest I would come to ever holding my child. Those evil bastards, I hoped they'd all rot in hell.

Matt seemed anxious for the train to arrive. Despite him embracing us, I sensed he'd been glancing over my shoulder, along the platform, eager for his trip to commence. Why so restless? He was leaving his son for the first time, for goodness sake. George was only six months old, and I was aware of how much Matt doted on him. The way they played, how he made him laugh. Sometimes, I would listen outside the bedroom door. The things he said, the visions he painted. 'I'll keep you safe,' he would vow. 'You're going to have a lovely life, son. A life full of dreams.' It never failed to make my eyes well and my heart heavy. Matt was a great dad and I couldn't wish for a better father for my baby George.

But still, I questioned whether Matt loved me too. Could he be clinging onto our relationship for the sake of our child, or for what we'd both been through, as if he somehow *owed* it to me? To us? I often considered confronting him, long before we stumbled upon our new house in my dream village, but the perfect moment never presented itself. Perhaps it never would. And that day, as we waited for the train, I truly considered if we were doing the right thing. Yes, he'd found himself a great job — a sales director, no less — but it made me uneasy, especially when he informed me he would stay in that bloody apartment in Earl's Court.

"Can't you commute?" I asked. It was on the day they offered him the new position, yet again threatening to dampen his already low spirits. He didn't volunteer a response. Perhaps he considered my question too stupid, beneath him and not warranting a reply. I only asked by way of a test. Of course, I understood a ninety-minute train journey into the city, followed by a second train out of the city, twice a day, every day, would be too much, but I harboured dreams he would sooner be with me and George, especially in our new house. If only he offered a little compassion, something to eradicate my nerves, anything to make me believe.

Shit! I suddenly realised I knew nothing about his precious apartment. We never discussed it, at any length at least. He told me he rented there. It was how he landed his new job because he worked for the same estate agents before, but apart from that, I didn't know the first thing about it. Why hadn't I asked him before? Simple questions: How big is it or how far from the tube station? Damn it, I had no idea about where he would stay during the week.

Attempting to raise my spirits, I asked Matt if he thought our house sale would go through by June, and I cheered myself momentarily whilst explaining our new adventure to George. However, as the train approached, I'd lost track of time and couldn't ask Matt anything else. The apartment would have to wait. Oh, that bloody apartment.

He hugged us one last time, a final embrace, before climbing aboard. Feeling myself shaking, I wondered if Matt detected it too. He quickly boarded the closest carriage and within seconds appeared at a window, waving to us on the platform. George giggled, oblivious to where his father might be going. I feared how he would react once the train departed, how I would react. Could I blame myself for becoming a nervous wreck?

Strange, because after we returned to Scotland following our house-hunting trip down south two months earlier, my antidepressants finally worked their magic. I felt calmer, as if we could finally bury the past. However, at that precise moment, alone on the platform, I felt the inner demons rising to the surface once more. Would George and I be safe? It would only be for two or three months until the house purchase went through. We were in the middle of nowhere. Scotland suddenly seemed extremely remote, and the prospect of Matt being hundreds of miles away threatened to swamp me with fear.

Will they find us?

Stop it, Lisa.

They were all locked away, well, apart from his wife. But DCI Small repeatedly informed us she'd fled the country and would be mad to come back.

But she is *mad. They're* all *mad.*

The detective was oblivious to what kind of people we were dealing with, only their crimes. Perhaps I should have told him, but what would he have done?

Nothing. You're on your own.

During the relatively brief journey to our remote house, I tried to cheer myself again, this time thinking of George. Growing up, starting school, even university? Maybe we should have another child? A brother or sister for my darling George. Yes. I decided to talk to Matt about it as soon as we settled. Surely he would agree to that idea? A proper family living in a lovely village with two perfect children.

But my foolish daydreaming only resulted in our new home to come crashing back into my thoughts. Not so much the house, more the village. Why did it bother me so damn much? Of course, it was perfect. I bloody well chose it, so how could I complain? Quintessential British countryside at its finest. Surrounded by rolling hills, complete with a cute little church and a thatched pub overlooking the village green. We had already made friends on our house-hunting trip too. Everything should be flawless.

However, although the location was idyllic, and the school sounded perfect for George once he reached the required age, the fact remained Matt had been the first to suggest that area. Why did he want to live so close to his old house? *That* house, *that* family. And the property he selected for us to view. He thinks I'm bloody stupid. As soon as he showed me online, I knew exactly why. It was the house he and Amelia were interested in. Hadn't they even put a deposit down? I often overheard Amelia and Tracy talking about it in the office. Amelia never stopped going on and on. She talked of growing vegetables in the extensive garden and acquiring custom-made furniture for every bloody room. Did he seriously expect me to move into a house that he and his crazy wife once contemplated buying together?

Yes, of course, I feigned interest when he showed me. I wanted to keep him sweet. But I already knew the village I desired, so I decided it was best to go through the motions of viewing *his* house as the perfect foil to view *mine*. My place made absolute sense, especially after seeing it in person and the aftermath of our trip to the pub to celebrate.

It wasn't just that house though; it was Matt himself.

He didn't appear to be recovering from our ordeal; his ordeal. Although I never blamed him for what he'd been through, instead of seeking help, he retreated further into his shell; eating less and drinking more. He religiously watched the news, and whenever I asked why, he would pretend he was waiting for the weather forecast because 'we don't want to get snowed in up here in Scotland'. And he spent hours in the spare bedroom where he kept his laptop. As soon as George went to bed, Matt would disappear too, implying he needed to job hunt or look for online courses to brush up on his skills. But he never told me of any new vacancies or how his expertise might be growing. So what did he do, and what was he looking at on that damn computer all the time?

Should I mention it?

No, I didn't want to upset him. He was volatile, but I couldn't afford to lose him. Matt was my rock, my child's father. How on earth would I cope without him? I could end up in one of those mental homes, or whatever the politically correct term is for them nowadays. Either way, I'd be locked away, protected for my own safety. And he would take George. Was that his plan, to take my darling baby back to that crazy, godforsaken family? Was that the intention, to send me mad?

Later that evening, I looked up the definition of being 'tipped over the edge'.

'... *to make someone feel so unhappy that they cannot deal with their life or situation any longer...*'.

Don't even go there, Lisa.

2

MATT

I soon realised Lisa was determined not to cry. We were at the station, waiting for my train to arrive, the day I left Scotland to start my new job. Hugging them both tight, I could feel her shaking in my arms. Although I realised she was struggling, I couldn't help but glance over her shoulder along the platform, praying the train wasn't far away. Why so anxious to get away?

"It won't be for long," I promised, holding Lisa at arm's length. "Two months will pass by so quickly." I ruffled George's hair, but he turned his head away and buried it deeper into his mum's shoulder. His punishment hit me much harder than Lisa's tears.

"Do you think the house will go through by June?" she asked desperately.

"Of course. Yes. I'll make damn sure it does."

Lisa attempted a smile whilst lifting George from his hiding place.

"You heard that, darling? We'll be living in our new house with Daddy in just a few months' time. It's going to be such fun. And Daddy is coming home in between, aren't you?"

Before I could reply, the station announcer informed us of the approaching train. The 10:17 to London.

George's expression altered immediately, and he pointed along the tracks as the first coach came into view. He appeared oblivious to whether I'd be back soon or what his new house is like or anything else. It's such a simple world at that age, brain resembling a sponge, absorbing so many new sights and sounds. It amazes me how the human mind can cope with so much at such a fragile time.

With a last embrace and kiss, I boarded the closest carriage. Quickly, I found an empty seat at the window adjacent to Lisa and George on the platform. And as I waved, the automated warning sound beeped before the train clunked into movement and smoothly pulled away.

George was waving frantically, giggling to himself, whilst Lisa held a solitary arm aloft. Within seconds, they disappeared from view.

Soon, I found myself out of the city and in the Scottish countryside. The trees and banks rushed by, occasionally broken by a row of cars waiting patiently for the barriers to lift. It became therapeutic, watching nothing in particular, leaving me and my thoughts.

I first met Amelia, my future wife, at an interview with a property consultancy firm called Opacy. The company was based near Covent Garden, central London, and held huge ambitions to become one of the largest such firms in the southeast of England.

And from the initial moment I caught sight of her, Amelia Reid took my breath away. Long, shiny black hair. The perfect physique, and the brownest eyes I've ever encountered. There was an immediate chemistry too. But little did I know she *chose* me before we ever met.

It all started during a so-called opportunist meeting with a woman called Julia at a hotel bar in central London. Nonetheless, I later found out it hadn't been a *random* encounter, and Julia was Amelia's older sister. She recommended I applied for a job at Opacy predicting I would be the perfect fit. A few short weeks later, I'd landed a new job and Amelia would be my *executive secretary*.

As I settled into the role, Amelia and I became close. We travelled to Harrogate alone for a prestigious conference. It would be where we first spent any intimate time together, as well as discussing extremely personal secrets. I informed her of my parents passing away in a devastating car accident and my ensuing continual battle to find inner solace. And Amelia dropped the bombshell: she would never be able to have children. I've since given that so much thought and why she told me so early in our relationship. Maybe a test. Would I want to commit to someone with whom I could never have children? To be fair, it didn't bother me either way. Perhaps that's why I forgot all about it. One of those things that goes in one ear, and out of the other, something which happens to me regularly. But had she been right? Could she have children, after all? Little did I know of the eventual consequences.

We spent many nights and weekends at my small flat

in North London; like two teenagers finding love for the first time. We were smitten. Head-over-heels. Crazy for each other, despite being in our middle to late thirties and far too old and civilised for such juvenile behaviour.

And then the time arrived to meet her family.

Tracy, her other sister, who also worked at Opacy.

Melissa, her mother.

Katrina, her niece, and Tracy's daughter.

And finally, Graham Meadows. The husband of Julia.

Eventually, I would find out what a crazy fucked-up family they were.

Graham was the driving force. Habitually around the house, despite possessing his own place with Julia in town. He questioned everything I said and did, from why I needed the internet, to what I found so interesting whilst speaking to the postman. He *instructed* me to look after Amelia. One day, early in our relationship, he told me her ex-boyfriend didn't *take care of* her, and he was no longer around. I never found out what 'not being around' actually meant.

But I did discover what happened to Tracy's husband; albeit far too late. Ryan Palmer was his name, and they buried him in the woods, which stood next to the family home. Graham murdered him with his bare hands; chased him into the dense trees, as he attempted to make his escape.

Graham also killed Lee Blackmore, an old friend of Ryan's. Lee always knew something was awry with Ryan's disappearance, but until I came along, he had no actual proof or knowledge of where to look.

And then there was Katrina. Strange teenager Katrina. She never attended school and never mixed with anybody of her own age. I liked and feared Katrina in equal measure. She somehow held the ability to see things, to know somebody was there, even if they hadn't yet made their presence known. Katrina spent most of her spare time in the woods, walking and playing alone, as well as visiting the grave of her father, Ryan Palmer. She had another grave too; a make-believe one for her grandfather, Patrick Reid. Patrick, Melissa's estranged husband, left home years ago, rendering Katrina heartbroken. So, the crazy family claimed he'd passed away and dug another grave for her to mourn. All Graham's ideas.

So, why did they do it? What was the motivation? Simple. Money and power.

Julia, Graham's wife and the person who persuaded me to join Opacy, was an ancestry expert. People paid her to dig deep into their family trees, and Graham eventually spotted an opportunity. Julia's passion allowed her to intricately piece together the roots and Graham became especially interested when she discovered one particular family who was due a large inheritance. They would need to remain patient until a rich grandparent met their demise and the cash would be theirs.

He broached the idea with the family. It wasn't so much they craved financial reward, although their house was in constant disrepair; it was more about greed and the ability to manipulate people.

Around the corresponding time, Ryan Palmer began working at the same hospital where Tracy was a nurse. Although she allegedly fell for him, the family put their new operation into practice anyway. And boy, did they hit the jackpot? Ryan's wife recently died of cancer. A brief illness. His friend, Lee Blackmore, was astonished Ryan went back to work so soon and was unable to understand why he started dating Tracy. To cut a long story short, they married, Katrina was born, and they moved into the family home. Years later, Ryan tried to escape, only to make it as far as the dense woodland.

Soon after, it would be Amelia's turn to find her true love.

Graham's new notion comprised matching curriculum vitae from prospective employees at Opacy to Julia's ancestry research. The ideal candidate would be required to meet two criteria. One, they were already involved in the property business to verify their authenticity, and two, they would come into money. Step forward my Aunt Edith. An aunt I never knew existed. But she did. Julia carried out all due diligence, and I became the perfect fit. Already in property, looking for my next career move and finally ready to settle down after years of drifting from job to job and relationship to relationship.

Again, cutting to the chase, I married Amelia, and we moved into the family home. She sold me the idea we could save a deposit for our own place much faster if we lived with Amelia's mother, sister and niece, and I fell for it. And so it all began.

Strange things happened. Threats from Graham if I didn't toe the family line. Advances from Melissa, presumably to keep me sweet. Inevitable postponements of buying our own house. And the longer it dragged on, the closer I inadvertently became to Lisa Ingram. Lisa also worked at Opacy but never fitted into the closed circle of Amelia and Tracy. We would sneak out of the office to a local café. Talk things through and share our secrets. And one day, with Melissa falling ill and Amelia having to care for her, Lisa and I attended a work conference in northern England.

Despite Graham unexpectedly turning up at the hotel,

we had already spent the night together. And we did the same the following evening.

Returning to the family home, I knew something was amiss. They realised I wasn't *accepting* them, and they made plans. Graham travelled north and killed my aunt, Edith, whilst I was drugged, tied to a bed and forced to sign over half of my inheritance in front of a solicitor. But with the help of Katrina and Lisa, I escaped into the woods, where we witnessed Graham killing Lee Blackmore before Katrina hit her uncle with the same shovel, presumably left for dead.

However, she didn't strike him hard enough and Graham survived, although he didn't escape. At a later trial, they sentenced him to a twenty-five-year prison sentence for the manslaughter of Ryan and Lee, plus the murder of an elderly aunt. He didn't quibble. I still believe he took most of the blame to protect the family. All should have been resolved, and I moved in with Lisa temporarily until I found my feet. But then Amelia hit me with her news, like a sledgehammer: she was pregnant.

Lisa put her house on the market, presumably moving into her mother's place and leaving me no choice but to leave too. I came across an apartment in Earl's Court, next door to a girl called Francis.

It didn't take long for that friendship to reach another level too, whilst I kept up a pretence and agreed to meet Amelia most weeks during her pregnancy. But something was amiss. Amelia didn't *act* pregnant. She wouldn't let me close or be involved, forever justifying her actions by the fact that Tracy was a qualified midwife and she would look after her instead. And Amelia never visited a doctor, never attended a hospital appointment. The whole thing came across as fake, even though her belly appeared to grow and eventually the big day arrived.

Amelia allegedly gave birth to a wonderful baby boy. In the meantime, I contacted Julia, and through spiralling depression, she took me to the woods. She showed me the fake grave where Katrina could mourn her grandfather, and she led me to an old shack in the middle of nowhere. The shack where I eventually found Lisa, two days after the birth of my son.

And Lisa claimed she was the mother. The family held her against her will for almost nine months, while Amelia and Tracy carried out the *fake* pregnancy with precision. Was it all a ploy to get me back into the family fold? Mother and father reunited with a new-born baby to raise in the world?

But I could never allow such a thing to happen. I wanted to protect Lisa and rescue our child. So, with Katrina's help once more, we revisited the house. Tracy, Melissa and Graham's brother, Andy, were arrested, but in a moment of madness, or was it something else altogether, I allowed Amelia to escape. She fled with her passport and mobile phone. We were the only two who knew what I'd done. How could I tell anybody else anything different?

So, weeks later, Lisa, George and I lived in a temporary home in remote Scotland, but always understood we would return south once the dust settled. And so the delay was over. It was time to move on.

The train pulled into Kings Cross station. The journey passed by so quickly, my thoughts ricocheting the entire trip. So much had happened in my life, so much grief, so much sadness, so much guilt. Yet now, a possible light at the end of the tunnel. A new beginning and a child to raise in this world.

But I still thought of her, and I still dreamt of how different my life could be.

It's been seven months since the baby was born, and I often wonder if they are sleeping together again. Of course, I hope not. No, 'hope' isn't a strong enough word. In fact, it repulses me to think of them like that. Cuddled up in bed, kissing, touching and God knows what else.

She doesn't deserve him either. She never did. Yes, I am biased, but he can do so much better. He will do so much better. Just like before.

I wonder what she looks like now. She was never the slimmest of women and had a tendency to balloon a couple of dress sizes just by looking at a bar of chocolate.

Ha! I laugh at my bitchiness. But that's the way I am. The way they have brought me up. We've always put each other first in my family.

Fair play, Lisa has a pretty face, and I know Matt always had a soft spot for her. The way he spoke about her left nothing to the imagination. But Matt is a ladies' man; much worse before marriage. Will the baby slow him down, finally prove to him he can't go chasing every piece of skirt he sets his eyes upon? Oh yes. I'll make sure he does; when the time is right. When I am ready.

Our future, our destiny.

And now, I'm sure I can feel his presence. For months, he has felt so far away. But recently, he was back in London, or somewhere close by, and now he's here again. Maybe she is with him? But my feelings for her are weak, for obvious reasons. We have no genuine connection, whilst Matt and I have spent many glorious nights locked away together under the same roof.

Yes, today, I can sense him. He's back, somewhere close. I'm tingling all over. It feels good to know he's near. And I can sense something else. Good news. Yes, he must be here for a reason, something to make him stay.

Can he feel me too? I know he can. My darling.

And now, I need to be patient, composed. I will have to wait, in hiding, biding my time. But for now, I will silently rejoice. Dream of our future together. A family once again, just the three of us.

Oh, my! Matthew is coming home.

3

MATT

Two months earlier, at the end of January, the three of us travelled south to view potential properties. It made sense to move back to the area we both knew, especially given my contacts in the world of property. And it pleased Lisa too, her drugs finally taking effect, doing their intended job. But I struggled, my mood swings making enthusiasm sound like a dirty word.

Ironically, and obviously not divulging the history behind it, the cute little cottage Amelia and I found all those months ago was still on the market. Lisa appeared to love it when I showed her online and was just as keen to view it. Her desperation to move back south turned almost obsessive towards the end of the year, but more than the house itself, she fell in love with the area again. She would be forever 'walking' the streets via Google Maps. The appointment I scheduled at the end of January couldn't arrive quickly enough.

However, once the day arrived, within moments of stepping inside, I knew Lisa didn't like it. She tugged on my arm as we made our way upstairs, following the agent who was full of the usual bullshit and exaggerated facts. Peering round at Lisa, she shook her head, and it hurt she didn't even appear disappointed. It was more of a *'just as I thought'* kind of look and, for the first time, I realised she may know why we were there.

What had I been thinking? I knew the layout of the house like the back of my hand. Amelia and I viewed it so many times before, planning where the furniture would go, maybe turn the tiny second bedroom into an office and what pictures would hang where. The place was our dream, our vision, and I suddenly realised I might be trying to replace Amelia with Lisa.

Crazy idiot.

"I'm sorry, it wasn't what I thought it would be," I lied, fastening George's seat belt. Lisa already sat in the passenger seat, flicking through some papers on her lap.

"Uh-huh," she replied, with no genuine commitment or acknowledgement she even heard what I said.

Once I joined her in the front of the car, I spun around to check on George. It made him giggle. Any sudden movement, especially accompanied by a silly face, inevitably ended up with him giggling. His zest for life momentarily lifted my spirits.

"You don't seem too disappointed. I thought you had your heart set on it."

Again, she *chose* not to hear me.

"What time is it?" she asked, looking up whilst confirming my suspicions.

"Sorry?" I snapped. "It's ten to eleven. Why?"

Lisa held up a sheet of paper and placed it on the

steering wheel, inches from my face, forcing me to take it from her.

"Because we're viewing this one at eleven thirty."

After quickly scanning the property details, my focus returned to Lisa and the broad grin stretched across her face. What was this?

"You know what, Matt," she said, so matter-of-factly it actually annoyed me, "I never thought that house would be for us. So, I've been checking online for anything else that might be available in the same area. And we're in luck." She tapped the details in front of me. "This one came on the market on Saturday and it's less than twenty minutes from here. It's with the same agent."

The entire situation felt contrived.

"But why didn't you tell me? I thought we—"

"You thought what? You thought we would come all this way from Scotland to look at one house? It's the area I love, and the village where this house is…" — she tapped the paper again — "…is adorable. We'd be silly not to consider something else within our price bracket."

The second house was indeed twenty minutes away. We arrived ahead of schedule, allowing us to drive through the village. Lisa was right. It surprised me that Amelia and I hadn't surveyed the area further. Properties flanked both sides of the street, a variety of shapes and sizes but all well in keeping with their surroundings. It was obviously an affluent place, and just admiring the vehicles parked by the houses, proved money wasn't in short supply. I caught Lisa gawking out of the car windows. Left, right, behind, in front. And not once did the smile leave her face.

Soon, the village pub came into view on the right-hand side. A lovely, thatched building with tables outside the front, overlooking the park and the green opposite. Even in the midst of mid-winter, and with my air of despondency, I could still picture myself sitting outside on a Sunday lunchtime with a cold beer and watching the world go by. Without admitting as much, Lisa's homework appeared justified, and it gave an initial impression of an ideal place to raise a family whilst being within touching distance of where I was hoping to find work. I wanted to keep myself in check, though. The prospect of returning home every night to a loving partner was never on my radar. I needed time to myself, time to think, so much so, I craved my own company, disappearing upstairs to *work* on my laptop and forever wondering if I should pick up my phone and make the call.

Lisa's *chosen* house was modest, but a separate kitchen, as well as a small third bedroom, made it a real possibility. She beamed as she walked from room to room before starting all over again. Tutting a silent apology to the young good-looking estate agent, Wendy, Lisa caught me as she unexpectedly returned from the living room.

Finally, after she inspected every single nook and cranny the property had to offer, we drove through the village twice more before Lisa suggested we call at the pub for lunch.

"You never know," she added, "Wendy might be in there to save you asking her if she'd like to go for a drink."

"Grow up, Lisa," I replied, the palms of my hands sweating against the steering wheel.

The pub was just as quintessential on the inside as it appeared from the road. Wooden beams crisscrossed the ceiling and deep red suede sofas and chairs were dotted throughout the lounge. A huge inglenook fireplace roared and crackled as the landlord added new logs to the flames.

"Wow!" I surprised myself. Again Lisa noticed, but this time nodded her approval.

Once I ordered drinks and fresh sandwiches from the bar, I joined Lisa and George on the far side of the fire. Lisa said it would be too hot for George to be so close, which annoyed me, as I had my eye on a table directly in front of it.

After we settled George down and discussed the house once again, the pub door opened, allowing a momentary chill to creep indoors. An older couple walked in, maybe in their mid to late fifties, along with a dog which appeared just as overweight as them. Studying them, they nodded their regards to other patrons, although nobody appeared especially pleased to see them in return. It felt good to be a stranger, somebody who wasn't interested in inane chatter about who's died or who put on the most weight over the holidays. However, I soon discovered that being a stranger in that particular village didn't stop people from approaching you.

Unbelievably, the couple ordered their drinks and looked around the pub for what I hoped was a spare table, before setting their eyes on us and casually walking over.

"A couple of new faces, Hannah," the plump guy said. "Mind if we join you?"

Yes, actually. Fuck off.

"Of course not," Lisa said. "I take it you're local? I'd love to pick your brains."

. . .

The following day, we offered the full asking price. The owners accepted it without quibble, and I suggested to Wendy I come into the office with proof of monies and any other documentation. She soon brought me back down to earth when she informed me we could do it all online. At least it made Lisa laugh.

Between my inheritance and Lisa's money from her house sale, we had enough to buy it outright. The majority came from me, but with a new job on the horizon too, I felt a twinge of excitement. Money has never been my motivator, but perhaps our luck was changing anyway.

The week before the house viewings, I'd made a speculative phone call to the estate agents in Earl's Court, where I'd worked part-time whilst living in the apartment. It had been during the period of Lisa's, or so I'd presumed, Amelia's, pregnancy. Incredibly, the owner, John Brookes, contacted me soon after we left the pub on our return journey to the hotel. The coincidence knocked us both for six and Lisa called it 'a sign'. He invited me to his office to discuss an opportunity he thought I may be interested in. After dropping Lisa and George at the hotel, I drove to Earl's Court in anticipation. John informed me his partner had left the business, and although he didn't offer me a partnership, he offered me the role of sales director. I couldn't believe my good fortune. Lisa was thrilled too, and that night we spent the best time together since George had been born. The only downside came when I suggested using my apartment in Earl's Court as a base during the working week. With several months remaining on its lease, it made perfect sense. To me, at least.

"Can't you commute?" she asked.

Her question didn't warrant a reply. The village was a ninety-minute train journey in and out of the city and I would need to catch one into the centre and another one back out. Having no intention of committing to that kind of daily grind, reluctantly, Lisa accepted.

During the following days, Lisa checked out the school in the village, although George wouldn't be starting for another four years.

Within days, her antidepressants finally helped with her ongoing anxiety. We began sleeping together again too. Having taken Lisa months to allow me to even hold her, I never did blame her. It made perfect sense, given her exploits of being tied up in that house, or worse still, the cabin in the woods.

But it isn't just Lisa who endures nightmares about that place. It still forces me to wake unexpectedly in the middle of the night. The doll in the corner; its eyes boring into mine. And I have the physical scars too, deeply embedded into my palms, where I jumped through the window and landed on my hands and knees. Often, I rub my fingertips over the smooth mounds of thick skin, contemplating the day I found Lisa bound in the corner of the shack on top of a sodden mattress, her face full of terror. The way she drank a bottle of water, as if she hadn't drunk for days. And then when she screamed out, *'It's my baby!'*.

The cabin was now gone. Demolished. Along with the makeshift grave, the family prepared for Katrina to mourn. Julia was right; there were no bones underneath. No traces of human life.

So, I allowed Lisa time to recover. It gave me time too. But my sleepless nights continue, and when I did sleep, it was frequently accompanied by hideous nightmares.

Occasionally, I scream out, often waking George, who inevitably screams out too. Lisa holds me and reassures me everything is in the past. And, after a while, I reciprocate. She asked me to take the same pills she was prescribed, but I've tried that before, with very mixed results. I do still carry a packet or two of sleeping tablets for an emergency, and a bottle of whisky is never far from my side.

But with the new house on the horizon, maybe things are finally moving in the right direction. George held us together during those initial tough months, but now, with the property in the village, a new job, and a brand new start for all three of us, I can pray for positive times and dream unimaginable thoughts. After all, it was what we all wanted. Wasn't it?

And there I was, disembarking onto the platform at Kings Cross station, emotionally closer to a new beginning, yet physically closer to my past. It also meant returning to my apartment in Earl's Court for the first time since late the previous summer.

Just two or three short months until they join you.

But experience told me that a lot could happen in just two or three short months.

4

MATT

As if it were only yesterday, the memories of living in Earl's Court came crashing back. As soon as I exited the tube station, the familiar sights and sounds greeted me, as if nothing had changed during the seven months I'd been away. The first thing I noticed was the *Police Box* on the high street, a replica of the time machine used in the popular British TV series, *Doctor Who*. Even though I barely watched the programme, it made me smile whenever I walk past, a tourist or two inevitably having their photograph taken alongside. The Courtfield public house stood opposite; the pub where I enjoyed many a pint of beer. Perhaps 'enjoyed' isn't the right word, 'endured' is more appropriate as it once became my go-to place to hide and reflect.

Farther along, I turned right onto Old Brompton Road, close to my apartment block now. My more upbeat recollections were replaced with doubt and fear; what or who awaits me? Maybe Francis had moved on? After all, she was an integral part of my private life and became entangled in the whole mess. Surely she had seen sense and started afresh? I hadn't heard from her since. Wasn't that proof enough she no longer wanted anything to do with me? But I'd developed this inner psyche, somehow able to predetermine what lies in wait. Perhaps down to my negative nature, always fearing the worst. Or maybe it was because of my connection to that family. Is it possible to inherit such incredulous behaviour?

The first person I recognised was my nosy neighbour. Of course, she hadn't moved on. The elderly woman lived in the apartment opposite, a lady called Claudia West. Before I even reached the final flight of stairs, I heard the distinctive sound of a door opening ahead and knew who to expect.

"Back again? It must be over six months since you were last here. Your mail has been piling up, and I've had to keep collecting it from your mailbox downstairs."

What a lovely greeting. You haven't died since I was here last time then?

"That's very kind of you, but how did you get a key? Those boxes are supposed to be confidential."

Claudia West had little time for my interrogations and defended her actions with confidence. She had this hidden ability to make you feel guilty even though you have done absolutely nothing wrong.

"If you had told somebody you weren't going to be around, then we might have known. The poor postman couldn't squeeze any more letters into the box. Besides, they have made me chief warden, what with all the cutbacks and stuff, and I have my own set of keys."

To everywhere?

"Wait there."

She held her hand aloft before scurrying back inside her own flat, leaving me standing on the landing, daring to peek at the door next to mine; Francis's door. A few moments later, Claudia returned with a wodge of envelopes, flyers and takeaway menus.

Why the hell have you kept all those?

"Here," she said, forcing me to drop my bag and retrieve the pile of junk mail.

"Thanks. But there really was no need."

"No, probably not. There isn't anything of interest in it, anyway."

So, you've been through it all, have you?

"I'll most likely just bin it then."

"Probably best. But we have recycling units outside. You never used them, did you?"

Seven months since I'd set eyes on that woman and you would think I only spoke to her the day before. But I had no time for her or her condescending manners. She spoke as though she owned me, as if she was the custodian of the entire apartment block.

Chief warden.

Leaving her standing on the landing, I bundled my door open and pushed my bag inside with my feet, clinging to the pile of mail in my hands. I heard Claudia mutter something else under her breath and I glared at her before shutting the door with a bang.

"It's been lovely and peaceful without you around," she shouted from outside. It took a lot of restraint not to rush back out, confront her and give her a mouthful. I had visions of finding her at the top of the stairwell and pushing her hard in the back, taking great delight as I watched her fly down the concrete steps with a satisfactory crack of the neck as she lands at the bottom.

What's wrong with you, Matt? Ever since…

Fortunately, I had the good sense to stop off at a convenience store nearby and buy a ready meal and a cheap bottle of own brand whisky. Dumping my bag on the bed, I returned to the kitchen and poured myself a generous measure. As I wandered through the flat, sipping my drink, I realised just how long it had been since I last lived there. It felt cold and damp, despite the arrival of springtime and the outside temperature indicating pleasant weather may be close by. Memories flooded back of the summer before. The hot days and warm nights. And thoughts of my next-door neighbour.

Is she still living there?

Right on cue, a knock at the door. Believing the nosy cow has returned to warn me not to have my television too loud or that she had banned all visitors from the premises without sufficient ID, it soon transpired it wasn't my prying neighbour at all. Instead, Francis stood nonchalantly in my doorway, complete with a baseball cap and the deepest dimples I'd ever seen. Her eyes were olive green, underlined by her pale skin and I noticed the tiny freckles across the bridge of her nose, which continued their journey a short distance either side. She smiled broadly and my heart instantaneously skipped a beat. She always could stir me from my eternally depressed state of mind.

"Welcome home, stranger," she said, placing her hands behind her back and offering me a sarcastic curtsey. It made me laugh, the first genuine laugh to escape my mouth in months, and it instantly felt wrong.

"Why, thank you," I replied, sounding quite pathetic

as I attempted to join in with the joviality. Feeling myself blush, I stood aside to allow her to pass.

"Nah, come around mine. I doubt you've got any food and your place smells damp." Francis exaggerated a sniffing action. "Put your heating on, air this place out, and pop round. Half an hour okay?"

Don't do it, you idiot.

"Okay. I'll unpack and make my bed up."

"Alright, but you won't be needing that tonight."

During the following three months, Claudia West never missed a beat. Ever since my first night back, every damn time I left Francis's apartment, she miraculously stepped out onto the landing. No doubt carrying a bag of rubbish, she maintained a pretence of needing to throw out her refuge. For a single woman living alone, she sure created a lot of trash. She would look at me and then at Francis's door and tut her disapproval with an exaggerated flick of her head, before disappearing down the stairs.

The satisfactory crack of her neck as she lands at the bottom...

It wasn't as though Francis and I were an item. We just happened to be there for one another. She was also enduring continual issues with her mum's health who still awaited a hip replacement. Francis even took her to Tenerife for four weeks over the winter, as the doctor predicted the warmer climate would help ease her pain. I assumed, without ever asking, Francis had all but frittered away the money she 'earned' for looking after me.

The previous summer, from the day I moved in, they paid her ten thousand pounds to 'keep her eye on me', made sure I stayed nearby and did nothing untoward. She reported directly to Andy Coleman, the local and bogus estate agent, who *found* me the apartment. But the apartment was part of the setup and Francis was part of the con. Andy Coleman's real name is Andy Meadows, the brother of Graham Meadows and he was an electrician by trade. He had no idea about selling houses and the family concocted the entire arrangement.

But Francis and I inadvertently formed a bond. We got on well and soon discovered we had a few things in common. Maybe we were just there at the right time for each other, or the wrong time, depending on which way you look at it. Genuinely, when I arrived back seven months later, I wished she had gone and I could have taken advantage of the apartment for its intended purpose but, as on many other occasions during my chaotic life, I fell for the charm and looks of a woman who showed an inkling of interest in me. However, deep down, I believed my *arrangement* with Francis was more than that. A replacement. Like using a reserve until your best player is fit enough to play again; if they ever do return from injury.

Realising I must put an end to it, especially now I'd completed my house purchase with Lisa, I had every intention of finishing with Francis once and for all. However, I never found the right time to do it.

Initially, she asked about my son and enquired about my wife, but at that time she knew nothing of Lisa. It wasn't as though she raised the subject very often and, as time passed by, she instead reverted to talking more about a future for us.

Put an end to this.

The situation was threatening to spiral out of control. I found myself digging and deeper by the day, and the more I postponed saying anything, the keener Francis believed I was becoming. I knew exactly why I allowed it to happen; to keep my mind from straying to the inevitable. Thinking I would be better on my own, I soon discovered company somehow kept the demons away. Any night I spent alone lead to unavoidable nightmares, cold sweats and an overwhelming feeling that what happened may catch up with me again. I was living through a combination of fear and expectancy.

But, in the arms of Francis, I felt relatively safe. Perhaps it's another reason I kept postponing the inescapable. Apart from Claudia West, how could anybody feasibly know anything was going on? Lisa didn't know where my apartment was, and even if she did, there was no possibility of her knowing who Francis Baker is.

5

LISA

FOR SOME BIZARRE REASON, I actually felt guilty going through Matt's pockets. Surely I should be expected to, especially if I'm putting *his* dirty clothes into *our* washing machine?

We moved into the new house just over a month before, and I had to admit, it was even more beautiful than I first recalled. Things were slowly taking shape. I fashioned brand-new curtains for almost every room, along with help from my steadfast friend, Hannah, and decorated George's nursery in vivid colours, before adding dinosaur stencils along one wall. Matt started on the garden on the weekends too, his lack of eagerness only strengthened by Tom insisting he helped. It baffled me why Matt wouldn't take to our neighbours. After all, they'd made us so welcome ever since that day we met them in the pub.

I recall them asking if they could join us and I said

we'd be delighted, especially as I wanted to pick their brains. We spent an hour together, and I enquired about the local school and the local playgroups as well as sports teams for when George grew older. Everything I could think of to reassure myself we were moving to the right area. As the conversation unfolded, Hannah and Tom confessed to being in the neighbourhood watch team, ensuring everybody stayed safe in the village. What better people to become friends with than a couple who could look out for us every single night and day? To me, it felt like a blessing.

On Friday night, the fourth weekend Matt returned home from his apartment, he had to dash straight back out, as he stupidly left his laptop on a seat outside the train station whilst waiting for his taxi. Fortunately, some kind person handed it in, and he drove our car to collect it. So, as I waited for his return, I loaded his washing into the machine, item by item. After we moved in, he brought his dirty laundry home, complaining of having nowhere to dry clothes in his stupid apartment. It would be easy to argue I wasn't his old spinster, there to carry out his chores and put hot food on the table, but I enjoyed keeping myself busy and was desperate for him to be happy, or more to the point, desperate for our new start in life to work out. The past was in the past and it was months since he'd mentioned Amelia or any other member of that family. Was it too much to ask he provided for me and his son in return? If I played my part, I would be happy, as long as he never took me for granted.

Once satisfied his pockets were clear, I poured detergent and softener into the machine, closed the door, turned the knob and pushed the 'On' button; like clock-work. But as I remained crouched down, I thought I spotted something on one of his shirts. Lipstick? Quickly, I pressed the same button, once, twice, rapidly in and out. But the machine didn't stop and instead I could only watch as his clothes spun and tossed and turned whilst I tried in vain to locate the same shirt.

Standing up too quickly, and suddenly feeling quite light-headed, I held onto a chair behind me. Surely it wasn't lipstick? We'd only lived in the house a month and he had George, a good job and all of our damn money ploughed into our future. He wouldn't put that in jeopardy, would he?

'…*and Daddy is coming home in between, aren't you, Daddy?*'

But he never did come back to Scotland whilst we waited for the house sale to complete. Instead, he spent every bloody weekend in London. So why did I never question him?

Looking down at my hands, I could see heavy imprints embedded into my palms. I'd dug my nails in too deep and my mouth felt dry whilst my breathing became erratic, just as it used to, all those months ago.

The doorbell made me jump. The television blared from the living room, and I panicked as I remembered I'd left George alone, playing on his mat with *CBeebies* on the TV. He must have grabbed the remote and turned it up louder. The doorbell rang again, twice, three times, as if whoever was there was holding it in and not letting go.

Storming through the hallway, the TV was even more deafening from there, so I swung the living room door open.

"Turn that racket down, George."

He sat crossed-legged, two feet from the screen with the controller pointing directly at it. He grinned broadly and made himself topple over onto one side. The door-bell rang again, so I ran into the lounge, prised the remote from his surprisingly firm grip and pressed down on the on-off button. George screamed, a high-pitched wail before the inevitable tears.

"Back in one minute," I said and rushed to the door, expecting to find Matt with his hands full and unable to get his key into the lock.

"What the hell…"

The smile on Hannah's face disappeared before I finished yelling.

"Everything okay, love?" she asked, walking directly past me before turning in the hall to face me.

Hannah and Tom lived in the middle of the village, three or four houses along from the pub, at number 264. They owned the largest house on the street and had resided in the borough for over thirty years. As I say, they made us most welcome, latching onto my troubled past and Hannah acting as a motherly figure. We'd formed a strong bond in such a brief space of time. It helped they were the neighbourhood watch team too, easing my mind to know they were so close by whilst Matt worked away during the week. Hannah also volunteered at the local library two afternoons a week; they really enjoyed being part of the local community and embraced all it had to offer. They even made themselves available to babysit and suggested it would do Matt and me good to get out for a meal or drink. Matt was keen, but I rebuffed her offers, although never sure why.

"Oh, sorry, Hannah. I thought it was Matt."

"And why would you be yelling at Matt?"

Before I could reply, she walked into the living room to see to George. His screams had dissipated, but been replaced with an incessant sob and the thrashing of his little arms on the carpet.

"Whatever's wrong, my darling?"

Passing Hannah the remote control, I said I'd be in the kitchen with the kettle on. She smiled and continued to tend to George. Remarkably, his crying stopped as fast as it started and I soon heard music from the television continue from where it left off, albeit at a much more acceptable volume.

"Well?" Hannah said, joining me, her face full of concern.

Peering over her shoulder, Hannah followed my gaze. Like a mind reader, she instantly knew why I was concerned.

"Oh, George. Don't worry, he's engrossed in his programme. Besides, I've told you before, you can't watch him *all* the time."

My cheeks burned at my over-cautious attitude. However, it wasn't just George making my mind do somersaults. I couldn't shake the image from inside the washing machine only a few minutes earlier.

The kettle boiled, and as I finished brewing a fresh pot of tea, Hannah sat down at our enormous kitchen table, willing me to explain whatever was bothering me. At least it had the required effect, and I soon calmed down. Even though I'd only known her for a few short weeks, I already realised how much I could trust Hannah Wells.

MATT

The moment I stepped inside the front door, the voices from the kitchen ceased, and I knew it would be our new neighbours yet again.

My paranoia had been working overtime during the past month, ever since we moved in. I'd promised myself to find a different apartment in London, without telling Francis. It struck me the previous weekend that if I just moved out with no fuss and left her a note, she would, in turn, leave me alone. Maybe naïve, and definitely extremely weak, I couldn't face the inevitable battle which would ensue if I attempted it face to face. However, I still hadn't contacted the estate agent to inform them I wished to run down my lease. And then, when I walked into my own house, I cursed myself, because there I was, on Friday night and another week had drifted by. Five more days of indecisiveness and a subsequent week when I spent two nights with Francis. The hole was getting deeper by the day and if I didn't act soon, there could be no way out.

"Hi," I said as politely as I could muster, placing my laptop bag on our ridiculously large kitchen table.

The pair of them turned to face me but not before I followed their eyes. Were they looking at the bloody washing machine?

"Not on there," Lisa said, pointing at my bag. "You don't know where it's been."

Instinctively, I picked it up, whilst my eyes remain focused on whatever they could be staring at. Just clothes tossing and spinning in the foam. What was so fascinating?

"What's wrong, darling?"

Lisa never called me darling. My eyes flicked from the

hypnotic turning of the laundry and back to Lisa. Hannah was now staring at me too.

"Nothing," I replied, kicking myself for sounding so high-pitched. "Why should there be?"

"Don't know. You appear mesmerised by the washing machine. Have I put something in there I shouldn't have done?"

Lisa stole Hannah a quick look and I'm sure Hannah offered a minuscule smile in return.

Thinking on my feet, I tapped the front pocket of my chinos.

"Ha, no. There it is." I retrieved my phone. "Thought I might have left it in my jeans," I said, nodding in the direction of the utility room.

"Well, that's alright then," Lisa replied, busying herself again. "You got your laptop, okay, I see?"

She nodded at the bag I was clutching too tightly under my arm.

"Yeah, yeah. All good," I said, tapping it like some kind of idiot playing out her game.

"It was decent of somebody to report it," Hannah joined in. "Nowadays, it's a wonder they didn't run off with it and put it up on eBay."

Exactly what I'd been thinking. The idea of a Good Samaritan is something which died out many years ago, ever since the country evolved into a 'look after number one' society. But that wasn't all. Twice since I began my new weekend travel ritual, I believed I'd seen somebody watching me on the train; once the previous Monday and again on the return journey. My *Good Samaritan*? But it was only a feeling, a sensation. I hadn't actually *seen* anybody. The train was full of commuters; men and women returning from a day or a week in the city. Nobody suspicious and nothing untoward.

But my paranoia was working overtime again. Ever since we moved in, something felt a little strange, and I'd had those premonitions before.

Of course, my sixth sense knows best. He had come home, and it took me no time to track him down to the village. Oh my goodness, Matt. You wanted to live in our village, didn't you? That way, you knew I would find you. And after you rejected our house, or more likely, she did, it only took one visit to the estate agents and they told me everything. I can still be quite the charmer. I've always kept my eye on the house, the one with the long garden where we could have grown vegetables. That should have been ours. But perhaps it isn't big enough for us and the baby.

And now you've bought another house in a nearby village. It was for sale with the same agents, they told me, and now I know where you live. So, I've started following you to work and to that apartment of yours in Earl's Court. I would love to get inside, see what it's like, see where you sleep during the week; and I will. You see, I'm clever and I can always find a way to get what I want.

Tonight you were silly, though. To begin with, why did you walk up and down the train? Did you think you had seen someone? Oh damn, surely not me? No. As I say, I'm clever. You wouldn't have spotted me. Maybe you 'sensed' me. Yes. I've always thought you would inherit our special gift, so I need to be careful until the day I want you to see me, of course. But not yet. That will be when I'm ready, not you.

Something agitated you on the train. Is that why you left your laptop on the seat outside the station? Good job I was watching.

These days, any old thief could have grabbed it, taken it home and put it up for sale on eBay.

I don't like to see you agitated, Matt. I wonder what's making you act this way? When I think about it, ever since I tracked you down, you haven't seemed your usual self. Oh, I know how much you've been through. We've all been through so much, but I expected my old Matt back. Fun-loving and free once again, even if you do have a baby.

And I was right about Lisa. She has got big. So much so, I think she'll struggle to shift that excess weight. But I like Lisa. She looks like she is a wonderful mother. I watch them in the park. Her eyes dart everywhere, but she's only protecting little George. I'll have to make my mind up about what to do with Lisa, but for now, *she is safe and the least of my concerns.*

No, it's you, Matt, who is bothering me. Something isn't right. You're acting quite peculiar. And I need to find out why.

6

LISA

MATT TAPPED me on the shoulder, jogging to keep up. "Did you see anybody up in the copse?"

Pretending I hadn't heard, I instead turned my attention to George. "Grip the ball, babe." Matt hated me calling him 'babe'. "If you drop it in the road, a big lorry will come along and squish it flat."

With my cheeks puffed out, I pushed them inwards between my finger and thumb, simultaneously allowing a farting sound to escape my mouth. It made George giggle. Silly noises always made him laugh. So much so, he often ended up with hiccups. Neither Matt nor I liked it when he got hiccups, but I was still angry with Matt, so I did it on purpose. It normally takes around ten minutes to walk home from the park, especially with George in tow, but that day, I pushed his buggy faster, eager to get inside, feign a headache and make myself scarce.

With the pathway only wide enough for one, Matt

hung behind, but I could hear his footsteps behind me. I clung onto the pushchair as if my life depended upon it.

"Did you hear me? I said I think somebody—"

A speeding van drove past, drowning out his words. Again, I ignored him, still irate I thought I'd spotted lipstick on his shirt. But that was two days ago, and he was due to travel back to London the following morning. I should have patched things up and been more amicable, but I couldn't bring myself to creep around him as if I were the guilty party.

The wind whipped up as a lorry hurtled past and I pushed George's new baseball cap firmly down on his head.

"Mummy!" he squealed. It made my heart melt every time he called me 'Mummy'. It was his very first word, and I knew it annoyed Matt.

After pulling his cap too far forward, covering his eyes, he slid it back up, higher than its original position, so it threatened to fall off his head altogether. Smiling, I left him alone, refusing to make a fuss.

"Make sure you don't lose that hat," Matt shouted. Looking down at George, I winked. He tried to wink back, both eyes blinking tightly simultaneously. I smiled again.

They say a mother is the glue which holds a family together, but in our case, George was the bond. Matt would reluctantly admit it too. George gave us a permanent excuse to focus our attention upon and therefore not on each other. It suited me fine, especially that weekend.

Finally, we reached the sanctuary of home and shelter from the strengthening July sun.

"Why did you ignore me?"

George was sitting on the bottom step of the staircase, desperately trying to pull his shoes off.

"Hang on, babe. I'll do that for you."

Matt tutted and stormed into the kitchen, leaving his trainers abandoned on the hallway floor.

"I'll pick those up for you, shall I?" I called after him. Winking at George again, he placed his hand over his mouth to stifle a giggle. Even at eleven months of age, he'd learnt quickly not to get on the wrong side of his dad.

Once his shoes were off, I carried George into the living room and put the television on. He could work the remote control better than me and soon the sound of *CBeebies* reverberated around the room. He sat crossed legged on the floor, about three feet from the screen, already engrossed by the bright colours and tuneful songs. Knowing I had little choice but to face Matt, I begrudgingly left my son with the door ajar behind me. Stalling for time, I packed the shoes away before joining him in the kitchen, my 'fabricated' headache rapidly turning into a reality.

"Tea?" I asked, filling the kettle whilst keeping my back to him.

He sat at the pine table. The six-seater table was far too big for our modest kitchen. You needed to wait for one person to pass before stepping from one side of the room to the other. I'd ordered it online a week after we moved in. But, of course, I got the measurements wrong. I recalled Matt arriving home from work and meeting him at the front door, realising my face was full of sheepishness.

"What's wrong?" he asked.

As always, I went on the defensive. "What do you

mean, 'what's wrong'? Why does something have to be wrong?"

He followed me into the kitchen and laughed. I admit the table and chairs looked out of place. Like a train set with a new locomotive. But the latest addition was a different scale to the others, towering ridiculously against the rest of the model.

"I think it's lovely," I lied in an attempt to hide my inadequacy. "Plenty of room for all three of us to sit around and have meals. Better than eating off trays in front of the television."

"There's enough room for us and all the neighbours," Matt quipped.

"Trust you to ruin it," I replied, before storming upstairs, leaving Matt to tend to George.

A week later, we reverted to eating meals from trays in front of the television. George's high chair sat between the two small sofas and we took turns feeding him. The oversized table remained in the same place and we never did use it for its intended purpose. Instead, it resembled a dumping ground for mail, keys and magazines, with George's books and toys piled at one end.

"Yes, please. If it's not too much trouble," Matt replied. "And can you make George a juice? I bet he's sat in there with his face pushed against the screen. It will damage his eyes, you know. Do you want him going blind? You just ignore us, don't you? It's me, me, me…"

Shut the fuck up.

"No, darling. Of course not."

Once I returned from the living room, having dragged George a few feet back from the TV, Matt was standing at the worktop, finishing the drinks.

"Not capable of that either, am I?"

Sitting down, I retrieved my phone from my pocket and scrolled through the news, paying no attention to any particular article. Matt placed a mug of tea in front of me, a little too forcefully, before taking a seat opposite.

"So, you didn't see anybody in the park?"

At least his voice dropped to a reasonable level. He appeared intent on a response to whatever, or whoever, he believed he noticed. Pushing my phone away, I swigged my tea before looking up to face him.

"Where?"

"Don't patronise me, Lisa. I'm only asking if you saw somebody. Jeez, you've been acting weird all weekend."

And so have you. For months.

The village park comprised a modest play area, two swings, a roundabout, plus a couple of climbing frames, fenced off from a large expanse of grass which once formed the local football pitch. Beyond that, a small copse created a boundary between the park and the fields beyond.

I often eyed the copse with suspicion. Deep down, I realised it was why I didn't want to hear Matt or his stories of someone following us.

"It's not just the park, though," he continued. "On the train, I thought somebody was watching me."

"But why would anybody be watching you and not make themselves known?"

Studying Matt scrupulously, he took his time, the cogs turning whilst searching for an explanation. He'd been struggling to hold himself together and his behaviour had been worrying me for a while. Why couldn't he just get his act together for everybody's sake?

"I don't know. I really do not know."

Silence enveloped us. He drifted again, miles away,

forever lost in his thoughts. He looked pasty white, and I'm sure he was losing weight.

"Are you eating enough during the week when you're in that apartment?" I said *that apartment* as patronisingly as I could, wanting to gauge his reaction.

He glared at me. "Of course I am. Do you think I'm some kind of teenager who can't look after himself?"

Matt shot to his feet, scraping his chair backwards and pushing his tea away. He mumbled something under his breath about going upstairs to pack.

It wasn't getting any easier. Something wasn't right. Not right at all. But I couldn't say anything, because I didn't want him to know how scared I felt too. Frightened, something bad could still happen to us, refusing to leave us in peace.

7

MATT

"WE SAW you in the park. Earlier today." I caught Lisa watching me out of the corner of her eye.

"Oh, right," she replied, still looking at me whilst answering on my behalf. "We didn't see you, did we, darling?"

Darling, again, and so patronising.

She knew I hated to be proven wrong or made a fool of, and right then I wanted the ground to open up and swallow me whole.

Our neighbours had joined us in the kitchen; Hannah and Tom Wells, the retired couple who lived in the village for several years. They worked in the city as IT consultants, self-employed, I believe, although I barely took any notice. I considered their life stories unworthy of my attention.

Nonetheless, however tedious I found them as a couple, they seemed harmless and Tom enjoyed a decent whisky, so we at least had that in common. And Hannah was being a good friend to Lisa, helping since we moved into our house. She occasionally volunteered to babysit for George too, but Lisa invariably declined, although she appreciated the sentiment. I always considered it a good idea. Give us a break, a night out, but convincing Lisa was an entirely different matter. She never appeared interested in spending time alone with me.

"We were out walking Charlie…"

What a surprise.

"…up near the copse. You know, in the park."

Tom regularly added, *'you know'*, in a mock cockney accent. It annoyed me more than it should have. And that bloody dog, Charlie. Some kind of Labrador cross, I think he said. Bloody fat thing always waddling after them. It lived on treats and scraps and a mountain of dog food. They were as soft as shit with it.

"Oh…" Lisa replied.

Is she actually smiling?

"Matt thought he may have seen somebody watching him. You should have said hello. Shouldn't they, Matthew?"

Suppressing the urge to kill Lisa, I remained composed, on the exterior at least, trying my utmost to ignore her sarcasm. I knew I saw somebody in the copse and it wasn't Hannah or Tom. Instead, a person alone, hiding, watching. Perhaps Hannah would be more sympathetic.

"You didn't happen to see anybody up there, did you?"

Hannah was smaller than her husband, and Tom was barely five foot six. I could only describe her as plump, like a snowwoman, her body and head equally round.

Don't get me wrong, Tom wasn't on the cusp of winning any male model competitions either. Like his wife, and their dog, Tom was overweight, but because of his broad shoulders, I imagined he would have once been quite muscular and strong. If they didn't take Charlie for a walk so often, I hated to think how big they would become. Hannah's hair was grey and curly, and she wore circular glasses, ageing her further. Studying her across the kitchen, I noticed her tight stonewashed jeans straining at the seams, whilst her baggy sweater hung over her breasts and belly like some kind of knitted sleeping bag.

Lisa was forever telling me not to be so cruel, but secretly I knew she liked the way Hannah looked. One, she realised I wouldn't be interested, and two, it made her feel better about herself.

Soon after we found our house in the country, and during our daily FaceTime calls, I noticed Lisa begin to regain her weight. Unsurprisingly, she lost over twenty pounds following her pregnancy and I regularly watched her push food around her plate, repeatedly complaining about a lack of appetite. Given the way Tracy *looked after her*, I knew she wasn't to blame, and it initially pleased me when she finally ate something like normal again. However, by the time she and George re-joined me in southern England, Lisa had ballooned. Once in our new home, she attempted to diet — 'a fresh start in life' she called it — but it didn't last long. Not that she tried *too* hard. Three days of relative fasting were undone by a pizza or a tub of Ben & Jerry's, or some other treat to help with a sudden anxiety attack. I never commented. Well, that's not entirely true, especially after a drink, but I generally kept my thoughts to myself. I had to remain in Lisa's favour. She was a great mum and upsetting her was certainly not in my interest. There were my feelings for Lisa too. I always had a soft spot for her. Even Amelia recognised that and would often remark on my *fondness* for our fellow worker. Little did she know.

"Like who?" Tom butted in. "The ghost of the copse?"

Tom did that 'woo-hoo' sound a ghost might make whilst raising his arms and wiggling his fingers. He appeared pleased with his little joke and I smiled as he looked at me for approval. Inside, I think 'what a dick'.

"Don't be facetious, Tom," Hannah said, turning her attention back to Lisa. Tom laughed heartily, now looking at Lisa for a reaction. She offered him an obligatory smirk, which at least had the desired effect of pacifying him. "What do you mean, Matt?" Hannah continued, evidently interested in my tale. "Did you see somebody?"

We'd only been there a month, but I already realised Lisa spoke to Hannah in private, and I strongly suspected Hannah relayed every detail to Tom. The mutual friendship between the three of them amazed me in such a brief space of time. Hannah and Tom inherited the title of neighbourhood watch coordinators some years ago after they carried out a similar role in their previous village. They were the ideal couple for such a position of authority; well, according to all the other nosy idiots living within the vicinity. Tom and Hannah took early retirement, therefore 'still having their wits about them', and both worked with computers; allegedly making them software whizz kids to keep their beady eyes on every house and street around. Tom liked to *dabble* with home security gadgets too. 'Nosy bastard', I described him, but Lisa rebuked me and often reminded me how grateful we should be.

"I'm sure I did," I replied, "but Lisa thinks I'm seeing things."

All eyes fell on Lisa, and she offered a wry smile.

"Well, you do have form, dear."

Tom smiled at her sarcastic response, which soon disappeared once Hannah shot him a look.

"That's true, darling," I responded sarcastically. "But now we know it was Hannah and Tom today, we can at least put a close to this one."

Hannah wouldn't let it drop.

"Just keep your eyes open, and let either Tom or I know if you suspect anything or anybody. We are the neighbourhood watch coordinators, after all."

Sighing inwardly, I wished Hannah would shut up, or better yet, change tack and talk about something else.

"We can put the word out, you know, on the neighbourhood website if you like?" Tom added, relishing his role within the community.

"That won't be necessary." I intervened, gathering the mugs from the table to bring the subject to a close, as well as prompt the nosy bastards to leave my house. I'd had enough for one day. Hannah leant forward to retrieve her own coffee, but she was too slow and I collected her half-drunk cup before pouring the contents down the sink. "We don't want to scare half the village, do we?" I added with a smile.

Lisa glanced sheepishly at our neighbours, secretly apologising for my behaviour. However, I knew Lisa sometimes believed that Hannah and Tom could go over the top with their inherited detective responsibilities, even though she would never admit to such a thing.

Tom looked taken aback by my abrupt response and pulled on Charlie's lead to get the fat dog up on its four legs. He had made himself at home under our huge kitchen table, soon settling down after a handful of treats for being 'such a good boy'.

"Well, it's lovely to see you both," Lisa said as we filed into the hallway. "And sorry George couldn't peel himself away from the television to say hello."

"Bless him," Hannah replied, air-kissing both of us. "I don't blame him for staying clear of us grumpy grown-ups."

I know how he feels.

We watched as they waddled along the road before disappearing from sight. Lisa shot me a look as she returned to the kitchen. Although I had a sarcastic comment lined up, I let it go and instead join George in the living room.

Ruffling his hair, his eyes don't leave the screen, so I sat on the sofa behind, contemplating whether I *did* see somebody in the copse. At first, I was adamant, but I doubted myself once our neighbours had sown a seed of doubt. But if someone had been watching, who could it possibly be?

Smiling at George, I stood and walked to the window. Lost in my thoughts, I stared at the dark, forbidding clouds overhead. A summer storm was brewing and I heard the distinct rumble of thunder somewhere far in the distance.

My mental state wasn't in a good place and the *sighting* only made me doubt my soundness of mind again. However, it suddenly occurred to me, if somebody said they thought they saw someone up in the trees, I would have responded with the most obvious question. *'What did they look like?'*

But if somebody had, how would I have explained she looked exactly like my ex-wife?

———————

Damn!

My first time watching him from the copse, and he has to look up at the same moment. I need to be careful. It's far too early for mistakes. I've waited almost a year, for goodness' sake. I can't blow it now.

However, it's a pleasant feeling to think he might actually believe he has *seen somebody watching but is unable to say so with conviction. A flash in the trees could be anything. A bird, a stray deer, or even the wind swaying the branches. After all, it is a blustery day and there is a storm brewing.*

And have those old folks spotted me? They mustn't see me either. But they're always walking that big fat dog and I've noticed how often they go around to their house, especially her, so I need to watch for them too.

George is growing up so fast. I saw him last week when they walked around the village. He looks so cute in his new baseball cap. I'll get Mother to buy him another one. She likes to know how her grandson is. It makes her happy, even though her health is deteriorating. I think they'll let her out soon, maybe to a care home. That Andy Meadows is taking full responsibility and Mother will soon be exempt from any serious blame and maybe Tracy too.

But enough about Melissa. It took all my inner strength not to run out of the copse, shove that Lisa out of the way and push George on the swing. He kept asking her to go faster, higher, but she ignored him. Scared he might fall off and crack his head open on the ground below. She always was so bloody boring. I would make him squeal with delight. Matt would like that too. He's braver and stronger. But obvi-

ously, I know that from personal experience. However, like I said after he left his laptop at the station, Matt is worrying me. Surely Lisa can see it too? Has she asked him, does she know something I don't?

I'm going to follow him to work again, and this time, I'm going to get inside his apartment. Perhaps something isn't right there? Something I can help fix.

8

MATT

EXPLAIN that she looked exactly like my ex-wife?

Jesus, Matt. What's wrong with you? It was purely a hallucination because of the stress you are under. Besides, it couldn't be Amelia. She doesn't even know where we live.

They have a sixth sense, remember?

'No, Matt, it's just you and your crazy mind playing tricks again. Perhaps I do need medication or professional help of some description. Are *sightings* an early warning sign of going mad?'

Ever since that day in the park, I'd been desperate to put what happened, or didn't, out of my thoughts. I avoided mentioning it to Lisa again, or our neighbourhood watch friends, who seemed to spend more time at our house than their own. Probably it was wise to keep things to myself and deal with what was happening the most suitable way I could, albeit remaining highly strung and liable to tip over the edge at any given point. The already over-generous measures of whisky before bedtime were creeping up too, especially during the week whilst alone in my apartment. Perhaps I should have spoken to Lisa, although I didn't know where to begin.

I was disappointed Lisa hadn't mentioned the incident in the copse herself. The day we returned home, she dismissed it as fantasy, ridiculing me in front of our neighbours. However, later the same afternoon, I caught her looking at me when I least expected. Once, whilst supposedly engrossed in a TV programme, and another occasion whilst I sat on the carpet playing with George. Her eyes flashed back to the film, but not quick enough for me not to notice. As well as my own fucked up mind, I found it impossible to gauge what was going on inside her head too.

On Friday morning, two weeks later, I packed my bag to leave the apartment for another long weekend at home. At least I had made the effort that week and begun the search for a new flat, even though I didn't get too far. My enthusiasm level for achieving anything productive was at an all-time low. It wasn't a case of feeling sorry for myself, it was downright depression, thrown in with a generous mix of fear. A lethal combination for somebody as vulnerable as me. It affected my work too, and now I'd been in my job for five months, the boredom had sunk in. Normally, I became disillusioned within weeks of starting a new role, but at least this position held my interest for a little longer. I never got bored at Opacy, but that's an entirely different story.

Working as a sales director wasn't my sole reason for any elongated enthusiasm. Jeez, it was as boring as jobs could be. Instead, it was always about the opportunity to get away during the week. Time to myself, to reflect, to think. I missed George, of course, but I hoped to have years ahead of me in his company, if things *ever* did return to normal.

As for why I never felt apathetic working at Opacy, well, that's because it's where I met Amelia. They could have employed me to clean the toilets out with my bare hands and I would have still been happy. Things obviously went awry in our personal lives, but I didn't blame Amelia. It's why I *allowed* her to escape from her house that night, the time when the police arrested Melissa, Tracy and Andy, and Katrina could finally start a new life with foster parents.

However, my mind often drifted back to Amelia. I know I never convinced DCI Small she broke free whilst I overcame the other family members, but that was his concern and he could never prove otherwise, even if his hunch was correct.

We watched them rush into the path of the awaiting officers, blue lights flashing in the torrential rain.

I held on tight to Amelia's arm, and recall turning to face her. She no longer put up a fight. The sight of the poker raised in my right fist and the sound of sirens outside told her all she needed to know.

But it wasn't the fear in her expression that struck me. It was the look of total despair and anguish. She fell limp, and I knew I could let go. Amelia had given up. The baby meant everything to her.

She collapsed into the chair, her eyes welling and never leaving mine. She attempted a smile; that same beautiful smile I'd fallen for the day we first met. Our very first road trip together flashed through my mind; the conference in Harrogate. When we first slept together and realised how much we meant to each other. The same road trip where we confessed many things. I'd explained about my parents dying, and of my continual search for happiness ever since. In return, Amelia admitted she could never have children.

'I have irregular periods and a failure to ovulate. I've been told it would be a miracle if I ever had children, Matt.'

That's why her pregnancy always intrigued me. The day she'd told me at the café she might be expecting a baby.

And then suggesting we give our relationship a whole new start.

'You never know, once we've had one, we'll probably want to adopt a baby sister or brother…'

'Adopt'. Why 'adopt' another child if you've just conceived naturally?

But I wondered if she could have been wrong about never being able to have a child of her own. Had the doctors been mistaken? Could miracles actually happen? I'd become so mesmerised by the whole charade that a part of me believed it. I'd asked the family doctor and visited the local maternity hospital. Secretly, I hoped it could be true; maybe even as much as Amelia did. After all, what kind of idiot would hang around that family after what they'd put me through? I could have run at any point; fled and started afresh. But no, deep down, I'd desperately wanted it to be true.

You've never stopped loving her, have you?

Wiping away the tear that fell from Amelia's eye, I dropped the poker and took her in my arms. We hugged with what inner strength we had left. She sobbed and clung to me. It felt like sheer desperation.

The sirens and flashing lights were now at the end of the drive-way; a commotion of noise and raised voices. Through the rain-drenched window, I could make out the figures of Katrina and Tracy. Police were with them, whilst three more marched towards the house; their heads bowed against the downpour.

Holding out the passport and mobile phone I'd taken from her bedside table, I pleaded for my wife to listen.

"Take these, Amelia, and run."

She looked at me incredulously.

"Now! Go! Out the back. Get away. But never come back. Promise me you'll never come back."

Amelia glanced out of the front window and then back to me.

"I love you, Matthew," she mouthed. "I promise with all my heart that I'll never come back."

She turned to go before hesitating at the door.

"And, Matt? Please look after our baby."

I gave myself a moment before leaving the apartment. Tears pricked at the back of my eyes and I silently prayed for Amelia, a part of me wishing it may have been her in the copse after all.

It took several moments to console myself as images flickered through my mind. Good thoughts and equally bad.

You have to banish all *the memories.*

The train was as busy as ever, but at least I found a seat with a table, and as we approached my last stop, I decided to call Lisa. "Tell Mummy I'll be home soon, mate."

Lisa put her phone on speaker whilst she busied herself in the kitchen, leaving me to speak to George. I could picture him sitting at the enormous table, kneeling on a chair and crouching over the handset to listen.

George giggled; aware his mum was cross with me.

At least his laugh momentarily lifted my spirits. The woman sitting opposite smiled when I hung up. "How old's your son?" she asked.

"Eleven months, going on sixteen years," I replied.

She laughed, showing off her uneven teeth, the imperfection somehow adding to her looks.

Unfortunately, the train came to a halt before we had the opportunity to talk further. I'm sure I'd seen her somewhere before. Perhaps the person I thought I'd noticed watching me on the same journey?

"Lovely to meet you. Er, I'm, sorry, I didn't catch your name?" I said, lifting my bag from the overhead luggage rack.

"That's because I never told you," she replied, smiling teasingly.

"Oh. Well, I'm Matthew, but everybody calls me Matt."

I noticed her glance at my bare wedding finger. The ring was elsewhere; I wouldn't be wearing that again.

"And I'm Sophie."

No wedding ring either.

Stop it, Matt.

Somebody tutted as I held up the aisle.

"We'd better get off," Sophie added, standing.

"Oh, is this your stop too? Don't fancy a quick drink, do you?"

A gentleman took it upon himself to attempt to barge past. Sophie said nothing, although her eyes widened, as if not dismissing my proposition altogether.

"Can I get by?" the man demanded.

"Yeah, yeah. We're getting off too."

Holding the irritated gentleman back, I allowed Sophie to squeeze out of her seat before we all shuffled along the narrow aisle. She paused once we reached the platform.

"It was nice to meet you, Matt. Maybe we can get that drink one day."

9

LISA

MATT CONTINUALLY RUBBED his finger where his wedding ring would have once been. He appeared to be in better spirits after arriving home from the station and I occasionally caught him smiling to himself. Perhaps he had an enjoyable week at work or did something else happen? More from the lipstick lady? I hated all the not knowing, as if he dealt all the cards. Did he believe I was just there to raise his child? It wouldn't hurt for him to realise my life wasn't a bed of roses. Maybe he would, sooner or later.

Although he hadn't mentioned it since, that *sighting* in the copse two weekends before really freaked him out. Could he have seen somebody, and if so, who could it be? Perhaps I should have probed him further; was it male or female? What did they look like and are you sure they were looking at you? But I didn't want to overindulge him, or more to the point, I didn't want to know.

"Good week at work?" I asked casually, passing him a cold beer. Following his lead, I opened one for myself and sat opposite him at the kitchen table. Matt was helping George with his dinner.

"Yeah. Why do you ask?" he replied, taking the bottle and swallowing half of it in one go. The usual half-hearted response.

"You just appear happier today. The last two week-ends you've seemed worried, so I thought something might have happened at work. Something to cheer you up."

One thing I did after his *incident in the park* was to beg him to go to the doctor. He'd begun to rely on whisky to knock him out at night and I believed he must be drinking twice as much whilst away during the week. But he wouldn't seek professional advice. He was too proud, or too scared. He carried two blister packs of sleeping tablets in his wallet; leftover prescriptions from previous night-mares, although I never checked if he used them. There was only so much I could do, but the anxiety pills helped me and I presumed they could help him too. Maybe I should start popping them in his last whisky at night? He would never taste the difference by that stage and they might just have the desired effect. I decided to ask Hannah what she thought. She was a good listener, and we were becoming very close. Matt thought she and Tom practically lived in our house, but he never stopped to think I needed adult company, too. Grown-up conversation with people who weren't involved with our past; someone who could offer a different perspective and be a damn good listener. Hannah fitted all of that criteria.

Of course, I didn't tell Hannah and Tom *everything*. They were good Christians and regular churchgoers, and

I knew they wouldn't approve of the time Matt and I slept together at the conference in Cheshire. Instead, I told them Matthew and Amelia had already split, gone their separate ways, before he and I got together. Hannah still didn't approve wholeheartedly, but she is a woman of the world and knows what goes on behind closed doors.

But I did tell them about that family, what they put me through, and what Matt endured the year before. Hannah and Tom considered the whole sorry story abhorrent and, like me, prayed they'd all rot in hell. Suggesting that was strong for committed Christians, Hannah grinned and said even the most dedicated of God's followers have principles.

"Everything is fine," Matt said, peeling the paper at the top of his beer bottle.

His failure to open up annoyed me. Did he genuinely believe I was incapable of thinking for myself? It's as though I should pin him down and physically force information from him. We were supposed to be a couple, for goodness' sake, and normal couples communicate. It wasn't just his private life though, or whatever thoughts occupied his mind during those dark days. It was normal, day-to-day conversation too. He'd been in that job for months and I still knew nothing about it. Worse than that, I still knew nothing about his apartment. Who did he see? Who did he speak to? After taking a swig of my beer for courage, I stood and walked through to the utility room and casually unloaded the washing machine.

"And your apartment," I said, my back to him, my voice indifferent. "Where is it again, Earl's Court?"

Unable to gauge his reaction, the pause informed me I'd hit a nerve.

"It's just a bloody apartment, Lisa," he snapped. "You

asked me if I'm eating okay the other week. Why the fascination?"

His patronising demeanour made me momentarily lose my self-control. Standing, I turned to face him, a pile of washing in one hand and a plastic basket in the other.

"Because you never bloody well tell me anything. If you just opened up, I might not have to keep asking. I know nothing about your job either. It's like we're leading two different—"

His phone rang, vibrating on the table. George laughed at the cheery, melodic sound. I tried to see the caller ID but Matt retrieved it too fast.

"Just taking this in the other room. Can you see to George, please?"

He passed me the plastic spoon, leaving me no option but to oblige. "Hello," he said, walking away, and in a tone suggesting he didn't know who it was. Watching him as he disappeared into the living room, he must have believed I couldn't hear his secret conversation.

MATT

"Hello?"

The caller ID displayed 'Unknown' and Lisa was peering over the table trying to see who it was. Quickly, I retrieved the phone and made my way through the living room. It at least got me out of her questioning about my job and what I got up to during the week. Her newly gained fascination made me uneasy, and arriving home in a better mood that day only appeared to have provoked her curiosity further.

"Are you still there?"

"Yes. Hello. Who is this?"

"Is that Matthew Walker?" The female voice was unfamiliar yet authoritative.

"Yes."

"Sorry to trouble you, but I'm WPC Wright, from Epsom Police Station."

What?

"I thought you should know that they released Melissa Reid from prison two days ago. They also moved Melissa to a local care home because she isn't well."

Unable to digest what I was hearing, the first thing I could think is why the hell were they even calling me?

"Who did you say you were again? You're not supposed to phone me. We specifically asked DCI Small not to keep in touch."

A few moments' silence ensued, and I became convinced the policewoman was walking around. Is she outdoors?

"I'm sorry, but we have no note of your request. However, don't panic. Melissa Reid's health has deteriorated significantly during the past twelve months."

Although we asked the DCI to keep us in the dark if they ever released any of the family, or if they even subsequently died in prison, I only did so at Lisa's request. Deep down, I wanted to know, especially if Graham was somehow allowed back into society, even though the chances of that were ridiculously low. He was serving a minimum of twenty-five years. But what about the others? Would they look for me, us? Would they entice Amelia back into the country?

"How could they release her? You can't get let out because your health is bad, can you?" It was a genuine question.

"Well, that's the thing. The courts decided that Melissa's health has deteriorated significantly enough to be sent to a care home." Again the WPC hesitated.

"Is there something else you're not telling me?" I asked.

Another moment's pause before she finally cleared her throat.

"Well, yes. I was coming to that. They reduced Tracy Reid's sentence too."

Tracy is out? Free? Free to find me, find my child?

"She's not out, is she?" The panic in my voice palpable.

Again, a slight hesitation down the line, almost as if whoever the WPC is, she didn't hold all the facts. "No, they have not released her. They downgraded her to an open prison."

"And what the hell does that mean?"

"Well, in short, it means they house prisoners who require minimal supervision. When the courts decided Melissa was so poorly, they agreed both hers and Tracy Reid's participation in the original crime was little more than aiding and abetting."

Aware that Lisa was in the other room, I still struggled to keep my voice low.

"We were told they were given up to twelve years each. How can—"

"Mr Walker," she interrupted. "They *were* given up to twelve years each, but all three sentences were never equal. They gave Andy Coleman twelve years for kidnapping. Melissa and Tracy were given minimal sentences for assisting. They are much less serious crimes."

You don't know them.

"Can she get out? You know, from this open prison thing?"

"Sir, you must understand that we rarely lock open-condition prisoners in their cells and they can even take up employment if their sentence is nearing the end."

They're clever. Very clever.

After hanging up, I sat on the edge of a chair with no recollection of walking across the room. Instead, I sat, staring at the blank TV set, my reflection, in turn, staring at me. And all I could think was this nightmare is far from over.

Will it ever be?

I heard from Mother earlier today, and I'm going to see her in a few days. I'm so excited. Yes, I went to see her in prison, but you can't really talk in there, can you? Not properly anyway. Besides, I hated it in that place. I'm so pleased Matt helped me escape from that. I don't think I would have coped at all.

Talking of Matthew, he's becoming quite forgetful. You see, last week, after he'd gone back to London, I let myself into their house. Matt always locks the front door behind him — I think he's becoming more paranoid by the day — but that day he forgot. That bloody Hannah woman was around again. I guess that's why Matt left in haste, to get away. So, I watched him leave, let myself in, picked up Lisa's set of keys from the telephone table, took them to the local ironmongers and had a copy cut for myself. She was still chatting away with her friend when I returned thirty minutes later. I put the keys back exactly where I found them. I just need to get the key to his apartment now.

One day, I will have to decide what to do with Lisa. She is the one person I've not been able to make my mind up about. Bloody plump Lisa and the baby. You see, I'm not that callous. She is good to Matt, after all. And I do believe in family values. Shit, it's been drummed into me all my bloody life that the family comes above everything else. You should kill for one another, Graham once said, and he should know; he did it three times. There was Ryan, Tracy's husband and then that silly Lee Blackmore guy who started interfering, so Graham almost knocked his head off too. And finally Matthew's aunt, some woman called Edith Weeks. She was worth a bloody fortune and Matt was due to inherit the whole lot! We can still be set up for life if he plays along.

Where was I? Oh yes, they released Mother from prison the other day. And now Matt knows too. I doubted whether the police would have told them, so I had to intervene. I'm sure he would have persuaded them to never inform him. Probably make Lisa even more paranoid so she had to pop even more pills. I often wonder what she would be like if she didn't take them at all.

So that's why I got WPC Wright to call him. She spoke nicely and sounded very authoritative and I persuaded her Matthew would love to know his mother-in-law is just fine.

He will visit the care home. I know he won't be able to stop himself, and that's exactly what I want. He'll realise how strong a family we are, and that he is a fundamental part of it. It's why I'm being so patient. Everything has to be in place.

And now I digress. Silly me and my stupid mind going into overdrive. I've always been like that. 'You're an overthinker,' Mother used to say to me, 'dissecting this and dissecting that.' Ha! She makes me laugh. She has always been so kind to all of us.

But now she is frail.

I have a distinct feeling Melissa might die soon.

10

MATT

As ALWAYS, as soon as I opened the door, that nosy cow from number 401 appeared from her apartment. She gave me a sharp look, not attempting to disguise our meeting could be coincidental.

"Going somewhere nice?" she asked, looking from me to Francis's closed door. A huge grin spread across her face, no doubt congratulating herself for such quick wit.

"I was just wondering how many steps you would hit if I pushed you down the stairs."

Her smile disappeared much faster than it arrived. "What a disgusting thing to say. I should report you for that."

Less than a year before, such a thought would never have entered my mind, let alone actually saying it.

What, or who, are you becoming?

"Go on, report me," I replied. She scuttled along the landing, a small black bag of refuse in her hand. "And guess what?" I called after her. "The day I returned; I threw all that mail into the bin. I didn't recycle one single item. Tell that to your authorities, too."

"There's something wrong with you," she muttered, scooting off down the stairs without looking back.

Waiting until she disappeared, I took a deep breath before knocking on Francis's door. It was only a few hours since I saw her, following another night in my apartment. We drank wine and ate an Indian takeaway, before inevitably ending up in bed. It must have been around three o'clock in the morning when I woke with a jolt and realised I simply *had* to finish it once and for all. The call from the WPC a week earlier had knocked me sideways, and I needed stability, plus a safe haven without added complications. If Melissa was out and Tracy was on the verge, could the past yet again catch up with me, with us?

And don't forget your sighting.

I had a son to protect and the last thing I could afford was to be caught screwing a neighbour. After agonising about it all day at work, reciting the words over and over, I decided now was the time to eventually break all ties with Francis.

"Oh, hi. I thought I heard voices out here. Who have you been talking to?"

With a glance over my shoulder, I asked if it would be okay if I went in. Francis immediately looked concerned.

"Of course. You're not usually so polite."

Once inside, Francis moved to kiss me. We hugged instead, her much tighter than any reciprocation. She buried her face into my neck, kissing it before moving to my lips, but I turned my face sideways so she had to peck my cheek instead. Her eyes were narrow, but before she asked the inevitable, I attempted to defuse the already growing tension between us. Holding her at arm's length, I smiled, desperately trying to think of something to say despite practising it all bloody day long.

"I was talking to that woman opposite. You know, the one who always opens her door at exactly the same time I do?"

Francis broke away, uninterested in my story, and instead walked towards the kitchen.

Great start, Matt, just great.

"Oh, I see. Claudia. Yes, she can be a right pain in the arse."

Although Francis attempted a jovial response, my abrupt entrance had obviously pissed her off.

"Yeah. I told her I would love to push her down the stairs."

Francis stopped in her tracks, as amazed at my quip as the old woman had been herself.

"That's awful, Matt. Did you actually say that to her?"

She continued to the kitchen without waiting for a reply. I stood still, not knowing what to say or do next. I'd gone round with the full intention of cooling things between us, telling her it was all over, but I made such a monumental fuck up within the opening minutes, it was going to take some effort to turn things around in my favour. Begrudgingly, like a lost sheep, I followed her.

"Wine?" she asked, already pouring me a glass.

"Erm, okay. Yes, that would be nice, thanks."

This is working out well then.

"So, who's going to push her, you or me?" Francis grinned as she passed me a drink. "I can't say it hasn't crossed my mind too."

"But you just said—"

"I was joking, silly. That nosy bitch deserves to be taken down a level or two if you forgive the pun."

She laughed, but it was false; exaggerated and unnatural. Had she guessed my intentions?

After we both took a few sips of wine, Francis moved to the living room, carrying a glass in one hand and the bottle in the other. She beckoned me to follow.

"I've got something to ask you, Matt. Please, sit down."

Great. This is supposed to be on my terms.

After placing the bottle on a small table, Francis sat cross-legged on the sofa, cradling her wine glass in both hands like a hot chocolate on a cold winter's day. I sat in the chair opposite. Without giving me any opportunity to speak, Francis continued.

"There's no easy way of saying this…"

Shit. Is she going to save me the trouble?

"…so I'll come straight out with it."

I'm not sure why, but I caught myself smiling and Francis took one look at me, got completely the wrong end of the stick and her face lit up.

"I'd like us to find an apartment together. Bigger than this, but somewhere we can call home. Without having to keep sneaking around to each other's place whilst a nosy neighbour watches our every move."

Oh fuck.

My silence and lack of enthusiasm knocked her off her stride, but no doubt having practised her speech a million times over, she wasn't giving up that easily.

"I'm aware you've got a baby and everything, and I know you weren't expecting this, but I thought you could bring him round and introduce him to me. I'm sure we'd get along great. And I'll spoil him rotten, buy him presents, play with him, take him to the park…"

She eventually trailed off, my expression informing her the big announcement wasn't going to plan. After taking a tiny sip of wine, I stood, clinging onto the glass for comfort before pacing to the window and turning back to face her. In just a matter of seconds, she appeared crestfallen.

"The thing is, it's my baby who's the problem here…" She had given me a get-out clause. "…and I need to bring him up in a stable environment. He already has a great mum, and I can't do this to her."

Although I initially kept Lisa from Francis, I eventually explained once we moved into the house together. I had to. Where else could I say I was at the weekends? When Lisa and George were in Scotland, I didn't need to bring them up, and I just informed Francis that George was with his mum. But since the move, I confessed to all, well, sort of.

"But you told me there is nothing between you and this, what's her name?"

Francis's usual unwavering demeanour was disappearing right in front of my eyes. I noticed red blotches forming across her collarbone and onto her neck as she uncrossed her legs and perched herself on the edge of the sofa.

"Her name's Lisa. And there isn't anything between us." I lied again. "But I stay there at the weekend. It's the only way I can see my son."

My lying made me feel sick, especially as it felt so natural, tripping off my tongue akin to a car salesman. Hell, I could even convince *myself* with some of the tales I'd begun to weave. Francis stood far too quickly, splashing some of the wine over the top of her glass. It landed on her expensive rug, immediately spreading like ink on blotting paper.

"Should I get a cloth?"

"Fuck the cloth, and fuck you!"

Oh shit, no.

The sound of shuffling footsteps on the landing alerted us both. Francis took one look at me before storming to the front door, wine dripping everywhere as she appeared oblivious to still be holding onto it.

"What the fuck are you listening to?" she shouted.

"That's it. I'm reporting you to—"

"Report me. And I'll report you for stalking, and for being a bloody peeping Tom too. You're deranged. Find somebody else to harass."

The door slammed and Francis stomped back into the room. She necked what wine she had left in the glass before refilling it to the brim. After drinking half of that, she wiped her mouth with the back of her hand and glared in my direction.

"What's all this then?" she asked, sweeping her outstretched arm in a semi-circle. "Just a bit on the side, am I? A midweek shag before you go back to your weekend retreat? Log fires, countryside walks. I bet you've got a fucking dog as well, haven't you?"

This is going much worse than I imagined.

"You know it's not like that, Francis. I haven't used you. We've just been here for each other. I thought we both understood that's as far as it goes."

She drained the rest of her drink so quickly that some dribbled down her chin. She wiped it off before fetching a second bottle from the kitchen. Standing in silence, I regretted ever setting sight on her.

"Top up?" she asked. I'd barely touched mine, and I refused with a shake of my head. Francis filled hers again before taking a swig directly from the bottle. She was fuming. I'd never seen her react that way before.

Following her lead, we sat in our original seats, the monotonous tick-tock of the clock on the wall the only sound to be heard. Even the London traffic appeared to have come to a standstill and I imagined a row of parked cars outside, their occupants standing in the road, looking up to our apartment block, listening, like some bloody reality soap opera. As I desperately tried to think of an escape plan, Francis broke the silence.

"Well, it's not going to be that easy, Matthew."

Her change of tone frightened me. What had I expected? I needed to stand up for myself.

"What do you mean, not *that* easy? Are you threatening me?"

"Maybe I am. Maybe it's time this Lisa woman found out what her precious partner gets up to during the week."

"You wouldn't dare…"

"Wouldn't I, Matt? Wouldn't I?"

She stood again and slowly walked behind me. I coiled, ready to defend myself. Once she stood at the back of my chair, she leant forward and spoke through gritted teeth, her mouth so close to my ear, I could feel the heat of her breath.

"Now, get out of my apartment, Matthew Walker. And don't *ever* come back."

11

LISA

MATT NEVER DID TELL me who the phone call was from, even though I did ask out of politeness. The call he took in the living room the weekend before, leaving me alone in the kitchen to feed George. He re-entered the room ashen-faced, like he'd seen a ghost, totally ignoring both of us before disappearing into the back garden. Studying him from the window, at one point his head kind of spasmed, as though he might be crying. Proper crying too, sobbing, but when he returned indoors, he showed no signs of being upset. But he looked properly scared. I never broached the subject, but again, I was livid that he didn't consider me worthy to discuss his private affairs with. Well, perhaps it was time I took care of myself. Did he really believe I could just carry on and be that bloody gullible?

But that was the weekend before, and when he returned from work later that week, a day early no less, his appearance had taken on yet another turn for the worse.

Has he received bad news?

Maybe a death, I thought, shocked at how quickly such a notion could enter my head whilst not even concerning who it might be.

"What are you doing home?" I asked, meeting him in the hallway, scared of what the answer might be.

"Not you as well," he replied, before dumping his bags and marching through to the kitchen, no doubt in search of his favourite bottle of Scotch. As I followed him, I thought of myself as an adoring spouse, the type who would do anything for their partner. I'd seen the documentaries where they even take the odd beating, but their allegiance to their partner held no barriers. I felt pathetic and weak and hated myself as I watched him pour a tumbler of whisky before necking it in one. How many times had I been there, worried about him, watching him suffer in silence, whilst my pain was just as strong?

"What do you mean, *not you as well?*"

When he turned, his eyes were moist. He looked like a little boy lost. But he didn't speak. Instead, he stepped over to me, still holding onto his bloody tumbler of Scotch. Unsure what to expect, it amazed me when he put his arms around me and pulled me in tight. Instantly reciprocating, I became lost in the moment yet totally bewildered by his actions.

And then I smelt it. On his shirt, no, on his neck. A distinct smell of perfume; expensive perfume.

It brought back memories of the lipstick I swore I'd seen on his shirt collar as it tossed and turned against the glass door of the washing machine. Did the same person whose scent I could detect now leave that on him? I held him tight, needing to be sure, although he made no attempt to release his grip anyway. It's as though he didn't want me to look at him, see how upset he was.

Eventually, I allowed my arms to become slack, and he saw it as his cue to let go. Holding his face in my hands, I kissed him gently on the lips. His eyes were bloody, red around the rims.

He has been crying.

"Do you want to talk?" I asked, his behaviour both worrying and scaring me in equal measure.

He shook his head before stepping away, back to the whisky bottle he'd left on the oversized table.

"Just a really shit day at work, that's all," he lied. Work *never* got to him like that. A job was a job to Matt, a means to earn money to do something much more exciting with his life. Work to live, not live to work.

"So bad you've come home twenty-four hours early?"

He looked at me, bemused, before taking his phone from his pocket. Was he really checking what day it was? If he did, he didn't let on and slid the mobile back into his jeans.

"Oh, I don't know. It's been building for a while. A problem that just wouldn't go away. But I've dealt with it now, but to tell you the truth, it's left me drained." He stepped back towards me and kissed me for a second time.

That waft of perfume again.

"I'm going to grab a shower. Take my mind off things."

I smiled and nodded, but I didn't really hear what he said. I only had one thing swirling around in my head.

'A problem that just wouldn't go away…'

79

. . .

MATT

I hid my face from Lisa. She couldn't see me crying. I could have kicked myself for allowing my emotions to run away like that. Why hadn't I got the taxi driver to drop me around the corner, or at the pub? Instead, as soon as I saw her, the ramifications of my repugnant meeting with Francis almost made me trip over in my haste to get to the whisky bottle. But she followed me. Sensing her eyes boring into my back, all I could think to do was to hold her, to keep my face obscured from view. And she reciprocated, burying her head into my shoulder.

'...*so bad you've come home twenty-four hours early?*'

I couldn't believe it. In my eagerness to get away from that apartment block, I hadn't even considered what bloody day it was. I'd have to phone in sick the following day, or call John that night and say something had come up and I needed to work from home. But John Brookes was the least of my worries. Besides, the following Monday, I had a two-day conference to attend in Birmingham, so I wouldn't be back in the office until the Wednesday. It also meant I didn't need to go to the apartment until Tuesday night. I prayed everything was quiet upon my return and I at least had some breathing space in between. So much was happening and none of it under my control. Thankfully, I hadn't heard from Melissa, although I had considered Tracy and where she might be. Would she jeopardise her downgrade in pursuit of me?

As I showered, I replayed the argument with Francis over and over in my head. I knew she would be hurt, and even a little angry, but I genuinely believed she felt the same as me. A bit of fun, somebody to talk to and some adult companionship. Not once did I consider Francis Baker would suggest we move in together.

Then the way she changed, that fury. The blotches across her neck and how she paced the room, slinging her wine everywhere. Shouting at our neighbour. Our neighbour. Shit. I'd forgotten all about her. What will she do next? She must have heard it all, her ear pressed tightly against the door. She said she would report Francis, and she had already threatened to report me too. Would she go through with it, and if she did, what would it mean for me, for Francis? Could they evict us or search our apartments?

Calm down. What would they find?

After showering, I tied a towel around my waist and collected my dirty clothes from the bathroom floor. And then I noticed a smell.

Sniffing my laundry, I pressed my shirt collar directly beneath my nostrils, the odour of perfume strong. Francis's perfume. She'd buried her head into my neck, kissed it, before moving to my mouth. And ten minutes earlier, Lisa put her head in exactly the same place.

Why is he home a day early? And why has he gone straight for the whisky bottle? Something has happened.

I'm watching through the kitchen window. As part of my daily routine, I walk up the hill at the rear of their house. I always like to ensure they're still there, some paranoia they might just up and leave one day and I'll never be able to find him again.

It's difficult to see too much from here, but I want to keep a safe distance. All I need is to see them to satisfy my curiosity, but I still see enough to know who's who and what they're doing.

I'm cross with Matthew anyway. It's a week since WPC Wright called him about Mother and I bet he has done nothing about finding out which care home she's in. You would have thought he'd have some compassion and want to know if she's okay. Well, she isn't okay, and he needs to see for himself. It's what I expect and what I demand. We're never going to reconcile if he won't accept he's family.

He's knocked that whisky back in one go. Bloody fool and his reliance on alcohol. That's one thing I should have made him stop doing when he lived at home.

Wait. Is he crying? Damn it for being so far away. But he's keeping his back to Lisa and now he's rubbing his eyes.

Whatever's wrong, my darling?

Finally, he steps over to Lisa, and they are hugging each other. It makes me feel ill just watching them, although I can't peel my eyes away. There is definitely something going on. He's been acting strange for a while, but this is taking it to another level. He's come home a day early, for heaven's sake, and I'm sure he was upset a moment or two ago.

No, that's it. This weekend I need to let myself in, find his set of keys and get them cut so I know I've got his apartment key too. And then on Monday morning, I'll get on the train, follow him to work and find out once and for all what is going on in his secret life in Earl's Court.

12

LISA

THE WEEKEND DRAGGED, feeling more like an entire bloody month. It didn't help that Matt worked from home on Friday, the day after his unexplained return. He'd made a mistake and obviously mixed up his days, but what could possibly have happened to get his mind in such a state? His erratic behaviour showed no sign of diminishing, but to forget what day of the week it was akin to an early onset of dementia. At first, I contemplated he'd suspected being watched again, or perhaps the phone call a few days prior was the catalyst. Nevertheless, the aroma on his shirt told me all I needed to know.

He phoned his boss, John Brookes, early on Friday and explained he wanted to work from home, citing a domestic issue the night before. During the day, I asked why he couldn't work remotely more often, but he soon dismissed the idea, claiming he would need special dispensation from his boss. Of course, it was bullshit, but how could I prove it?

Finally, Monday arrived, and Matt left early for a two-day property conference in Birmingham. He didn't want to go, believing it a complete waste of his, and the company's time. But John insisted they were represented, and Matt drew the short straw. It meant Matt wouldn't return to his apartment until Tuesday evening and was the perfect opportunity for me to investigate his instability. After searching through his bank statements, I made a call to the housing agency he paid monthly and acquired the address. Finally, I knew where he lived.

So, George and I set off for London in the back of Tom and Hannah's car. They were adamant they should come along, primarily for my safety, but I knew of their intrigue into Matt's personal life, especially Tom. Perhaps I'd told them too much, but I found it nigh on impossible to cope on my own. My anti-anxiety pills could only handle so much, and if Matt would never open up, I needed to confide in somebody.

Tom observed every speed limit to the law and would forever allow cars to exit junctions or turn in front of us. It grated as I just wanted to get to London, see where Matt lived, and return home. Occasionally, I noticed Tom peering at us in his rear-view mirror, and after a while, it made me uneasy, particularly when I believed he'd been looking at my chest.

He's just checking behind him. You know what a careful driver he is.

Kicking myself for being over-sensitive, I knew I needed their help much more than they appreciated. I also realised it would be a long journey for George and I hoped the momentum of the car would enable him to sleep the majority of the way.

Desperately, I tried to relax, but couldn't shake the feeling Matt would somehow know where we were heading, even if he couldn't possibly have an inkling. Allowing myself a further glance at Tom in the mirror, I sighed with relief as he concentrated on the road ahead.

Finally, we arrived in London, and after Tom located a parking space nearby, Hannah and I found ourselves outside Matt's apartment in Earl's Court. The realisation hit me of where we actually were.

What am I doing here?

The building didn't look much, but he had mentioned the exterior was a little shabby, in addition to the communal areas inside. It's one thing he divulged, giving in to my incessant questioning. I lost count of how many times I asked if I could visit, but he always dismissed me, declaring there was nothing to see and it was just a place to crash out during the working week. His behaviour, as well as the unmistakable signs of another woman, told me differently.

Forcing myself to pick up courage, I retrieved a large letter from my oversized handbag and stood outside the communal entrance. Hannah held onto George, and although I realised that could be a problem, I at least had an alibi. Tom remained in the car, at my request. We didn't all need to go charging in.

After what felt like an eternity, somebody appeared from behind us and nodded a 'hello' before placing her key in the lock.

"Mind if I deliver this to number four-oh-three?" I asked politely, stepping forward whilst holding the envelope aloft. The elderly lady stopped and turned to face me. She looked me up and down, immediately putting me on edge.

"Number four-oh-three, did you say?"

"Yes. Four-oh-three. Is that a problem?"

The way she said 'number 403' made the hairs on my arms stand on end. She knew the occupant. "I can take it up for you," she declared with a sudden air of authority. "I happen to live just across the landing."

Shit. I hadn't expected that response. "Erm, thank you, but it has to be delivered by hand, and with all due respect, I have to ensure it reaches the correct address personally."

She appeared offended and eyed the envelope suspiciously. "Well, he's not in. He'll be at work."

"Oh, yes, I know that. I can let myself in. I'm from the letting agency. I just need to put it inside so I know he gets it."

Showing her my key, I soon realised she still wasn't finished.

"Then why don't you have a key to the front door? And why do you have a small child with you?"

Nosy fucking bitch.

"I forgot the other key, okay? And I'm not supposed to be working today, so I have my mum and son with me. Now, will you please let me in? I have a lot to do."

Her reluctance was almost palpable, but she realised she had little choice in the matter. Leaving Hannah and George at the bottom, I followed the woman upstairs with a nervous glance over my shoulder. Once we reached the fourth floor, she led me to number 403.

"It's this one," she said, nodding. "Do you need me anymore?"

"No thanks. I'm more than capable of opening a door on my own."

She tutted her disapproval, and I watched as she stood outside her own apartment. Matt had mentioned a neighbour who revelled in gossip and I discerned it must be her. Almost in slow-motion, she removed her key from her handbag before looking back at me. My hands shook as my temper rose by the second.

"Do you want me to help you open your door?"

Again she tutted loudly before finally letting herself in. But she didn't close the door completely. I thought how useless she would be at playing hide-and-seek.

"Is there something else?" I asked. Without replying, she shut the door with a click, but I knew she would be standing on the other side, listening intently. Quickly, I pulled a pair of latex gloves from my handbag and let myself in.

Matt was right. The apartment was indeed nicer on the inside than the exterior suggested. However, it could have been much better laid out, and it lacked a female touch. An enormous television, mod cons and gadgets everywhere. It was a bachelor pad, a home from home for Matt. The perfect place to shack up with whomever he desired. And my suspicions were confirmed as soon as I entered the kitchen. Two used wine glasses stood next to the sink, both containing the tiniest dregs of red wine. Upon closer inspection, I spotted traces of lipstick around the rim of one of them. Turning to the dishwasher, I silently prayed it hadn't been switched on. Yes! Why was I congratulating myself? Two dirty plates, two knives, two forks, two of every bloody thing. With my anger increasing, I scrambled for the bin, promptly faced with empty silver food cartons. Chinese or Indian? Matt preferred a curry, so I guessed the latter. I wasn't going to fucking sniff them, was I?

With my blood boiling, I cursed myself for not bringing my medication along. I needed to get it over and done with, so returned to the lounge before my eyes were drawn to what I feared the most, the bedroom.

Should I leave it at this? Isn't this enough evidence already?

I began the dreaded walk towards the closed door. Surely they weren't in there? No, as the nosy bitch across the landing had said, 'He'll be at work.'. It struck me he might be with the cow at that precise moment, at the conference in Birmingham, discussing house prices or whatever the hell he did for a living.

With an outstretched arm, I gave the door a push and allowed it to swing effortlessly open. After two or three more delicate steps, I found myself inside and instantly felt my stomach churn.

The bed was rumpled, unmade and the duvet slung to one side. The sheets were creased and both sets of pillows were indented. But the thing that made me struggle to hold down my vomit was the packet of condoms on the small bedside table.

Running over, I grabbed the tiny box and hurled it across the room. The remaining contents spilt over the bed and onto the floor. "Bastard!" I shouted, immediately regretting raising my voice.

I grabbed the condoms and replaced them in the packet. A door clicked outside, and I instinctively knew who it was, no doubt my swearing not meeting her approval.

"Hey, you," I said to the crack in the door, one foot propped behind me. Her door opened ever so slightly. "Yes, you. Get out here, now."

The confidence of the nosy neighbour evaporated before me, but I was conscious she still wanted to pry. She was one of those people who just couldn't help themselves. Tentatively, she stepped outside her apartment whilst keeping her fingers wrapped around the door handle, ready to dart from the crazy woman with the made-up job from the made-up letting agency.

"What is it?" she asked, lacking any of her previous cockiness. I needed to calm down or she wouldn't be any help at all.

"Erm, sorry to bother you, and sorry I shouted, but I'm angry as I believe my client may have someone staying in here with him. It's a lease in just his name, you see, and if he has somebody else living here, he needs to declare it to both the agency and the council. He's paying single residency tax and gets further reductions off his heating as well."

I was more surprised by my fast thinking than the woman standing in front of me. I'd no idea if you got discounts for heating, but I knew from living on my own that I got twenty-five per cent off my council tax bill. The nosy cow regained some energy. After all, this was prime gossip time. She took a step closer, allowing the door to shut behind her. She spoke in a lower voice, determined to keep the conversation between the two of us.

"It's her," she whispered, pointing towards another door.

"Eh? Who's her?"

"Her. Number four-oh-four. Francis Baker is her name. They often sneak into each other's apartments. They're at it like rabbits. And you should have heard the noise coming from there last week."

What kind of noise? Do I want to know? Hold on, last week? Thursday night?

Yet again, I felt bile rise from somewhere deep in the pit of my stomach, but I needed to stay strong.

"Are you sure? So they're not living together as such, just having some kind of affair."

My voice faltered on the last word.

"Oh, yes. Ever since he moved in. But it's only now and then, when it suits, if that makes sense? I'm going to report them to the police."

The police? What the hell have they done wrong?

"Hold on," she said, taking a bundle of keys from her apron pocket. Making light work of the sheer amount of metal on the ring, she unlocked Francis's door.

"Not now," I said, improvising. Offering to buy her a coffee, I implied I needed more information, but it would be best to get away from the apartment in case one of them returned. She looked as though all of her birthdays had arrived at once and quickly disappeared to fetch a coat and handbag. With a quick glance over my shoulder at number 404, I promised myself to come back later to see Francis Baker.

The following evening, in our own kitchen, I opened a bottle of wine and poured Hannah and me a generous measure each.

"Cheers," I said, clinking her glass.

After a good chat and a subsequent refill, the sound of my mobile phone ringing from the living room interrupted us mid-flow.

"I'll have to take that. Won't be a minute."

Hannah raised her drink and smiled widely. I think she was pissed after one and a bit glasses.

"Hi, darling," I said, immediately regretting my enthusiasm.

"Hi, somebody's in a good mood."

"Yeah, sorry. Hannah's popped round and we're having a glass of wine." The sound of a car in the background diverted my attention. "Is that traffic I can hear? I take it you've got back from the conference?"

"Yes, yes. The conference was boring and I've been counting down the hours to get back. I'm outside the apartment block now. A police officer just stopped me to tell me something."

"Oh, right," I replied, biting on my bottom lip whilst contemplating fetching Hannah for support.

"Yeah. You'll never guess what's happened."

Bet I can.

"Go on." His newfound enthusiasm scared me.

"A woman fell down the stairwell in our apartment block yesterday afternoon. Killed instantly, apparently."

"Really?"

"Yeah. And it's someone I know."

I'm sure it is.

"Who?"

"It's that nosy bitch from across the landing."

13

WHERE ON EARTH IS HE? *It's early Monday morning, and Matthew always takes the seven thirty train to London, but there's no sign of him. All of this on top of him arriving home a day early last week. Has he left his job?*

Well, I'm still going, anyway. I'm not travelling to see him in particular, even though I do like it when we ride on the same train. The last time we did, he walked up and down the carriages, convinced somebody was watching him. Then he left his laptop on the seat outside the station. Luckily, I handed it in. But now I'm disappointed he isn't here. Oh well, I've got the keys. He left them in the usual place when they went out over the weekend, so I got them all cut and now I have the full set so I can let myself in without fear of anybody catching me; not that they will. I'm far too clever for that.

Finally, I arrive in London, and after taking the underground to Earl's Court, I cannot believe what I'm seeing. That's Lisa, standing on the pavement outside Matthew's apartment block, and she's carrying George. And if I'm not mistaken, it's that nosy neighbourhood watch bitch with them. She's pushing George's empty buggy.

I've done some further research. Can you blame me? That Hannah and Tom are invariably around their house. So, I made some polite enquiries, asking who they are and the woman in the pub was most helpful. Sophie is her name. Nice lady. I'm surprised Matthew hasn't tried it on with her yet. Well, apparently, this Hannah and Tom have always been the neighbourhood watch coordinators, and although I'm not sure what that actually entails, I realise it makes them incredibly nosy in everybody else's affairs. Sophie told me as much. She doesn't like them.

Anyway, I can't let them bother me, not after I've travelled all the way to London. I'll just have to be patient, something I've become really good at.

What's that? Lisa's passed George to her friend and is holding an envelope in her hand and talking to an old woman. This is getting weirder by the second. What *is* she doing? Lisa looks agitated until finally, the woman opens the front door and allows them all inside. The nosy bitch stays with George whilst Lisa disappears upstairs with that old woman.

Now I want to follow them, but I doubt there's much room inside. No hiding places. This isn't what I planned today. It isn't supposed to be about her. This is about me finding out where Matt lives and what his apartment is like. I need to know everything about him.

Wait! Lisa's coming back out with the same woman and she takes George from her friend, puts him in his buggy and the three of them walk off, leaving whoever it is waiting outside. What is going on?

Ten minutes later, they're back. After a few words, the four of *them start walking towards the shops. Well, intrigue has got the better of me, so, keeping a safe distance, I decide to follow them.*

The two older women sit outside one of those Costa cafés with George in his buggy, whilst Lisa goes inside. There is a spare table next to them. Quickly, I pull my hoodie over my baseball cap, tuck my jet-black hair up inside, cross the street with my head bowed and grab a chair so my back is to them. Fortunately, the table hasn't been cleared and I snatch one of the purple printed cups and drag it in front of me. I hold on tight as a member of staff arrives and clears the rest of the empties away. She's looking at me suspiciously, so I offer her a sarcastic smile before taking a sip of my newly acquired drink. The coffee is stone cold, and I gag as I allow a tiny amount to trickle down my throat. Still, it's enough to make the young girl leave me alone. Oh, how clever I am.

I'm in luck. Lisa sits directly behind me, leaving the old woman closest to George. I allow myself a quick glance over my shoulder and see he's asleep. Once the old woman says thank you for her drink, Lisa scrapes her chair forward and begins to talk. I can just make out what she's saying, and her opening line almost makes me choke.

"So, my client, Matthew Walker, has been having intimate relations with his next-door neighbour? What did you say her name was again?"

'Intimate fucking relations'? What the hell does that mean? And 'my client'; he's your fucking partner. Why are you calling him your bloody client?

Lisa didn't ask politely, and I can tell from her voice she is livid.

"Francis Baker is her name." The old woman is much calmer. She sounds as though she's loving her own importance. "She lives at number four-oh-four, next door to your client, if that's what you want to call him."

The old lady laughs, adding to Lisa's anger.

"Okay, he's not my client. He's the father of my child and we live together in a village west of here. Does that satisfy you?"

"Hey, don't take it out on me. It's not my fault they're at it like rabbits."

Lisa goes quiet. I so wish I could spin my chair around and study her face. Maybe it resembles mine, full of disappointment and rage. How could Matt do this to me, to us? I need to ask this old woman questions of my own and see how true it is. Could she just be a jealous old busybody, keen on stirring up trouble? Perhaps she's made a pass at Matthew, or he's pissed her off in some other way, and now she's set on revenge, trying to make his life hell in return?

I've heard enough. I already hate the old woman, but I can come back for her later. She'll be easy to manipulate. Maybe I'll push her under a car or something, fabricate it to look like an accident. She doesn't deserve to live anyway, gossiping old bitch. Standing up, I keep my back to the now silent table and walk away quickly, towards the apartment block.

Once I arrive, I take one last glance over my shoulder and fumble with the set of keys in my hand until I find the right one to gain entry. It's quiet in here, warm and stuffy. After taking a quick look up the stairs, I slowly make my way up to the fourth floor. My anger is threatening to boil over and I realise I need to keep my emotions under control.

Number 401, 402, there, number 403. That's his apartment. And next door, number 404. Isn't that where the old woman said this Francis Baker lives?

Cursing for not knowing which key is for what door, it takes several attempts to find the right one, but I'm in his flat, and it's exactly what I expected. All mod cons, a huge television — he always did like a big TV — and barely any pictures or photographs to be seen. It needs a feminine touch, so why hasn't this Francis tart offered to help if she's so bloody fantastic?

His dishwasher door is open, the bottom tray pulled out. There's *two of everything in there; plates, knives, forks. And on top are two wine glasses and one has got lipstick around the rim. I want to pick it up and throw it against the wall. Tiny pieces of glass all over his lovely little bachelor pad kitchen. And then I'll make her walk bare-foot across it, crunching the fragments into the soles of her feet until there are trails of blood and chunks of skin everywhere.*

Keep it together.

How can I keep it together? I've waited a year, been patient, and all this time he's been screwing some slapper in his pristine little shitty apartment block. Imagining him with Lisa is bad enough, but at least she is helping to raise his child; for now.

His bedroom door is open too. He never left the bedroom door open at the family home.

As soon as I step inside, I spot the packet of condoms on the bedside table. I take them out, count them, before stuffing them back into the container. And now a click of a door on the landing outside.

Slowly, I walk through his apartment. Listening intently, I open the door an inch or two until I can see outside. There is no move-ment, no sound.

Then I notice number 404, and the door is slightly ajar.

Clicking Matt's door shut behind me, I remove my hoodie and baseball cap before untying my hair. It falls loose, long, and halfway down my back. It's jet-black and shiny, the way Matt loves it.

Clearing my throat, I stand directly outside Francis Baker's apartment. I glare at the number '404' until I pick up enough courage to knock.

Tap, tap, tap.

There, you've done it. No turning back.

My heart is thudding.

Keep it together.

Knock, knock.

This time louder and I'm amazed as the door opens ever so

slightly. It's eerily quiet. Slowly, I push it further ajar, trying to see inside.

"Francis Baker?" I ask. Still no sound.

Gingerly, I step inside.

"I'm a friend of Matthew Walker. Do you mind if I come in?"

14

MATT

ALMOST TWO WEEKS after my nosy neighbour met her untimely demise, I found myself on the train ride home again. Despite all my best intentions to start afresh, I'd drifted back into the familiar uneasy state of mind; pensive, disillusioned and often scared. Having barely slept since, my thoughts always wandered back to the same people: Francis, Claudia, Melissa, Tracy, and dare I add, Amelia.

As I walked into the house, the sound of authoritative voices seeping from the kitchen threatened to submerge me. I hadn't seen or heard from Francis since our infamous argument. She'd gone away, I *knew* it.

'...*Get out of my apartment, Matthew Walker. And don't ever come back...*'.

Perhaps she'd be the one who never came back?

Tentatively, I stepped along the hallway, conscious

that the talking had stopped and I anticipated all eyes would be upon me as soon as I came into view.

The sight of two police officers took my breath away. Propping my arm against the doorframe to steady myself, I realised how unnatural I looked. Lisa noticed too and her eyes narrowed, adding to the guilt which threatened to engulf me. Had one of the officers noticed as well?

"Expecting somebody else, sir?"

I shot Lisa a look; was I looking for sympathy or help?

"Sir?"

"Erm, no. Sorry. I wasn't expecting anybody. What's all this about?"

My eyes hadn't left Lisa's and the expression across her face informed me she felt just as uncomfortable. Quickly, I crossed the room, kissed her on the cheek, and clung to her side. One of us was shaking, maybe both.

"Where's George?" I asked, desperate to sound as natural as possible. Lisa replied in a slightly high-pitched voice.

"He's in the living room, playing with his train set."

"I'll check on him, say hello…"

As soon as I take a stepped forward, the same officer spoke again, holding his hand aloft. "That won't be necessary, sir. Your partner has seen to him, haven't you, Lisa?"

Lisa nodded. I thought she might be sick.

"Tea, coffee?" I asked, my hands shaking as I picked up the kettle.

"No, thank you. We're just here to chat with you about your neighbour in Earl's Court. It won't take long."

Francis?

I tried to buy myself a few moments to steady my racing heart.

"How well did you know Claudia West?"

I sighed heavily, replacing the kettle. They're here to talk about *her*, not Francis.

"Are you okay, sir? You seem somewhat nervous."

Turning and grabbing the back of a chair, I finally fixed my attention on the police officer. He glared at me in return.

"I'm fine. Yes, I'm fine. It's just a shock when you know there's been an accident so close to where you live, and then discover it's one of your neighbours. I guess I'm still a little shaken up, that's all."

They glanced at one another, unconvinced by my stuttering response.

"Yes, well, I can see you're somewhat traumatised by it all. With it all happening almost two weeks ago, you must have got on well with Miss West?"

"Miss West?" I paused. "Oh, yes, Miss West, my neighbour. No, not necessarily. She was often outside on the landing, so I would say hello now and then, but apart from that, I don't know her at all. I mean, *didn't* know her at all."

The other officer spoke for the first time.

"Then why are you so shaken, sir, if you don't mind me asking?"

Desperate for a whisky, I clutched the back of the chair. The whites of my knuckles protruding.

"As I say, I'm still a little shaken up. And I've had an incredibly tough week at work. To see two police officers in my kitchen when I eventually get home, I guess it's all kind of hit me at once. Can I ask why you're here, by the way? You're a long way from Earl's Court."

"We've been attempting to contact you all week, but you didn't return our calls. Not trying to avoid us, are you, sir?"

They laughed in unison. Lisa tried to join in, although she sounded pathetic.

"No, no, nothing like that." I floundered. "As I say, I've just been extremely busy at work."

The knowing look between them told me to shut up and stop digging myself deeper into the shit. I'd ignored at least four phone calls during the week and erased two voicemails without even listening. I knew it was stupid, but I couldn't face answering any more questions.

"So, you were at work a week last Monday, erm, let's see…" He flipped over a page in his notebook. "…between noon and four o'clock?"

My eyes darted from one officer to the other. Why were they asking me that? Aren't they the questions you ask when you're some kind of suspect?

"Yes, yes. I was at work. In Birmingham. You can ask my boss. John Brookes. I'll get you his number."

My rambling wasn't helping, and I sounded as guilty as sin.

"If you don't mind, sir. We just need to rule every-body out."

After fumbling with the keypad, I spun my phone around and let the officer take down John's contact details.

"Thank you, sir."

They turned to leave, and I finally allowed myself to relax. I gladly saw them to the door, Lisa following and clinging to me. But one of them paused and turned to face me again.

"There is one other thing…"

Of course there is.

"We believe you know a Miss Baker from next door at number four-oh-four."

Oh, God.

"Erm, yes. I know her. It's difficult not to know most people in the block."

Lisa tensed by my side, but I didn't have the courage to face her.

"You don't know where she is, do you?"

Both the officers glared at me. If I'd never set eyes on her in my entire life, they would still have made me feel incredibly guilty.

"No idea. Why, should I?"

"Just asking. She seems to have disappeared around the same time as Miss West died."

"I'm sorry. I really don't know."

Whether they believed me, I couldn't be sure. They exchanged another glance before one opened the door.

"Thank you both for your time."

"So," I called after them. "When you said you need to rule everybody out, what does that mean, exactly?"

Why have you asked them that?

The one who did all the talking took a step towards me.

"I don't think I'll be telling you anything that you won't be able to find out for yourself on the news or the internet. You see, we're not convinced it was an accident, sir."

"Oh?" I replied, in the form of a question. My heart was doing somersaults even though I knew what's coming.

"Yes. Miss West died from a broken neck…"

Oh shit.

"…which would be consistent with a fall from the top of the stairwell to the bottom."

There's a 'but', isn't there?

"But she also had a blow to the back of her head. And

it doesn't look as though that was sustained during the fall."

Nodding, I just wanted them to shut up and go away.

"Which can only mean it happened before."

My whole body shook as I walked to the end of the pathway to see them off our premises. Once we reached the gate, they stopped again and looked over my shoulder. Lisa had stayed inside — is that what they were waiting for? — and the officer spoke, so quietly I had to strain to hear.

"Do you really not know Miss Francis Baker as more than a *friend?*" he asked.

Realising they must have noticed how guilty I'd looked before, I silently thanked them for having the decency to ask me out of Lisa's hearing. Struggling to find my voice, I nodded instead.

With a knowing look at one another, the other policeman spoke up. "And when did you last see her?"

Straining my eyes and rubbing my forehead, I said it must have been on the Thursday night. They explained Francis's door had been left unlocked and some of her clothes appeared to be missing.

"Do you have any inkling where she might have gone?"

"I've no idea, sorry. As I say, she was fine the last time I saw her."

"That's not all…"

Shit.

"Forensics had a quick look around after they finished at Miss West's…"

Please go away.

"…and they've dusted for prints in there too. If she's left of her own accord, then it obviously doesn't matter, but until we can make contact, we need to keep all avenues open. Of course, it might mean nothing, but if you have been in her apartment, it would be in your interests to admit it, just so we can rule out your prints."

Once they left, I returned to the house and sat on the small wall by our porch. Closing my eyes, I took deep breaths, desperately trying to calm myself.

"Daddy!"

George made me jump. They were standing in the open doorway, Lisa hugging him tightly. How long had they been there?

"Hey, mate," I replied, relieving him from Lisa's grasp.

"Is everything okay?" Lisa asked, her arms now folded. I found it difficult to read her expression.

"Sure, why?" My focus remained on George, and I tickled his tummy to make him laugh.

"You seem very nervous, that's all."

You can talk.

"It's been a shock, okay? You don't see a dead body every day of the week."

Lisa walked to the kitchen, leaving me to carry George after her.

"You *saw* her?" Lisa said, retrieving two beers from the fridge.

Shit.

"Well, no. I didn't *see* her, but I saw the police tape the following day, and when I realised it was somebody I actually knew, well, I guess it kind of hit me."

She popped the top off one beer and passed it to me. I nodded my appreciation before taking a huge gulp. George watched me intently.

Lisa drank a generous amount of her beer too. I

didn't like her questioning me when she appeared to be just as apprehensive.

"Lisa?"

"Huh, huh?"

"Did they ask you anything else before I got home?"

LISA

Why would he ask me that?

Taking another long swig of my beer, it felt good, hitting all the right spots. I'd intended the conversation to remain within my remit, under my control, but the way he asked immediately put me on edge.

"The police? No, nothing. Why should they? I don't even know where your apartment block is." He looked sceptical, and I realised I was rambling. "Do *you* think her death is suspicious?"

He paused and gripped the neck of the bottle between his teeth. "I'm not sure," he eventually replied, releasing the bottle from his mouth. "To tell you the truth, I don't want to talk about it anymore. It's just a nosy old woman who has somehow got herself killed."

And what about the other woman in your apartment block?

It was agony trying to keep everything concealed. It still made me feel sick, ever since Claudia told me about those two sneaking into each other's apartments.

But could that be my fault?

Of course, I knew what kind of person Matt was. A womaniser, a drifter who'd spent his entire adult life hopping from one bed to another, so what did I expect? I'd been popping pills like candy from a jar, scared to be touched, keeping him at arm's length. I hadn't so much as allowed him to share my bed for the first few months, not until we found the house and I could finally see a future for the three of us.

My fault or not, it was all over. And there's no way he can know I visited his apartment. I left no clues. I even wore gloves. And I watched the news. His neighbour died on the stairwell before Matt arrived home, so she couldn't have told him anything about my visit, either. I checked his phone, and he didn't have her contact details stored; why would he? I asked her if she knew his number and, of course, she said no. I know she was telling the truth. The only thing I had to worry about was if any witnesses came forward who saw us walking along the street. But London was busy, and I made sure I remained a few feet behind her. Besides, I was with Hannah, and we chatted together.

Matt drained his drink and carried George through to the living room without saying another word.

Unable to help myself, I smiled and turned to the window. The way he'd acted when he initially saw the police officers standing in our kitchen told me all I needed to know.

It wasn't Claudia West who was playing on his mind; it was that slag at number 404.

15

MATT

THE WINE ALLOWED me to momentarily forget my troubles and I admit I had fun with Lisa. We drank outside and chatted and drank some more, followed by kissing and more laughing. After the police left, I spent some time alone with George. We ate off our trays in the living room and soon after, Lisa bathed George before putting him to bed. She seemed happier after the officers disappeared, somehow more upbeat, and suggested opening a bottle of wine and taking it outside to drink in the warm, late summer sunshine.

Neither of us mentioned the police, Claudia West, or my apartment in West London. As the alcohol worked its magic, I contemplated bringing Francis into the conversation and telling Lisa what I'd told the police. But each time it was on the tip of my tongue, I lost my nerve and talked about something else instead.

But as I say, it was a fun night, and we chatted and

laughed more than we had for an age. And we carried on in bed, but the talking turned to kissing, and the laughing was replaced by something much more intimate. If only things could have always been like that. Simple, everyday living, the way the majority of the population live their lives. I consistently defied convention, believing there is more to life than what we were taught in school or by our parents, who, to be fair, only passed on what their own parents had taught them and ad infinitum. But that evening, convention was exactly what I craved, and I promised myself to make more of an effort with Lisa. That night, Lisa was just what I desired.

However, the following morning, I woke with a raging hangover. Lisa's side of the bed was empty, but it felt warm to the touch, so I figured she'd gone to see to George. Reaching for my phone, I noticed a new message; an unknown number. Groggily, I held the mobile at arm's length and, as soon as I focused on the words, my heartbeat rose rapidly.

> Hello, Matthew. It's Melissa here. I've got a new mobile, so you might not recognise the number. Anyway, I've been released from prison after they eventually realised I did nothing wrong. Andrew has admitted to everything, so I'm hoping my darling Tracy will be out soon too. Won't that be nice for all of us? Can I ask you a huge favour, Matthew? I would love to see you again and I have something really important to ask. Come to think of it, I'm not asking you to come and see me. I'm telling you to. Looking forward to it already. Love, Melissa

"George is still asleep. What's that you're reading?"

I hadn't heard Lisa walk in. She carried two mugs of steaming coffee and placed one on my bedside table. With a smile, she walked around to her side before climbing back in.

"Just the news." I lied, turning my screen off and placing the phone upside down next to my drink.

"Anything interesting happening?"

She knows you're lying.

"Erm, no, nothing of interest."

Sitting upright, my head throbbed and I slurped the boiling hot beverage. Lisa tutted her disapproval.

"There must be *something* happening?"

Why is she doing this?

"Why don't you look for yourself if you're so interested?"

Lisa smirked before sipping her drink, followed by an exaggerated 'ah' sound.

LISA

He was such a lying bastard. Reading the news. He never reads the news. I doubt he even knows who the prime minister is. So what *was* he looking at? Reading a text or composing one himself? I knew I could no longer trust him, not that I ever could. But the night before helped. I had fun, and I know Matt did too. Outside on the terrace was the most I'd heard him laugh for months, and he appeared genuinely content to be in my company. We clambered into bed, laughing and kissing whilst undressing each other. It brought back a lot of happy memories. I recollected the time at the hotel conference in Cheshire; the night George was conceived.

But then he was being nasty again. A snide little remark asking why didn't I look at the news for myself if I was so damn interested. I admit, I pushed him, enquiring what was happening in the world, but he had no answer. He may as well have said, 'I'm a born liar and I can't help myself'. A bit of honesty wouldn't go amiss.

You can talk, Lisa.

He caught me smiling to myself but didn't ask why. Instead, he slurped his coffee, knowing I hated it when he did that, before getting out of bed and making his way to the shower. I watched his naked body disappear, wishing he would turn around and come back and join me. The sound of the water running informed me that would not happen, and I begrudgingly got up again to see to George.

Once downstairs, I flicked the kettle on and remembered Matt asking if the police had asked me anything else before he returned home. I'd lied and said, of course not. But they had. They'd asked me if I knew of a Francis Baker. I felt the blood drain from my face as I told them I'd never heard of her. When I questioned what it was in connection with, they told me she lived next door to Matt but had gone missing, along with some of her clothes.

"Maybe she's gone on holiday, or to visit somebody."

"Yeah, maybe," one replied. "But we need to rule her out of our enquiries."

That made my heart skip a beat.

"Enquiries?"

"Yes. It may all be totally coincidental, but with Claudia West's freak accident and her immediate neighbour going missing, we have to keep an open mind."

He air-quoted *freak accident*, again implying they didn't believe it was any such thing.

I kept telling myself I'd done nothing wrong, and that's the truth. Well, kind of the truth. I went to their apartment block, and I spent time with Claudia West. But I'd been careful.

As the police left, Matt showed them to the garden gate, but he didn't know I'd collected George and sneaked behind the front door to listen. They asked him again if he knew Francis Baker, and he reluctantly admitted to it. Not that he had a choice, especially when they said they'd dusted her apartment for prints.

Dusted for prints.

That's what they do at a crime scene. I allowed myself a pat on the back, as I'd had the foresight to wear gloves. You can never be too careful.

As the kettle boiled, I looked out of the window, along the garden and to the patio where we sat laughing the night before. There were two empty wine bottles. Contemplating collecting them and putting them in recycling, another thing crossed my mind.

'You don't see a dead body every day of the week…'.

Why did he say that? Had he seen Claudia's body, or was he talking about Francis? In either event, he let it slip and he tried to stammer and stutter his way out of it, babbling about police tape or something. So, did he see a body? Obviously, I meant lately. Matt had seen dead bodies before. We both had. But he was in Birmingham, at a conference. He was confident enough to give the police the contact details of John Brookes, eradicating his involvement.

But Matt was so bloody cunning and secretive.

Then again, aren't we all?

My blood has been boiling for two weeks now. Ever since I visited that bloody apartment. Claudia West and Francis Baker. Well, they've got exactly what they deserve. But I don't care about those two. I can't even shed a tear for either of them. Sometimes, I have to stop myself from laughing, the way that nosy bitch flew down the stairs. I can still imagine her bones cracking as she fell like a rag doll.

And Francis Baker has gone too, and now that she has, Matthew is my problem.

Last night, I followed him home, and about ten minutes later, two policemen came out. What were they doing there? That doesn't matter, though. I have no worries as far as they are concerned. It was what happened later that really irked me. On top of finding out about him and that Francis. I now believe he and Lisa are getting close again. You see, they were in the garden; I think around seven o'clock. George would have been in bed, and they sat outside, drinking wine, and a lot of it. I don't like Matt drinking. I never did. Alcohol is very bad for you. Fortunately, my family banned it in the house, which used to annoy him, but that's his tough shit. Doesn't he know what damage it does to your brain and your body? All those different cancers. I don't want Matt to go that way. I remember when Graham used to reward Matthew with a bottle of beer if he helped in the garden or chopped up some wood for the family fire. Matt used to pull a face behind Graham's back, and I always thought that was really cruel and ungrateful.

Anyway, why do I keep digressing?

Yes, they were drinking wine and laughing and talking and kissing. I was crouched down behind their garden fence, so close I could almost touch them. And he was saying how much he wants to start afresh, put everything behind them. And Lisa agreed and giggled and kissed him more. They kissed so loudly I could hear their lips and mouths touching each other. I thought I might be sick.

I bet Lisa wanted to bring up the subject of Francis and I know Matt would have been dreading her doing so. That made me laugh, both having their own little secrets. But I know the most. I'm aware they are keeping things from each other and that may help me.

And I'm also furious Matthew hasn't contacted Mother. She wants to see him again, but he's pretending he doesn't know. Does he honestly not realise what this family is all about? After all this time, you would have thought he would have learnt. I'll send a message from her phone later. That might make him understand he can't just ignore us.

Eventually, they stopped drinking and kissing, but it didn't stop there. He asked her if she wanted to go to bed, have an early night. She giggled and said she'd love to. And now I've had enough. Had enough of being Little Miss Nice. Had enough of tiptoeing around him, making sure he's okay and ensuring baby George is being brought up correctly. One day, he will comprehend why I must take my time, why I can't just spring out in front of him and say 'ta-da, I'm back darling. Let's start all over again. You, me, George. Just like old times'. But I can't, not yet, although it won't be long. The problem is, he can't keep his grubby little hands to himself. If only he realised I'm his guardian angel, albeit from a distance, allowing him to lead his life whilst guaranteeing he'll come to no harm. And I always believed I only need to bide my time, wait a little longer, and he will realise that he belongs to me, belongs to the family.

But as I say, I've had enough of being Little Miss Nice.

16

MATT

EVER SINCE IT ARRIVED, I kept reading the same message over and over. Even as a text, I found it difficult to comprehend Melissa could be so malicious. For all her faults, and there were plenty, she always spoke well and politely, and the threat sounded somehow alien.

'*…I'm not asking you to come and see me, I'm telling you to…*'

And could the news they might release Tracy be true? I knew they had downgraded her, but released? Maybe I should call DCI Small and get an update. I cursed the time we asked not to be informed of any developments. Even if this WPC Wright let slip vital information, I would have still felt more comfortable hearing from the detective who was involved in the case all along. But wasn't that particular line of enquiries now closed? I doubted he had any knowledge of who may or may not be let out. However, DCI Small reassured us if the day did arrive, we would be in no further danger. They electronically tag them and place them under some kind of licence, and they would be crazy to dare to come within miles of us.

He doesn't know them. They are crazy.

Graham's brother, Andy, would always serve a longer sentence than Melissa or Tracy, as he admitted to the majority of charges, but now he'd taken the blame for *all* the allegations. He kidnapped Lisa and threatened and blackmailed Francis. He even got physical with Francis, punching her, resulting in a black eye, as well as restraining her and bruising her arms. The truth was, or so I'd been led to believe, Melissa, Tracy and Amelia had all 'gone along' with these schemes rather than implement them themselves. And now Melissa was unwell, or so WPC Wright said, and was in a care home in Epsom whilst Tracy could be on the cusp of being let free too.

During the day, I hit *reply* to Melissa's text several times and composed my own message, before deleting it and starting over. The sound of the doorbell made me give up for good. Lisa had already informed me Hannah and Tom were coming over after dinner. Another reason the promise of a decent weekend had descended into the usual cacophony of deafening alarm bells ringing in my ears.

An hour later, I found myself sat in the local pub alongside Tom. His idea of leaving Lisa and Hannah to have a good gossip had enabled me to give his friendship momentary consideration. We were both nursing a large whisky and as Tom savoured his, I just wanted to neck mine and order a refill.

"Is everything okay?" Tom asked, continually spinning his glass between his fingers, whilst occasionally taking a delicate sip of his drink. "You know, with all that's going on?"

Do you really need to ask that?

"Sorry, what?"

Although I heard Tom perfectly well, if he hadn't added his usual 'you know', I may have given him a direct reply.

"Just asking if everything is okay? I mean, you seemed pretty convinced you saw someone up in the copse a few weeks ago, and now you've had this terrible incident inside your apartment block. You don't think your family has anything to do—"

"Whoa," I interrupted. "*My* family? That's all in the past, Tom. And I don't know how much Lisa has told you, but it's private, if it's all the same with you?"

Tom sipped his whisky and sighed outwardly. He smiled his appreciation at his choice of single malt. It was difficult to disagree he knew his stuff when it came to my favourite tipple, but I couldn't help but think the smile wasn't just for his gratitude towards the distillery.

"No, Matt, no. I'm not *blaming* you. You know, you have always been very fair in your assessment of whatever happened in your previous life. I'm talking about now. What happens next? You have a beautiful son and an adorable partner. Perhaps you should appreciate Lisa a little more."

Was he winding me up or was he making small talk for the sake of it? No doubt he found the situation as difficult as I was, unsure what to say whilst trying to find a common subject. Lisa, George and his neighbourhood watch duties exhausted the list and we covered all of those within thirty minutes of arriving at the pub. But why mention Lisa again? Not wanting to give him any satisfaction, I tried a different tack.

"You know what?"

I smirked to myself, pleased I got in a 'you know', even though it's unnecessary.

"What's that?" he replied, finally taking his eyes off his whisky tumbler. He momentarily appeared lost in his thoughts.

"I don't think I've ever been to your house. Well, I mean inside. I'd love to see your infamous whisky collection."

Tom returned to his drink, spinning it round and round between his fingers. I couldn't believe I was sitting in a pub with somebody as bloody boring as Tom Wells. Not many years ago, I would have been in my local with a few mates necking pints of strong lager whilst eyeing up anybody of the opposite sex who dared to enter the building.

"Yes. That would be grand. I'll get Hannah to organise something."

Silence ensued once again. Tom occasionally broke the emotional strain, either talking about a recent gadget he received from Amazon or a new Highland single malt he ordered online from the *Whisky Club*. In truth, I zoned out. After a while, I offered to take Charlie outside for his call of nature as Tom shifted his enormous backside to go to the bar to replenish our drinks.

"Are you sure? You, Matt Walker, take my Charlie for a walk?" Tom asked, faking the need to hold on to the table to stop himself from falling. He chortled heartily at his joke. I offered a token smile in return.

"My pleasure. Could do with cooling down. It's very stuffy in here tonight."

It wasn't stuffy at all. I just had to get away for five minutes. The boredom was exhausting and I struggled to conceal the yawns which were arriving at alarming intervals. But it wasn't only the apathy; I had a million thoughts preoccupying my mind and I was desperate for my own space. Charlie struggled to his feet and looked as though he couldn't believe it either when I tugged on his lead instead of his usual tubby master.

"Come on you. Let's go for a little walk."

The cool still atmosphere prickled my senses, immediately invigorating me. As I breathed in deeply, the taste of whisky filled my mouth before warming my chest as the air spiralled down.

"Ahh, Charlie, smell that. Doesn't it feel good?" Charlie continued to look at me. However, he knew where we were and what we were there for, and pulled on the lead, towards the road and across to the park. "Okay, okay. Hold on, fellow, I've never seen you move so fast."

Allowing the overweight canine to drag me across the deserted road, we reached the desolate and somewhat intimidating park. It was the first time I'd been there at this time of night, and I suddenly felt quite alone. The swings looked especially haunting, motionless and jet-black against the moon. Charlie obviously knew the score, and I let him off the lead to wander around sniffing and doing whatever he needed to do. Tom had given me a *poop bag* to pick up any mess, but the thought of that made my stomach churn, so I stuffed it in my pocket instead. As if he would come over and check.

After a few moments, I called Charlie, expecting him to return, just as he always did whenever Tom did the same. But Charlie didn't return.

"Charlie," I shouted, a little more nervously. "Come on, boy, let's go back."

Something caught my attention to the left. A swing appeared to move, ever so gently, swaying, back and forth, yet I couldn't feel a breath of wind.

A rustling sound from a nearby hedge. I spun to my right. "Charlie? Is that you?"

Suddenly, it went very dark. The moon, which had been in full view when we left the pub, disappeared behind thick clouds. A chill washed over me. Glancing over my shoulder, towards the pub, it looked somehow darker too. Apart from a solitary light at the far end, the car park entrance, it appeared closed, with no sign of life, inside or out.

"Charlie!" I shouted, spinning back to the park. "Come on!"

Something else caught my eye. Up past the silhouette of the climbing frame and swings, beyond the old football pitch and up towards the copse. *That copse.* A figure. Motionless. Arms by their side. The person looked distinctly female. Her long hair blew in the breeze. The gentle wind picked up some more and both swings swayed, now with more energy. Back and forth. Back and forth.

What the…

Another movement from the hedgerow to my left. My eyes strained in the pitch dark.

A bark.

Thank fuck.

Charlie came into view, faster than I'd seen him move before. He clung to my side, and as soon as I fastened his lead, he pulled me towards the road, back to where we started. His panting was erratic and I was scared he might have a heart attack. I allowed myself one quick look behind. The figure had gone, and the copse lay empty once more.

"It's okay," I said, stroking Charlie's head.

In one quick movement, he snapped his head backwards, opened his jaw and bit down on my hand.

"Fuck!" I screamed out. "Let go, you shit."

Grabbing my wrist with my spare hand, I pulled hard, trying to release the one stuck in his mouth.

"Let go you fat—"

"Charlie!"

It was Tom, standing at the side of the pub. Charlie took one look up, let go of my hand and bounded across the road to his owner. I stared after him, not only in relief that he let go but also at the pub. All the lights were on and a hub of noise escaped from the small open windows at the front.

Spinning around, whilst cradling my half-chewed hand, I looked back towards the copse. The moon lit up the entire park. The swings were motionless, and there wasn't a soul to be seen.

I've just followed them to the pub; Matthew, his fat neighbour and his equally fat dog. They're not walking very fast; probably as quick as that hound can go. No doubt they've force-fed him with a load more treats. Bloody thing will die of a heart attack soon. Maybe that's something I can help with.

Ha! I do make myself laugh. So cruel, yet I'm having such fun. Well, I was until I found out about Matthew and that Francis. And last night, that giggling and kissing in the garden with Lisa.

After they disappeared upstairs, I made myself sick by sticking two fingers down my throat. I stayed outside their garden until all the lights went out downstairs, and the lamp went on in their bedroom. 'They're undressing each other', I thought to myself. 'They're kissing and touching and... oh God... I don't even want to think about it.' And so I walked around the front of their house and made myself vomit over their wall, into a flowerbed.

The copse looks scary to some people, but it intrigues me. We always lived next to the woods, and they never scared me; scared none of us. Matt always used to ask about them, how far they go back and things like that. I could tell they intimidated him.

And now I'm standing in the copse, looking down the hill, beyond the park and at the pub. The noise from inside drifts up the slope. Jovial, raised voices escape from the small open windows at the front. Maybe I should go in? It's Saturday night and I'm guessing it's full. But what if it's one of those pubs where everybody goes quiet when somebody fresh opens the door? I can just imagine it, every single set of eyes on me. Maybe that's how I'll reintroduce myself. Ha! Yes. That will be fun.

Hold on, what's this? Matthew has just walked outside with that fat fucking mongrel. Where's Tom? Matt hates dogs. It's too late for me to move, but I don't care. He'll never be able to make out who I am from down there.

I whistle, a high-pitched sound from somewhere deep in my lungs. I didn't even know I could do that. The fat dog runs, well, I say 'run', I mean 'amble faster than normal'. Matt's struggling to hold on to his lead and now they're in the park and Matt lets the dog go, and it runs along the hedgerow, up towards the copse. It pauses and whines in my direction. I growl back, enjoying my game. I want him to come all the way up here so I can slit his fucking throat.

But now Matt's calling him. He looks as though he's swaying. He's staring directly at me, but the thick cloud makes everywhere go pitch dark and I lose him again.

There! The dog is back by his side. I whistle again and the dog grabs his hand. "Bite the bastard," I'm saying under my breath, trying to communicate with the canine. Ha! Matt is yelling out.

And then everything stops. Tom's calling Charlie. The cloud disappears and everywhere lights up again, as if somebody has flicked a switch. Quickly, I dart for cover and watch as the three of them disappear down the street.

Matt glances back one last time.

"It's started, darling," I whisper. "It's started."

17

MATT

"WHAT HAPPENED?" Tom asked, cradling his overweight dog as though I'd injected it with rabies.

"It bloody bit me. Look." Holding up my hand to the outside light, I couldn't believe my eyes. There was no blood, no teeth marks, just wet slobber dripping from my palm.

Tom turned away without another word and walked along the road in the direction of my house. Frantically, I checked my other hand, thinking I'd somehow got them mixed up. As expected, there was nothing to see.

"Hey, Tom. Wait up." He stopped in his tracks and Charlie obediently sat by his master's side, mocking me as I approached. "Honestly, I'm not making it up. Something freaked Charlie out in the park and he came bounding out of the dark and latched onto my hand. He was biting hard, seriously. I can't believe he hasn't drawn blood."

Tom let one of his pathetic laughs escape. "Charlie, *bounding*, are you sure, Matthew? You know what? Charlie hasn't *bounded* anywhere for years."

Looking down at the fat lump, I could understand how incredulous my story must have sounded, but I'd just been in the park and Charlie was definitely freaked out and he'd bitten hard on my hand. So why was there no blood? I couldn't even see any teeth marks. It made no sense.

The pub lights.

"You know when we were outside?" He nodded, pulling Charlie to his feet in anticipation of getting home. He'd obviously heard enough. Ignoring him, I continued regardless. "Did the lights go out in the pub? Just for a few seconds?"

He looked at me and then at the pub behind.

"Matt. I'm not being funny, but have you taken something? You know, some kind of drug or smoked some cannabis or whatever you youngsters do? It's why I changed my mind at the bar and didn't get us another drink. I think you've had enough already. In fact, I think you've been drinking far too much. Lisa told me so."

Oh, did she now?

Although momentarily delighted to be called a young-ster again, I could tell Tom was being deadly serious. It pissed me off he used Lisa as a continual subject to riddle me with guilt. But his face wasn't just full of accusation, he appeared genuinely concerned. Opening my mouth to respond, he cut me off before I can say a single word.

"Come on. Let's get you home. I think both you and Lisa are under a lot of pressure. Maybe you have been ever since you arrived in this village. I'd suggest laying off the Scotch for a bit."

As far as Tom was concerned, the conversation was over. He pulled on Charlie's lead and the dog put all his effort into getting his legs moving again. I'm sure he looked at me and chuckled in his own crazy dog world as if he knew we had our own little secret.

As soon as we stepped inside, I heard Lisa and Hannah laughing. They were in the kitchen, at the rear of the house. Charlie heard too and ambled off towards his other master's dulcet tones.

"You know, I'm guessing that's Charlie 'bounding' off again, eh?" Tom suggested, followed by another mock punch on my arm. It took all my effort not to step up to him and knock his bloody lights out.

"Yeah, I guess," I replied, suddenly desperate to be alone. Letting Tom go ahead, I studied my hand under the bright hallway light. Not a hint of a mark or indentation. I couldn't have made that up, could I? The pain was real, and I tried to wrestle my hand free from the grasp of Charlie's mouth. And the dog's saliva was left behind, so it must have been in his jaw at some point. And what about the figure in the copse, two months after my first *sighting* up there? It was definitely real. I'd seen it with my very own eyes. Hadn't I?

Shit, was I losing it? If I was an outsider looking in, I'd agree with Tom and deliberate if I was indeed taking illegal substances.

A figure. Motionless, arms by their side. The person looks unmistakably female. Her hair blowing in the breeze…

I'd been desperately trying to block out what I saw, or believed I saw, in the copse all those weeks ago. Believing they looked distinctly like Amelia, I still realised I had to blank it. Having nobody to mention it to, ironic really, because a couple of years prior it's just the thing Lisa and I would chat about on our rendezvous at the local café but then, I had to protect her from any such pretence. Maybe even safeguard myself too. I could see what it was doing to me and I was unable to stop it. Once I made my intentions clear with Francis, I thought I would finally move on. The police thought her disappearance as suspicious, but what did they know? She told me to get out of her flat and never come back, and now she'd gone. Some clothes were missing from her wardrobe too. I had nothing to worry about, and alongside Claudia bloody West, neither of them could testify differently. But what about the silhouette in the copse?

The hair, her height, her figure, her stature. Surely not?

It made no sense. Why wouldn't she let me recognise her? Contact me rather than keep appearing as some apparition. Was she waiting for an opportune time, but when *was* the opportune time? Was it because of Francis? I recalled the *person* on the train. Another *sighting* or a genuine observation?

Laughter from the kitchen brought me back to the present. Taking a deep breath, I reluctantly realised I had to join the others and pray I'd walk into the kitchen and find Hannah putting her coat on. No such bloody luck.

"Ha! Here he is," Tom mocked me. "The guy who Charlie almost licked to death."

The three of them laughed in unison. Hannah was crying, faking it like an imbecile, begging Tom to stop. It wasn't even that bloody funny.

"Whisky, Tom?" I asked, ignoring their little joke whilst ridiculing his suggestion that I cut back on my drinking. Squeezing past the pointless oversized table, I grabbed a tumbler, poured a generous measure and necked it in one. The laughter from behind stopped abruptly as if being operated by an on-off switch.

"What's wrong?" I asked.

"Don't you think you've had enough?" Tom spoke on behalf of all three, like a group of concerned grown-ups looking after a troubled child.

"I don't think I've had anywhere near enough, Tom."

Charlie growled, picking up on my aggressive manner.

"Maybe we should go," Hannah said, standing. "It's getting late."

Lisa shot me a look, but I had no intention of backing down. Instead, I poured myself another shot and took a seat at the table. I offered our neighbours a solitary nod as they bid me goodnight. Lisa followed them into the hallway and I could hear a muttering of voices. I didn't even attempt to listen in. No doubt Tom was advising Lisa to watch my drinking and filling her in with my incredulous tale of his ferocious dog and pub lights randomly switching themselves on and off. I was pleased I didn't mention the figure in the copse too. That's all I needed, a further grilling. I drained the whisky and poured another.

18

LISA

THE FOLLOWING TWO DAYS, I felt incredibly guilty. We should never have laughed at Matt like we did when they arrived home from the pub. As soon as I saw his face, I knew something was seriously amiss, but by that stage, Tom had made us howl with laughter with his impersonation of Matt being licked to death by Charlie.

Matt continually looked at his hand, turning it over and over, inspecting it. Is that where the dog supposedly grabbed him? I couldn't see anything, although Matt appeared convinced. But then my concern evaporated when he became so rude, pouring himself a large drink and knocking it back like that. What must our neighbours think?

Matt didn't even come to the front door to say goodbye, and Hannah took the opportunity to tell me how worried they were about Matt. Tom again suggested he'd been drinking too much and thought he might have been hallucinating when he took Charlie outside to the park.

"He believes this poor thing bit his hand." Tom patted his dog on the head, who reciprocated by rubbing himself against his owner's leg. "And then he asked me if all the lights had gone out, you know, in the pub."

"That's strange," Hannah followed her husband's lead by keeping her voice to only a whisper. "Why would he think that?"

Tom shrugged. To be fair to Matt, our neighbourhood watch friends appeared to be enjoying the exchange. Matt says they take their responsibilities too far and revel in the gossip and the opportunity to pry into everybody else's business.

"Do you think what happened in London has tipped him over the edge?" Hannah asked me, her hand resting on my arm, her face full of concern. "He wasn't exactly stable before, was he? And you know what I said to you during the week, Lisa? Please give it some serious thought."

With the sound of a chair scraping in the kitchen, Hannah and Tom quickly said their goodbyes and dragged a reluctant Charlie outside. After walking with them to the end of the footpath — I needed some air — I noticed Tom looking at me, just as he had in his car. He smiled, and I reciprocated out of politeness. Closing our gate, I returned indoors and shut the door with a bang. Matt was already in the living room, so I took the opportunity to tidy the kitchen in peace. When I returned, Matt was sprawled out on the sofa, stinking of booze and drifting in and out of consciousness. Fetching a spare duvet from upstairs, I laid it over him. He looked so tranquil, his eyes closed and his breathing regular. Kissing him on the forehead, I silently prayed the demons would allow him a peaceful night's sleep before praying the same for me.

On Monday morning, Matt returned to London. Summer seemed reluctant to let go, and it was a fine day with crystal clear skies and the sun still offering significant heat. Deciding to spend some time in the garden, I waited until George's mid-morning nap, put him in his buggy and wheeled him outside the front of our house. Positioning him in a shady spot, I fetched some garden tools from the shed and clipped away at the overgrown bushes. I've always found gardening therapeutic, and when I was married, I loved my moments of tranquillity outdoors in the fresh air. My ex-husband hated it, but he would forever be away playing golf, or whatever else he got up to, so I had plenty of time to myself. Gardening allows my mind to drift, to dream of better times, something I'd contemplated so much during the past year.

I'd barely seen Matt the day before; his hangover was reluctant to let go, so he spent most of it in bed. When he did eventually surface, he made it quite clear he didn't want to talk about the previous evening. It felt as though I was caught between a rock and a hard place. I wanted to know everything that was going on inside that mind of his. After all, it took a visit to London to discover what he'd been up to the previous few months but he was still obviously traumatised. He hadn't mentioned the sighting up in the copse since the day it allegedly happened. Could that be what he was bottling up? But surely one thing wouldn't be enough to leave him so unsettled? Yes, he'd had the shock of his neighbour falling, and then his 'bit on the side' vanishing. But he couldn't stand that Claudia woman and surely he could see we were all better off without him having an affair behind my back? Come to think of it, he didn't appear too upset about Francis moving out. That pleased me. So what else could it be? If only he would open up and discuss what was going on. Or perhaps I didn't really want to know? My medication helped me cope and the opening of old wounds would inevitably have me spiralling back into the dark places that I so hoped I'd left behind for good.

Hannah and Tom couldn't believe what I was putting up with, but they have never been in my shoes. Jeez, I can't think of anybody who has ever gone through what I have. So how could anyone suggest they know best or offer advice?

"Lisa, you can't stay with him," Hannah suggested after the trip to his apartment. "He's been having an affair whilst you raise his child. And his behaviour is so erratic."

But what did she know of *my* thoughts? What was continually reverberating through my head? I'm not stupid. Anybody who came across my story would yell at me to leave, calling me all the names under the sun for even contemplating staying put. But what do they know? Have they been tied up in a shack for months? Have they had their child taken away at birth? And who rescued me from all of that? Yes, Matthew. People make me sick, judging others when they have no comprehension of what's going on beneath the surface. Just take a moment to scratch at the edges and see what you find. I'd been to hell and back, and so had Matthew. Despite his errors, and I knew there were plenty, he was a good man and a wonderful father.

Standing up to straighten my back, I noticed a pile of twigs and clippings on the ground beneath me; I couldn't even remember cutting the damn things off. Taking a moment, I glanced over at George and smiled to myself.

No, it wasn't that easy. Bollocks to Hannah pretending to know how I felt. Bollocks to everybody who judged me. I needed Matt, he needed me, and George needed us both. We were a team, despite all the flaws, and I was determined to get through it together. And it would get better, I'd make sure of that. Now that Francis was out of the way, it should be a fresh start. I doubted Matt had the energy for another fling. That's all it was, Lisa, a fling, despite Hannah calling it a bloody affair, and I doubted any *normal* woman would take him on, given the state of his mind and erratic behaviour.

Talking about his state of mind, I wondered if he could hold down his job for much longer. His boss didn't seem keen on him working from home a few Fridays ago, and Matt appeared worried after the call. He mumbled something about needing to keep him happy, but I knew Matt didn't care about the job. Perhaps now his fling was over and done with, he could look for something more local. Yes, why hadn't I thought of it before? There was nothing in London for him anymore. Would he be able to get out of his apartment lease? I've never rented, only owned my property in Ealing with my ex, and now we'd bought the house together, I have no comprehension of how a lease works. Yes, we rented in Scotland, but that was an Airbnb, or whatever they're called, and Matt organised all that anyway. Probably I could ask Hannah and Tom if they were aware of any local jobs. They knew everybody, so they were bound to hear news of people looking for help.

I felt a renewed spring in my step. The rollercoaster of emotions was unbelievable, but the pills helped level things out and keep me on the straight and narrow. I wondered how long I'd have to stay on them. The thought of not popping them made me shudder. I so wished Matt would try them too. The local doctor gave me a repeat prescription within seconds of reading my notes and said I didn't have to see him for another twelve months. Asking if there would be any long-term effects, he laughed and said not nearly as many as the short-term ones if I stopped taking them. *I'm pleased you find it so bloody funny,* I thought.

With another quick check on George, I gave pruning a break and instead decided to pull up some weeds along the front wall. The exercise and fresh air were helping, and I realised I should spend more time outdoors. The back garden required a lot of attention too. They weren't enormous spaces, but they were large enough to keep me occupied. Maybe I should ask Hannah if she'd like to visit the local garden centre with me?

"What the…"

As I knelt down, I put my hand in front to balance and immediately felt it squelch into something cold and sticky. The stench hit me at the same time. Slowly, I lifted my hand from out of the bedding plants and reluctantly turned it over. Yellow, gooey liquid dripped from my palm. There were little chunks of food interspersed. Loathe to inspect further, I parted the flowers with my spare hand. A few flies buzzed up from underneath, one in particular pissed off with me disturbing it, and it landed directly on my neck. Swatting at it, it didn't move, and I could feel a tickle as it crawled its way across the back of my head. And then another landed on my face, writing across my cheek, pursued by several more, buzzing around me, some landing in my hair.

Struggling not to retch at the vomit dripping from my hand, I stood up, swatting at the incessant humming around my ears. Quickly, I ran to George, grabbed his buggy, swung it around, and darted for the front door. Panic rose as I thought the flies might get to my baby too.

Slamming the door shut, I stepped to the mirror, expecting at least a hundred flies to be crawling silently through my hair, across my face and around my neck.

But there were none. Not a single bug. Just the stench of sick emanating from my right hand.

I didn't follow him to London today. I didn't feel the need, especially now that tart is off the scene for good. Come to think of it, does he have to go to London anymore? I can tell by his face, his demeanour, that he detests his job, so what are his reasons for wanting to be there during the week? I've overheard them saying he's a director, but it's only an estate agency, for goodness' sake, and with his experience, Matt can find a similar role anywhere. Yes, I need to stop him from venturing there altogether. It's tiresome getting on that train for all of us. I'm going to change it. I'm going to call his boss.

So, instead of following Matt to London, I'm watching the house. And what a lovely surprise. She's brought George outside into the front garden. But now where's she going? She's only left her precious baby boy asleep in his buggy and wandered off around the back. Anybody could walk past and snatch him. He's strapped into his pushchair, and it would take no effort at all to open the gate and wheel him away. Perhaps I should? Teach her a lesson that she's not the perfect bloody mother she believes she is. We all know who the perfect mother is, don't we? And talking of mothers, I know he hasn't replied to Melissa's text message yet. Does he think I'm bloody simple? He can't just ignore us, hope we disappear. But I happen to know he doesn't want that anyway. He's part of this family, and there's no letting go. It's why he came back here. Near us. Near the house. In search of the family and his future.

His lack of enthusiasm for contacting Melissa makes little sense. She wants to see him. She's told me so. In fact, she's desperate to, but she won't tell me why. And that annoys me too. We are supposed to be in it together, one extended family who look after each other. But Melissa is keeping secrets from me. I know she is. I have so much to do, so much to sort out, and I'm getting angrier by the day at the way people are treating me; as if I don't exist, as if I'm not important. Don't they all realise I'm the only important one?

Oh, hold on, Lisa's back, carrying some tools. Trust me to over-think things when Lisa left George all by himself. If she ever does that again, I'll grab him and run.

She's clipping a hedge now, and she actually looks as though she knows what she's doing. Is she a keen gardener? Hmm, that could be interesting. So many thoughts swirling through my mind. Oh look, she's smiling to herself, a sure sign that she's going crazy too. Shit. I'm smiling to myself as well. Then it can't be a sign of going crazy. Nobody could ever accuse me of that.

Lisa stops cutting the damn hedge, checking on George, before reverting to her precious gardening and kneeling behind the wall. Ha! Now what? She's standing up and is looking at her hand. Oh shit, that's my vomit! I'd forgotten all about it. But this is so funny. Look at her face. Is she about to throw up herself? And now she's swatting her hair, slapping the back of her neck. She looks fucking demented.

She's grabbed the buggy, spun it around and is darting for the front door. It shuts with a bang, and I so want to see her inside, panicking and rushing around like a deranged lunatic.

And to think, I've just made all that happen.

Oh, you are a clever girl.

19

MATT

ON MONDAY AFTERNOON, Lisa called me at work. I'd asked her not to bother me there unless it was an emergency. The sight of her name on my screen made me hit the green phone icon after a single ring.

"What's wrong?" A couple browsing the house listings looked towards me because of my raised voice. John glanced over too before walking across to the prospective clients, fixing on a smile.

"Take that in the back, Matthew," he whispered as he deviated by my desk, but Lisa spoke again before I had a chance to move.

"Have you been sick in our front garden?"

Is she for real?

"What did you just say?"

"I said have you been sick over our front wall, in the garden?"

Lisa's incredulous suggestion caused me to wonder if I

was even hearing correctly. I darted out of the office and through to the small yard at the rear of the building, the smoker's area, even though nobody smoked from our office. Perhaps I should have taken it up, it might have helped with my nerves.

"What did you just ask me?"

Lisa repeated the question, which I denied, although a slight doubt entered my head. Was I sick on the way home from the pub or did I sneak outside during the night after Lisa threw a duvet over me on the sofa? No. Admittedly, I drank far too much, but not enough to make me forget doing such a thing. Or could I have somehow blanked it from memory like some kind of coping mechanism? I'd seen somebody in the copse, the lights go out in the pub, and a dog apparently gnawing my hand, so why not throw up in the bushes to add to my delirium?

Half listening, Lisa explained she and George were out the front doing a spot of gardening when she put her palm in a pile of stale vomit. It made me retch to hear her recite her tale.

"And you're accusing me?" I eventually asked, both angry and extremely concerned as to who the culprit might be.

The figure in the copse.

"No. Oh, I don't know. Maybe it was just a gang of lads on the way home from the pub?" Lisa was backtracking. She believed it was me, or at least hoped it was. And her other theory was bullshit too, but she was desperately trying to advocate a viable explanation. Gangs of lads never used our village pub and I couldn't think of anybody else who would be so irresponsible.

It isn't irresponsibility. It's intentional.

"You obviously believe it was me, Lisa."

She hung up without another word.

Remaining outside, I gave myself a few moments to reflect. Lisa's tone annoyed me, more of an accusation than a question. But if it wasn't me, then who and why? My thoughts returned to the call I made to Epsom Police Station and the infamous WPC Wright. Somebody wanted me to contact Melissa. Could the same person be responsible and was the figure in the copse the connection? It was obvious what I needed to do. A combination of fear and confusion reigned in my mind again and I wanted to be anywhere else but stuck behind a stupid desk at work pretending to be interested in selling houses.

Ironically, later in the afternoon, my wish came true, even though it wasn't on my terms. Just after I locked the agency door to close for the evening, John popped his head around the entrance from his office cubicle.

"Matt?" His face told me all I needed to know. "Have you got a minute, please?"

LISA

Of course he denied it, although he didn't sound convinced. I wish I'd never left him downstairs on the sofa now. If he had been with me, I would have known if he had roamed in the middle of the night. However, even with all the medication, I've always been a ridiculously light sleeper and I'm convinced I would have heard the front door opening.

No, I didn't believe Matt did it, and I certainly didn't

believe my own bullshit that a gang of lads were responsible whilst walking home from the pub. Gangs of lads don't use the pub in the village. It was far too quiet for anybody of that age. So, who could it be? It's a respectable neighbourhood, with respectable residents. People don't just go around throwing up in each other's gardens. Do they? Could I relate it to the person who Matt spotted in the copse? And didn't he mention being followed on the train too?

Shit. Is somebody stalking him, stalking us?

Soon after I called Matt, I popped a couple more pills. George was wide awake, looking at one of his books at the table whilst I prepared a juice and an afternoon snack. Seeing him so content always had the desired effect, allowing me to relax and realise all might not be so bad in this world.

Who are you kidding? It's a living hell.

Matt wasn't happy when I called him at work either. He perpetually ordered me to only call him in an emergency. Goodness knows why. It's a bloody estate agent, and he hated working there anyway. Anybody normal would be pleased to hear from their partner to break up the monotony of the working day. But not Matthew. Him and his precious little second life where he escaped during the week. I thought of Francis. She wouldn't come back, but I wondered if Matt would have attempted to contact her. Wanting to resurrect what they had between them. Well, tough shit, Matthew, I don't think she'll be bothering you again.

A snap of a small branch, or maybe a twig, alerts me to someone outside. Then another breaking sound, a crunching underfoot.

Ignore it. It's nothing.

George dropped his juice container onto the floor and immediately whined.

Retrieving it, I placed it on the table, but as soon as my back was turned, I heard it crash to the floor again. He giggled, enjoying his little game.

Well, I'm not enjoying it.

Bending down to pick it up one last time, I told him I'd take it away for good if he threw it once more. But as I stood again, George stopped giggling and instead, a huge grin spread across his face. He stared straight past me, towards the window, before giggling uncontrollably.

My eyes widened, and I held my breath. Reluctantly, I turned to see what, or who, he was looking at, my hands trembling. I didn't want to, but George kept laughing, the onset of hiccups already disrupting his breaths.

But as my view of the outside world eventually matched his own, there was nobody or nothing to be seen. Just an empty garden and a clear blue sky.

Turning back to George, my heart thumping, he at least stopped his incessant laughing. He'd appeared so animated, to be staring at something which held his attention and made him laugh wildly.

"What was it, sweetheart?" I asked, passing him the juice. Deep down. I prayed he didn't reply.

George's eyes met mine, the smile now completely vanished. He only said two words, but it was enough to scare the wits out of me. His voice dropped a couple of octaves too, only adding to my hysteria.

"Pretty lady," he said, before grabbing his drink and gulping down its contents as though his life depended upon it.

She hasn't seen me, but George has. I'm crouching underneath their kitchen window. If she comes outside, I've had it, caught red-handed, nowhere to hide, nowhere to run. But I need to take some risks now. If I'm ever going to get my Matthew back, then I have to up my game and scare them, especially her. Francis Baker has gone, and Matt is refusing to see Mother. And then that intimate night with Lisa. Well, that was the straw that broke the camel's back. I need Lisa popping pills like there's no tomorrow. I need her addicted. An absolute mess without them, unable to cope, unable to look after baby George. Yes, I always knew I would have to deal with her at some point.

And as I said, I need to get Matthew back home under the roof of his own house, so I can manipulate the pair of them and put the last pieces of the jigsaw into place. He will *lose his job and he* will *go to see Melissa.*

It's on my terms from now on.

I'm shaking, crouched underneath this bloody window now, desperate to hold my Matthew once more.

20

LISA

IT WASN'T GETTING any easier. It was supposed to be better, returning to some kind of normality, so why were things still happening to us? I now believed Matt was telling the truth a few nights before, despite laughing at him alongside Hannah and Tom. Something definitely occurred outside the pub, and now this. Vomit in our garden and George coming across as though he were momentarily possessed. I thought I'd fixed it all after his 'bit on the side' disappeared from the face of the earth. He left me with little choice but to get him home under the roof of our house. The only place I could keep my eye on him, know where he is, understand his intentions and, most of all, track his movements.

"Something is going on, Matt. I know it and I'm scared. You owe it to me to tell me what's happening."

Matt arrived home from work around an hour earlier. I'd been counting down the days until he got back. It was seven o'clock Thursday evening, four days after I called him at his office. On the previous occasion he arrived home a day early, he'd lied to me, blaming it on some work issue.

'*...it's a problem that just won't go away. But I've dealt with it now, but to tell you the truth, it's left me drained...*'

But this time, there *was* a genuine problem at work. I should bloody well know, because on Monday after I hung up on Matt, I phoned his boss instead. Matt made me so angry, dismissing me as a child when all I did was ask if he knew who could be responsible for a pile of vomit in our front garden. He thought it was an accusation and maybe it was but it was also a valid question.

"What's happening? You tell me. Why should I have the answers?" he retorted, his face ashen, tiny beads of sweat clinging to his forehead. If I didn't know better, I could have sworn he had arrived home carrying a fever.

"Come on, even you have to admit that a pile of sick in the garden isn't exactly normal. And then George giggled at somebody in the window. You should have seen him. He scared the hell out of me."

Matt stood and crossed the kitchen to fetch his Scotch. To my surprise, he collected two tumblers before returning to the table. He poured two very generous measures — I'll never drink all that, I wanted to say, but wouldn't dare — and slid one across the table towards me, as if we were starring in some kind of clichéd Western movie. He raised his glass without a hint of expression before slinging the contents down in one. Matt twisted his neck at a funny angle and breathed in deeply. He nodded at the tumbler in my hand. Taking a hearty sip, knowing how strong that stuff was, I coughed as the burning liquid hit the back of my throat. But it tasted good, and I soon took another swig, followed by another. It had an instant and desired effect, soothing my insides and relaxing my mind.

"Are you sure he said pretty lady?" he asked, offering me an approving nod of his head at my drinking escapades.

"Of course I'm sure. I couldn't make *that* up."

Matt stood again, irritating me he wouldn't sit still, and walked to the window. He must have looked out of it a hundred times since I relayed my story. He'd also been out the front of the house and inspected the pile of sick. Observing him from the front window, he bent down and parted the plants before standing and glancing up and down the street. Did he expect somebody to be watching him?

"Anything else?" he asked, turning back to face me.

At least he finally appeared as concerned as me. It was the first time he showed any genuine interest in what I said for months. I understood he was going through a lot himself, and I knew from experience he bottled it all up, but surely he realised he wasn't the only one suffering. Would a good talk help us both get things out into the open? Of course, I couldn't mention my trip to London, as I doubted he would ever want to raise the subject himself. But I had to know if he had anything else to hide. If I put *most* of my cards onto the table, maybe he would too? Or was that just wishful thinking? His job, another woman or something else altogether? I felt confident I could rule out another woman, despite his reputation. He couldn't have been seeing anybody else at that apartment complex, not with Claudia West living across the landing. She would have busted a gut to tell Francis, and I know she would have told me and Hannah too when we met.

And I felt confident once Francis disappeared, he simply didn't have it in him to begin another relationship.

My phone call with John Brookes did at least reassure me when he disclosed Matt was acting weird at work too, but John couldn't believe for one second it had anything to do with 'being under pressure'. "We just sell houses for goodness' sake, and we're not exactly struggling," he explained. He reported their year-to-date figures were smashing all expectations and Matt's sales were still okay, despite trailing off over recent weeks. "But now you've called and told me this, it gives me greater cause to be concerned," he added, before ending the call rather abruptly. Perhaps I said too much, knowing Matt would go crazy if he ever found out, although John promised to keep our conversation confidential, and even though I'd never met the guy, I knew I could trust him.

"No," I lie. "I can't think of anything else." Collecting the two tumblers, I placed them in the dishwasher. With a wry smile, I kept my back to him, knowing my next words would be like an arrow through his heart. "Now, get yourself ready. We're going to Hannah and Tom's for drinks."

MATT

Me and my big mouth. Why did I have to say anything?

'...*I don't think I've ever been to your house, and I'd love to see your infamous whisky collection...*'.

The last thing I needed after losing my job and arriving home to a delusional Lisa was having to endure an evening with those two. Protesting, Lisa said I only had myself to blame. At least I could avoid telling her I'd been sacked, for a while anyway.

. . .

Hannah and Tom's house wasn't what I was expecting. I imagined a pristine, albeit old-fashioned interior, straight from one of those housekeeping magazines. Maybe draped curtains, a patterned three-piece suite and thick carpets which your feet sink into, after removing one's shoes, of course. Instead, as we stepped from the hallway, through the living room and into the adjacent dining room, I soon discovered how unkempt and in need of thorough modernisation it was.

Catching Lisa's eye, I spotted a glimpse of one-upmanship, a *well, well, you're not as posh as I thought you were* kind of look. It surprised me she hadn't been to their house already. Or was I misreading her and it was all an act?

So many bloody secrets.

The walls were covered in woodchip wallpaper, painted magnolia, which now resembled a pub from the early seventies: yellow and peeling. The carpet fared no better, frayed at the edges and falling an inch or two short of the skirting. The exposed floorboards beneath were dark oak or some other similar wood, and I couldn't help but imagine how beautiful it would be if they stripped the flea-ridden carpets away altogether. And the furniture didn't help. An antiquated dark mahogany sideboard with chipped brass handles. Sofas and chairs decorated in floral patterns, large pink roses faded and worn. Noticing a tear down the back of one chair which they had crudely stapled together, it looked as though it had been through radical surgery.

Tom offered us a seat at the round and shiny dining room table. On closer inspection, the surface was full of tiny scratches around the edges, no doubt caused by an overzealous dog begging for attention.

"Thanks," I said, actually enjoying acquainting myself with their shithole of a house. Lisa shot me a look and I wondered why she always took their side.

The chair Tom pointed to looked as though a person of a certain weight could go straight through it, but looking up at our host, I realised Lisa and I would be safe. I caught myself smiling. Maybe it was just the evening I needed to distract my mind from the inevitable.

"Wine for the ladies, and I think I know what Matthew might want, even if I suggested you take it a little easy." He extended his arm and shook his hand uncontrollably, a pathetic impersonation of an alcoholic in desperate search of his next drink.

Dickhead.

Tom laughed at his little joke.

"Erm, Tom," I called after him, twisting my torso. "Any chance of seeing your collection?"

I was making polite conversation for the sake of it. Shit, I would have sooner been scraping that vomit up with my bare hands than wasting a Friday night in their company but I was genuinely interested in examining all those single malts which Tom had bragged about since the day I first met him. And now we are in their house, curiosity gripped me and I wanted to explore more.

Tom and Hannah exchanged a look which I couldn't decipher.

"The thing is, Matt, I keep them all down the cellar, and it's a bit of a mess down there at the moment."

No shit.

"Ah, come on. A bit of a mess doesn't bother me."

Standing to follow him, Tom's expression changed.

"No," he said in a raised voice. "I wouldn't want you to fall or anything. Health and safety and all that."

His attitude was like a red rag to a bull to me.

"Nonsense. If I trip, I promise not to sue."

Tom stood perfectly still and Charlie dragged himself to his feet from behind the sofa. He growled in my direction.

"I said no, Matt," Tom concluded. "I'll fetch the drinks and you sit with the others."

Charlie barked, slobber dripping from his jaw, his eyes set on mine. Taking another step forward to follow Tom, Charlie barked louder and manoeuvred himself closer. Hannah shouted from behind, startling me.

"Charlie! Quiet!"

The dog stopped barking and emitted a low growl instead, his teeth appearing sharper than I'd noticed before. It felt like some kind of stand-off. Tom at one end of the room, Hannah at the other, and Charlie and myself in the middle. Who dare move next?

"Come and sit down, Matt," Lisa pleaded. "Tom is about to fetch the drinks. I'm sure there will be another time you can see his collection. Right, Tom?"

Turning back to Tom, I saw his hand clenching in and out of a fist.

"Right," he replied, his breathing shallow and quick. He smiled at Lisa — is that a flirty smile? — and I looked at her, and as I did, she blushed.

"I won't be long." Tom flicked the back of his hand towards the dining room table, leaving me with little choice but to re-join the others. Lisa's eyes narrowed as I sat down. A *what the hell was that all about* kind of look? Shrugging my shoulders, I noticed Hannah glaring at me too, her face full of contempt. On the brink of saying something facetious, the sound of Tom returning with clinking glasses made me bite my lip.

After Tom poured the wine, he passed me two bottles of Scotch to examine.

"Take your pick," he said, smiling as if our encounter from moments earlier hadn't occurred at all.

"Is that it?" I asked. "Two bottles? I thought you had a collection?" I air-quoted *collection*, watching Tom squirm as he stood above me.

"The *collection* is in the basement, Matt. You know, I thought I just made that perfectly clear?"

"Come on, just choose one, Matt," Lisa intervened, desperately trying to defuse the situation.

"Either. I'm sure they're both as good as one another."

Again, Tom and Hannah exchanged a glance. Hannah's neck had come out in blotches.

"What were you doing at home today?" she asked, catching me off-guard. "Don't you have to be in the office every day?"

"I've worked from home," I lied, catching Lisa watching me. She suddenly looked as nervous as I felt.

It wasn't a complete fabrication as I did spend most of the day in our third bedroom, the makeshift office, scanning websites for similar positions, but this time more local. Finding nothing suitable, I widened my search to non-skilled jobs as I realised our savings wouldn't last forever.

"This John Brookes fellow gave you permission, did he?" Tom asked, smirking.

"How do you know my boss's name?"

"Lisa told us," Hannah replied. "Didn't you, Lisa?"

Lisa blushed again before taking a long sip of wine.

"Yeah, I may have done." She looked at me. "It's not a secret, is it?"

My paranoia cranked up another level.

Is everybody in cahoots against me?

We stayed around an hour. Sixty minutes of boring conversation about nothing in particular, the underlying tension in the room almost palpable. Charlie growled each time I made the tiniest of movements and Tom regurgitated his joke about me being licked to death by his ferocious canine. Hannah laughed wildly, but Lisa was finding it more difficult to join in than she did the previous week. Eventually, we made our excuses to leave.

Lisa collected George in his baby carrier, who had slept throughout the entire encounter and followed our hosts to the front door. Purposefully, I strayed behind.

Between the living room and the kitchen was a doorway to my left. A long rusty key dangled from the lock.

"This the infamous cellar, Tom?" I called after him.

Quickly, he scooted back and positioned himself between me and the door. He turned the key and put it into an adjacent chest of drawers.

"Yeah. As I said, it's a tip down there. You know, next time I promise to tidy it so you can go down and have a look. You seem pretty keen to see it for some unknown reason."

But Tom was blabbering, his words tripping over each other. He glanced at his wife as if seeking reassurance he was saying the right things. Remarkably, she nodded, like he'd been a good boy.

"I look forward to it," I replied, and the dog immediately barked again. "Want me to take you to the park, Charlie?" Unbelievably, he slumped down onto his belly and whined, as if I threatened him with a trip to the vet. Did he see something that night too?

"Perhaps he's scared about what you might accuse him of," Hannah quipped, making Tom fall into pathetic and false laughter. He propped himself against the cellar door, holding his ribs with his spare hand. But I wasn't interested in him or his antics.

Instead, my eyes focused firmly on the cellar door behind him.

21

MATT

WE SPENT the rest of the weekend tiptoeing around each other, both on tenterhooks recognising that any kind of spark could ignite the flame. I was conscious Lisa's incident at the window was still playing on her mind. She continually looked outside, along the garden and up the hill beyond, and I knew I would do the same. Had George *really* seen someone at the window? *Pretty lady*. But even on her medication, Lisa's anxiety levels had soared. However, she was faring better than me, and I was aware that the slightest of things could tip me over the edge. I needed to keep my latest text message hidden from Lisa too. If she found that...

It arrived the day before whilst I tidied away the mess Lisa had created in the garden. Although I didn't particularly want to do it, it enabled me to get outside and have a few precious moments to myself. The feel of my phone vibrating in my pocket made my heart sink before I even retrieved it.

> Hello Matthew. It's Melissa again. I'm quite annoyed you are not replying to my messages, and I'm very annoyed you haven't been to visit me. What is it, Matthew? Why won't you come? I'll give you a week, Matthew. One week, starting... Now! Love always. Melissa

What the hell is that supposed to mean?

Peering up, I caught Lisa in the kitchen, staring directly at me. Her eyes drifted to the phone in my hand. She turned away though and hadn't mentioned it since. Perhaps she didn't see?

Quickly, I hit 'reply' and told Melissa I'd be in to see her on Monday.

On Sunday night I knew I could no longer put it off. Neither of us had alluded to the night at Hannah and Tom's house. Lisa's face when we left told me all I needed to know about her feelings on the subject. Sometimes I wondered just what they have in common and how quickly they formed such a strong bond. They were becoming inseparable and I admit to feeling a certain amount of envy creeping up inside whenever I saw them together. If they aren't around each other's property, or meeting in the park, they were forever messaging each other, most likely inane chatter about George or the weather. Or could it be something much more sinister?

Tom's irreverent attitude towards me, taking me for a simpleton who should just sit still and be quiet, was beginning to really piss me off too.

"I've got something to tell you."

Lisa looked up at me from the sofa. I'd just put George down for the night and I carried two glasses of red wine, like some kind of peace offering.

It took me all weekend to gain the confidence to broach the subject, but as soon as I spoke, the words threatened to get stuck in my throat.

"What is it?" Lisa asked, showing a surprising lack of interest. She took a glass from me, and without a 'thank-you', placed it on the coffee table in front of her before going back to her magazine. I wanted to snatch it from her, rip it in two and demand she gave me a moment's attention.

"It's about my job, at the estate agent's."

She replied without looking up.

"Well, what other job do you have?"

My cheeks burned. The need to mock me was totally unnecessary. After giving myself a moment, I sat on the chair and held on to my wine, taking intermittent sips to calm my nerves.

"You know what I mean," I proceeded with a hint of sarcasm myself. "The job that brings in the money." Her expression didn't change, but at least she faced me. "Well," I continued, my self-belief diminishing by the second, "last week, I handed my notice in."

Lisa smiled before collecting her glass. She took a long swig and allowed the soothing claret to slide effortlessly down her throat. She smiled again before eventually closing the magazine and placing it on the table.

"I see."

Does she know I'm lying?

"What do you mean, *you see*? Is that all you've got to say on the subject?"

"Why, is there something else you're not telling me?"

The conversation was heading in a direction I hadn't even contemplated. I expected Lisa to go crazy, ask why I would leave such a good job and worry about where the money would come from. Those questions I was prepared for and had answers lined up for each. So why was she expressing such disdain for the situation? Standing, I paced to the front window before returning to my chair, realising I was showing all the traits of somebody riddled with guilt.

"I've left my new apartment too. I just need to go back tomorrow to get my gear. Then I'll stay overnight, as I can't square up my rent until Tuesday."

The second part wasn't a lie. It also played into my hands, as I could use the car whilst making a detour en route.

"That's good then. I'm surprised they let you just give your apartment up like that."

She showed no animation, just sarcastic remark after sarcastic remark. Teasing me, attempting to get me to bite. I had to hold it together. The weekend was almost over, and I'd made it this far.

"Yeah," I replied, my voice gaining strength even though I continued to spout lie after lie. "I gave them some sob story about a sick relative and I couldn't do my job anymore. And if I didn't have a job, I wouldn't need the flat."

I did actually tell the agency the same story, and they amazingly allowed me to pay until the end of the month. They said they would have no problem re-letting the apartment and were happy to part on good terms.

"And your boss didn't want you to serve your notice period at the estate agents?"

Just let it go. Don't you want to talk about money or where else I might find work?

"He was really good, actually. I gave him the same story about a sick relative."

"Hmm," Lisa replied before taking another sip of her wine. "My mum always used to say you shouldn't make up stories about sick relatives in case it comes true."

Lisa's weird attitude finally made me snap.

"What are you trying to say?" I asked, standing again to somehow give me a feeling of supremacy. "Do you know something I don't?"

If she knew anything, I needed to see her reaction. But she stood too and momentarily left the living room. I heard the opening and closing of a drawer. The small table in the hallway. She returned seconds later with an envelope in her hand.

LISA

The weekend dragged and the thought of the vomit in the garden and George's *sighting* at the window played havoc with my mind. But Matt barely mentioned it. He did at least tidy the mess I'd made outside, but I soon discerned that was more of an excuse to get away from me rather than any actual enjoyment in the task. Finally, Sunday night arrived and the conversation I'd been anticipating for three days took place. Matt ultimately grew the balls to confide in me. I couldn't help but be sarcastic in reply. Maybe I overdid it, but he couldn't keep taking me for a fool. Hannah and Tom said he was forever taking the piss out of me, but they didn't know him as well as I did, and I've already explained why I needed to keep him close. However, a little fun made me feel better, and it didn't hurt to remind him two could play at his game.

The wine tasted good too, and I savoured every drop whilst listening to Matt squirm his way through his bullshit and lies. The bit about his apartment sounded genuine though, and he suddenly got a spring in his step, as if on safer ground. I couldn't help a little dig about John Brookes not asking him to work his notice period though, and the way Matt blushed almost made me laugh out loud. But then he became angry, and I realised I'd taken it too far. We were supposed to be on the same side, but dishonesty has always been one of my pet hates. I took his mood swing as an opportunity to get away for a few moments, and I turned my back to him as I left the room.

As I fumbled in the small chest of drawers in the hallway, I heard Matt clearing his throat. He wasn't making it easy for himself and I allowed myself a few extra seconds to listen to him struggle. Finally, I returned with an envelope in my hand and dropped it on the chair arm where he sat.

"That arrived for you during the week," I said, returning to my chair and collecting my wine glass. Matt's hand shook as he tried to open the letter addressed to him.

Why hadn't I opened it before? The answer is obvious. Because I already knew he had been sacked, and John Brookes informed me he would put his reasonings into a letter. The postmark indicated it was from the estate agency, so I didn't even contemplate reading the damn thing myself.

Eventually, he looked up and a pang of guilt jolted through me as Matt appeared to be close to tears.

"So, why didn't you say something? Why put me through all this if you've already read the letter and you know he has fired me?"

His voice was cracking, and he halted a couple of times to keep his emotions in check.

"Because I needed to know how long you would conceal it from me," I fib, "and if you can lie about this, what else have you been lying about?"

He stood, walked to the window again, and then back to me. His pacing up and down made me want to scream. He sat on the sofa, reached across and took my hands in his. Tears welled in his eyes and his lips were crimson from the wine. He resembled a forsaken clown, and I kicked myself for being so cruel.

"There's nothing else I'm lying about," he declared, his voice breaking as the words tumbled out. "I just didn't know how to tell you. Once I've collected all my belongings from the apartment, I'll return and find another job."

"Okay," I replied, "clear your apartment, come home, and we'll discuss where we go from here. Deal?"

"Deal," he said, before kissing me on the cheek, resting his chin on my shoulder and holding me tight. Even though I could feel him shaking, and despite my pangs of guilt, I knew I could never trust Matthew Walker as far as I could throw him.

22

MATT

I'm unsure whether Lisa believed me about needing to empty the apartment. At first, I thought she had believed my lie, but as I held her tight, the tone of her voice carried no genuine conviction.

'...go and clear your apartment, come home, and we'll discuss where we go from here. Deal?'

The way she said, 'go and clear your apartment' came across derisively, like a teacher giving a pupil another opportunity to do their homework even though their original excuse sounded pathetic. And her sarcastic attitude to everything else I said left me in no doubt she knew something. But the envelope from my boss was still sealed and, if it hadn't already been opened, how could Lisa know I'd been sacked?

To save her any embarrassment, I let it go and instead allowed my emotions to overflow to keep her on side. It had been a genuine struggle to hold back the tears, and at least it helped with the authenticity of the situation. And I had other things on my mind. Monday morning was fast approaching and my upcoming visit to the care home in Epsom and coming face to face with Melissa for the first time in over a year.

Why are you even going?

The threats in the second text message left me no choice. Besides, far too much was happening and I needed to know what Melissa might know.

The care home looked like some kind of converted mansion house and in need of general repair. White paint peeled away, exposing the original dark red brick beneath. The metal window frames were desperately clinging to an occasional patch of white gloss, giving them a grey and miserable appearance. The garden didn't look as though they had tended it to in a while either; weeds amongst the bedding plants and the lawn several inches overgrown. A large conservatory stood at the far end, by far the cleanest and most modern aspect of the building. But overall, the structure gave me the creeps and the steady drizzle which has replaced the late autumn sunshine, added further to the gloom. *What a place to see out the final chapter of your life*, I thought, and immediately regretted allowing death to creep into my psyche.

As soon as I stepped inside, the heat hit me, like stepping into a furnace. What kind of temperature do they run these places at? Are they scared they might lose one or two occupants to hypothermia?

"Is she expecting you?" asked the elderly receptionist after I informed her of the reason for my visit.

"No, I thought I would surprise her. You do allow surprises, don't you?"

She glanced up whilst turning the visitors' book to face me. She either didn't understand sarcasm or felt it beneath her to comment. Picking up a phone, she pressed two digits and I could hear the ringtone along the line. After a few moments, she hung up and addressed me with her usual charmless etiquette.

"Melissa is not in her room. I suggest you try the conservatory at the far end of the lounge. She's always in there. Go through those double doors and walk straight ahead. You can't miss it."

Resisting another sarcastic response, I completed my name and date of visit and looked in the direction she just pointed.

The nurse returned her attention to the visitors' book and her expression became even more sour. She peered up at me, her mouth open, as she tried to comprehend who she has allowed in. Of course, I was back in Epsom. Back in the town where the shit hit the fan a year before. The news would have rocked the local community. The Reid family were like celebrities around these parts, and so was Matthew Walker.

"When did you last see her?" she called after me. I'd increased my pace before she could change her mind.

"Over a year ago. Why?" I replied, walking backwards.

"You might notice a difference, that's all." She somehow looked pleased with herself.

The open-plan living area was even warmer than the entrance hall. Wishing I'd worn a T-shirt and shorts, I continued straight ahead in the conservatory's direction. One or two of the residents smiled as I meandered through. A couple were playing dominoes at a table, whilst the majority sat in a semi-circle watching an old TV set. The presenter on the afternoon quiz show blared out his inane repetitive lines at a volume far too loud, given the proximity of those viewing it. It amazed me to see at least two of the audience were fast asleep.

Must be the heat. It could knock an elephant out in here.

As I approached the end of the communal living area, I had an overwhelming sensation to turn around and march straight back out. Something suddenly felt very wrong. Hesitating at the conservatory doorway, I saw a solitary person sitting in a soft cushioned, high-backed, wicker chair at the far end. Although she had her back to me, I instantly recognised Melissa's hair, now complete with even more grey streaks. The room was otherwise empty and I noticed how the temperature had dropped too.

Again, I contemplated leaving it there. I'd seen her with my own eyes and I was suddenly aware it was just the two of us.

But, as I adjusted my stance, that crazy, inexplicable recognition the family possess allowed Melissa to speak without even turning.

"Matthew? Matthew Walker. Is that you?"

Has she got a bloody mirror?

Still, she didn't move, her head fixed ahead, staring outwards.

Attempting a reply, the words were stuck in my throat. As I cleared it, Melissa extended her arm and, with a slight wave of her fingers, beckoned me forward. My already rapid heartbeat turned itself up another notch. Clearing my throat once more, I steadily walked forward until I was standing adjacent to my mother-in-law. And as soon as I saw her, I couldn't believe the transformation.

'You might notice a difference…'.

Her ever-greying hair paled into insignificance in contrast to the rest of her. Melissa looked so gaunt, as though she had barely eaten a thing since being locked away. Her cheekbones were incredibly hollow, as if she was purposefully sucking and holding them in. Likewise, her eye sockets were sunken and blackened, her eyes red around the rims and contained several burst blood vessels. Completing the transformation, I noticed her lips were so dry they split at various points, creating tiny scabs.

Melissa wore a thick fleece dressing gown, but I could still determine how much weight she had lost. Her arms and bony hands protruded from the sleeves and dark blue veins continued down to the knuckles. Red bruises darkened the back of both hands.

Is that where the intravenous drip goes in?

I always admired Melissa's appearance, the way she carried herself, the way she dressed and remained young looking, despite being in her early seventies. Yet I struggled to recognise any of those redeeming features from only a relatively short time ago. It's as though she was a different person, despite her demeanour informing me it was definitely Amelia's mother sitting in front of me.

"Oh my," she said in an incredibly shallow voice. The words emanated from somewhere deep inside her chest, and she struggled to reach them before they eventually escaped as some kind of croaky whisper. Melissa pointed to the chair next to her.

Half in shock and half petrified, I did as instructed. Desperate to keep my distance, it pissed me off when she beckoned me closer still.

"To what do I owe the pleasure?" she asked.

Why won't you look at me?

"You told me to come, Melissa, in your messages."

Again, I strained to hear as her words escaped as no more than a deep whisper.

"Messages? I have sent no messages. I don't even own a phone, Matthew."

What? Why are you lying to me?

Before I could respond, Melissa continued, "But I knew you would come. I sensed it."

Of course you fucking did.

All I could do was nod and attempt to smile.

"We've missed you, Matthew."

We?

The call from WPC Wright entered my head.

"Yes, well, the police called and said they had let you out…" Melissa smiled as I struggled to find the right words. "No, not let out, I mean, allowed you to come to this care home. They said you were poorly and that Andy Meadows had taken all the—"

She raised her hand ever so slightly, a sure sign for me to stop rambling. I was pleased she did, as I had no words left anyway.

"You live close by now, don't you?"

How does she know that?

"Well, kind of. In a village not far from—"

"In the village where you and my Amelia almost bought the house. The house with the long garden."

You need to leave, Matt. Get out of here. This isn't right…

"Yes. That's correct. How did you…?"

She smiled again. Her chapped lips made me cringe, although she appeared oblivious.

"We knew you would come back."

Melissa broke off, breathing hard, the effort of talking taking its toll. There was a jug of water on the table next to her and I took it upon myself to fill a plastic beaker and pass it to her. But Melissa didn't hold out her hand.

"Pour it into my mouth, Matthew. I want to feel you close to me."

Oh shit.

And then I noticed. Her eyes still hadn't moved from their original position. She stared directly ahead, through the glass, out into the overgrown garden. Without thinking, I waved my free hand in front of them. Melissa didn't even blink.

"You've noticed then," she remarked with a grin. "I lost my sight a few months ago."

What the…

"Undetected glaucoma. You see, we never visited an optician. Tracy used to do it for us. She's qualified, you know." I'm convinced they would believe Tracy could perform brain surgery if she'd told them so. "It's one of the main reasons they let me out, I guess."

"I'm, er, sorry, Melissa. I didn't know."

Placing the plastic beaker to her lips, she sipped delicately. After a few moments, she lifted her hand for me to stop.

"Sit back down, Matthew."

Why the hell am I here?

Melissa read my mind, freaking me out even more, if that's possible. "You must be wondering why you came to see me now, mustn't you?"

I gave up trying to respond. I had no words, no explanation for any of it. She smiled whilst staring straight ahead.

"Let me help you," she continued. "You want to know

why you received that phone call, don't you? Why would the police tell you I was out of prison? You want to know if I could know anything?"

My face burned and my hands were drenched in perspiration.

"Something bad is going to happen, Matthew."

"Bad? What do you mean, *bad*?"

My voice rose several octaves and I was pleased she couldn't see what a quivering mess I'd become, but I assumed she knew anyway.

Then, for the first time since I arrived, Melissa moved her head. Her neck slowly twisting towards me until her face was adjacent to mine. But her eyes didn't meet my own. Instead, they stared straight through me, as if she was watching somebody else outside.

She can't see, Matt.

"Something very bad. I can sense it."

Her arm propelled sideways, and she gripped my hand before I had an opportunity to withdraw it. How the hell did she move so quickly? Her fingernails dug in deep and I felt my skin pierce.

"I don't know what you're talking about, Melissa. Honest."

She smiled, a sign to inform me to stop making a fool of her. And then her eyes retracted and, instead of glaring straight through me, she stared directly into mine.

"You're lying, Matthew Walker, and you know how I feel about liars."

23

LISA

Not only did he lie to me, he also thought I'm bloody stupid. Last month, when he received his phone call and sneaked off into the living room believing I couldn't hear, well, I gave George a spoonful of food and quietly made my way to eavesdrop from outside the door. He was talking to a policeman, or woman, and he kept mentioning Melissa's name. Then he asked what care home in Epsom she was staying in before he began asking all other kinds of questions, such as 'can she get out of this open prison thing'. I found it difficult to keep up, given his muffled voice and lack of any detail. Finally, I dashed back into the kitchen when the conversation was obviously concluding. I deciphered they must have released Melissa Reid, or she was on the verge of being discharged. Well, she had me to deal with too, not just her darling Matthew.

"Who was that?" I asked casually, feeding George once again.

He looked in a total daze, lost within himself.

"Eh?" he replied, still staring at the mobile in his hand.

"I said, who was that, on the phone?"

Finally, he peered up, and I noticed all the colour was drained from his cheeks; not that there was much there to begin with. Matt looked permanently haggard, carrying the weight of the world on his shoulders.

"Erm, wrong number," he lied.

Deciding to let it go, I didn't want another row in front of George, but his constant covering up was beginning to take its toll on me. Matt left the room without a word and I contemplated why the police would inform him that his ex-mother-in-law was now living in a care home. Epsom he'd said, the place where Matt lived with them, and the place where they kept me hidden in the woods during my pregnancy. There can't be many care homes in Epsom, can there? He could easily track her down if he wanted to, but would he seriously want to rekindle the past? The *hideous* past. It played on my mind ever since, but I somehow stored it away, alongside numerous other dark thoughts. But later that Sunday night, following our *conversation* regarding his job, I found out where he was really going the next day. You see, I watched him from the kitchen window during the weekend. He was in the garden, tapping away on his phone, and he looked up and caught me spying on him. Neither of us said anything, but we didn't have to. I'd seen enough.

So, he's planning to clean out his apartment, is he? Well, the night before, after I'd shown him the letter from

John Brookes and his fake tears, I plied him with whisky. He could never resist. Later, as he lay on the bed comatose, I held his phone to his face and opened it using facial recognition. Sneaking into the en suite, I read his messages and found out he intended to visit Melissa the following day. I can be quite the little detective when I put my mind to it. I tracked down his 'bit on the side' in Earl's Court, and now I knew he'd contacted Melissa. The one thing I couldn't work out was why he would pursue that family, unless it was for the obvious reason.

Maybe I should find out where she is for myself and pay her a visit?

If Matt appeared shaken up when he returned home from work the previous Thursday night, on Monday afternoon, he looked emphatically spooked. Meeting him in the hallway, he stumbled indoors, after I'd heard him struggle for several moments with his key in the door.

"Oh, hi. What are you doing?" he asked. If I thought his cheeks had been devoid of colour before, then he was positively translucent that day. His veins protruded from each temple, dark blue, and I'm sure I could see the blood pumping through them.

"What's wrong? You look awful. You said you weren't home until tomorrow."

He glared at me, daring me to say more whilst appearing perplexed at my suggestion.

"Just a heavy day, that's all."

He put his holdall down and marched right past me. No hug, no kiss. He smelt of stale sweat and again I noticed the sheen of perspiration across his forehead. George had the TV on in the living room, but Matt walked straight past. Never had he failed to make his son the first port of call when he returned home.

Following him into the kitchen, he made straight for the whisky. With his back to me, he poured himself a hefty measure and knocked it back in one. Exhaling a deep breath as the Scotch hit the spot, he quickly poured another.

"Not going to say hello to George?" I asked.

He spun around, the sheen of sweat on his forehead now a multitude of droplets, threatening to run into his eyes. What the hell was wrong with him? What *has* she said?

"Eh? Yeah, sure. Sorry, I'm not feeling too good. Think I've got some kind of fever."

"Oh, well, maybe it's wise to stay away from George then."

He looked at me as if I'd suggested he never see his son again.

"Hmm, yeah, good idea. Maybe that's best." He attempted a wry smile, somehow oblivious to the bottle of whisky in one hand and the tumbler in the other. He walked towards the door. "Listen, I'm going to grab a shower. Try to freshen up." He lifted an arm and sniffed underneath. "Jeez, I stink." Attempting another false laugh, he addressed me directly. "Don't mind, do you, babe?"

Babe? He's never called me 'babe'.

"Of course I don't mind. I think it's for the best. I noticed the odour in the hallway." Desperately trying to keep the conversation light, I also wanted him out of the way. "Let me take those off you, and you shower."

Matt passed me the bottle and tumbler without thinking and, as he did, I spotted some marks on the back of his hand, half-moon shape, as if made by fingernails. Deciding not to say anything, I waited patiently for him to leave the room. Standing perfectly still, I listened as he ascended the staircase, his footsteps heavy. He paced above in our bedroom before I eventually heard running water from the shower. I gave him a minute to undress before guessing he must have stepped inside.

Quickly, I grabbed my phone and Googled care homes in Epsom. There were at least five listed and I became conscious of time once I'd had no success with the first three. The third one especially took an age, the woman allegedly looking on their system for any matching name. Don't they know who is residing there? Finally, on call number four, I was in luck.

"Hi. Do you have a Melissa Reid staying with you? I've been informed she's in a care home in Epsom, but my husband didn't tell me which one."

"Hmm, yes we do. And I have to say, Melissa Reid has become very popular in recent days."

MATT

As I stood soaking in the shower, I contemplated how I must have looked to Lisa. I couldn't even recall the drive home from Epsom. The image of Melissa was ingrained in my mind and I could not shift it. Her skin, her bony arms and hands, her sunken cheeks. Those darkened eyes. And losing her sight, yet somehow it felt as though she could still see me.

Shuddering at the thought, I turned up the heat until the water scalded my flesh. Lathering myself in shower gel for a second time, I scraped the sweat from my body. I noticed the marks on the back of each hand where Melissa had dug her nails in. Did Lisa see them? No, surely she would have said.

As soon as step out of the cubicle, I heard Lisa's muffled voice from downstairs. It didn't sound as though she was speaking to George, not in that tone. Instead, it was much more authoritative. Shit. Did she just say, 'care home'?

The shower at least freshened me up and the smell of my visit evaporated alongside some of the initial shock. But what had Melissa meant, and how could she possibly know something bad *might* happen?

After dressing, I tentatively descended the stairs, my hand gripping the rail until the perspiration made it squeak. George's face lit up the room as he sat at the enormous table, momentarily taking my mind off things. I kicked myself for not going to see him as soon as I walked in, I knew he should always be at the forefront of my thoughts.

"Hello, mate," I said, trying my utmost to fix a grin on my face. George smiled broadly in return.

"Daddy!"

My heart melted and I struggled to contain my emotions. Fortunately, Lisa smiled too and passed me an ice-cold beer before clinking my bottle with hers.

Leaning forward, I kissed her, which made George giggle. Lisa kissed me back and I couldn't stop myself from embracing her.

The sound of her phone vibrating on the table forced her to release her grip, and she snatched the device before I could see who it is.

"It's only a text from Hannah," she said, reading my

mind. "We're going to get together tomorrow and have a little ride out to the shops. You don't mind, do you?"

He looks absolutely petrified as he leaves the care home. What could she have said to him?

Maybe it's not what she said. Perhaps he didn't expect her to look the way she does. You see, after visiting her in prison, I'm accustomed to it. Her deteriorating eyesight and losing so much weight has made Melissa look so old, so frail, but could her appearance alone have left him in that much of a state? Maybe he has something else to be scared about, something I know nothing of, but Melissa does.

Even though I've become angry with him for not returning Melissa's messages, well, my messages from her pretend *phone, I always knew he would visit, eventually. He can't let go; you see. You can never let go once you're part of this family.*

One thing I do hope is that she is secretly pleased he's been to see her. Matthew was always her favourite. She didn't like that Ryan Palmer, and I've never been convinced she liked Graham. But Matthew Walker is the son she never had, which makes it more baffling why he looks so frightened now.

As he walks past, I can sense a strong feeling of guilt. He's sweating, his forehead is glistening despite the drop in temperature over recent days. And his eyes, they're darting everywhere. Is he expecting somebody?

The need to follow him is now paramount. Perhaps I've made a huge mistake setting up this meeting? The intentions were admirable, but I hope they've not backfired on me. It was supposed to bring us closer, but if Mother hasn't played ball, then perhaps I will have to deal with her instead.

24

LISA

THE CARE HOME wasn't what I expected. Then again, I'm not sure what I'd anticipated. I can't recall ever being in one or paying any attention to what they actually look like. Hannah and Tom persuaded me to go after I explained about Matt's message exchange with Melissa. They thought it strange that he would consider further contact with any member of that family. One thing I didn't confess was that Matt's infatuation with the Reids never really surprised me. And when I say Hannah and Tom 'persuaded' me to go, I'd only been seeking an acquaintance. Once I plied Matt with whisky and read his messages, coupled with the state he returned home in, there wasn't a chance in hell I wouldn't be visiting.

"Why would he want to meet her again?" Hannah asked on the phone. After he'd showered, Matt took George to the park. I told him to get some fresh air after his *heavy day* clearing his apartment. As I say, did he think

I was bloody stupid? As soon as they left, I picked up the phone and called my friend. "Her ex-husband got away when he could," Hannah continued, "so I don't know why Matt would want to reacquaint himself with her. With them." Had I mentioned Melissa's ex-husband before? I couldn't recollect doing so, but then again, we'd discussed the subject over and over, and it all became a bit of a blur.

We sat in the car park, just Hannah and I. Tom had to be somewhere else, I think he mentioned it was an important meeting with another neighbourhood watch coordinator.

We both took in our surroundings, the paintwork shabby, exposing dark bricks beneath. The windows needed replacing too; modern uPVC double-glazing instead of the old metal frames which were almost devoid of paint.

"It looks a bit dilapidated, doesn't it?" Hannah commented, leaning forward in her seat to check the roof.

"Yes. Imagine coming here to see out your days?"

"Lisa Ingram!" Hannah laughed. "What a wicked thing to say."

I loved Hannah's sense of humour. I found her both cultivated and down to earth at the same time. You could be posh in her company or equally discuss more trivial subjects such as soap operas or reality TV. And like Tom, Hannah was well educated. Politics, travel, movies and much more. I always presumed they would be a magnificent pair to team up with at a pub quiz; now there's an idea.

"You know what I mean," I chuckled in return.

"What else do you go to a care home for? Few come out unless it's in a wooden box."

We began laughing, Hannah grabbing my arm to control herself. It was more from nerves than the subject being that funny, and when we finally restrained ourselves, I turned to check on George in the back seat. That's when I spotted somebody sitting in the conservatory at the far end. Having not noticed that part of the building before, my focus became firmly fixed on the modern extension which stood in stark contrast to the rest of the neglected care home. Hannah stopped laughing too, and her eyes followed mine.

"Is that somebody looking at us?" she asked, now unable to stop staring either.

"I'm not sure. They're too far away. But there's definitely someone in there."

Hannah had already made her mind up.

"Why are they staring at us? I feel like marching over there and asking what their problem is."

Her change in attitude caught me off-guard.

"Probably don't see many people. Just being nosy."

Hannah glanced at me.

"Yeah, yeah, you're right. Sorry, it just sends a shiver down my spine to think of anybody watching me like that. But you're spot on, this is a place full of old folk and doubtless, most of them are senile."

She twirled her finger round and round her temple and made herself go cross-eyed. I couldn't stop myself from laughing again.

"Hannah Wells. What a wicked thing to say," I repeated her words.

Although we both laughed, I couldn't help but peek

over Hannah's shoulder. The person in the conservatory hadn't moved an inch since I first noticed them.

"Go on in and see if you can find this Melissa Reid," Hannah said. "I'll look after George. He's still fast asleep, isn't he?"

George was indeed out for the count. He always was on a car journey, dropping off within a mile of leaving home, whatever the time of day.

"You sure?"

"Hell, yes. It was my idea for you to come. You don't want to be subjecting your poor child to all those old farts in there. Could scar him for life."

With another laugh and a squeeze of my arm, Hannah nodded towards the driver's door to get me to hurry along. She was right; I hadn't come this far not to see Matt's mother-in-law. Ever since I read the text exchange between them, I was intrigued and scared by what she could want. Realising I was being irresponsible and could put myself in danger, I still simply had to know. DCI Small promised me, promised us, that the family could be of no further risk, yet here I was, outside a care home, less than an hour from where we lived. Did that mean anything? Did it put us in some kind of peril? Surely not. I'd discussed it over and over with Matt, as well as with Hannah and Tom, and even if Matt dismissed it, our neighbours were tremendously supportive and reassured me none of us could be in any kind of danger. They should know. They ran the local neighbourhood watch and attended police meetings with like-minded coordinators. Tom even discreetly asked if anybody mixed up in any such case would be allowed back into the community if they posed a threat, and he received a definite 'no' as an answer. So why was I there? As I say, I didn't trust any of them, and I didn't trust Matt. Not only that, I had personal scores to settle with that family and I couldn't guarantee how I would react.

"Hi. I'm here to see Melissa Reid, please."

"Do you mind removing your scarf please?" the stern-looking receptionist asked.

I'd purposefully chosen attire to disguise myself from cameras or prying eyes. It was Tom's idea, but I felt ridiculous in dark sunglasses, a wide-brimmed hat and a scarf half covering my face.

"I'd sooner not. I've had a cold recently, and I don't want to pass on anything to the residents. My eyes are still bloodshot too. I look like Freddie Krueger."

My attempt at humour fell on deaf ears.

"Is she expecting you?" She looked as though she wanted to be there about as much as me.

"I called yesterday. Whoever I spoke to said that would—"

"Yes," she rather rudely interrupted. "That was me. Just sign the book and go through. She'll be in the conservatory. She always is."

The conservatory? Where the stranger just glared at me?

"Thanks."

Quickly, I tried to scan the visitors' book, searching for Matt's name. But the nurse tutted at my hesitancy and as soon as I signed it, she snatched the pen and dragged the book back to her. She read my entry before looking up at me. There was no way she could trace me with the name I used.

"Straight through. You can't miss it," she said, pointing.

The TV lounge was depressing. Dark, soulless and boiling hot. For the second time, I regretted my choice of clothing. One or two people looked up at me and a gentleman wearing pyjamas wolf-whistled in my direction. Another man laughed and I could feel my cheeks burn. Hastening my pace, I soon found myself at the conservatory door where one solitary resident sat with their back to me. They were overlooking the garden, and at first I didn't believe they had noticed me arrive.

"Hello," I said edgily, feeling my entire body tremor. "I'm looking for Melissa Reid."

"Has he sent you?"

The person's voice was weak and croaky but I immediately knew it was her.

"He? Who is he?"

She laughed, triggering a cough. I gave her a few moments to compose herself.

"My son-in-law. I take it you're the so-called mother of my grandchild?"

Cautiously, I proceeded forward. She was freaking me out, but I needed to remain strong.

"With all due respect, my son is not *your* grandchild."

Melissa laughed again, more of a cackle. It wasn't until I stepped alongside her that I could see the transformation. She looked so weak, so fragile. Her sweatshirt hung loosely from her tiny frame, and her bony arms and hands protruded from the sleeves, exposing bruised skin. And Melissa's face was so sunken, skeletal like, and those eyes, shit, those eyes.

Why wouldn't she look at me? She continued to stare straight ahead. And when she spoke, her tongue was just as evil as her appearance.

"If the child belongs to Matthew, then the child is a Reid. One day soon, you will give him up, back to whom he belongs."

My blood boiled, and I positioned myself until I was directly in front of her; my face only inches from hers. But still, she didn't move, and her eyes did not blink.

Can she even see me?

I had to hold my nerve.

"You will never get your filthy hands on my child. Never. And another—"

Melissa's arm snapped like the tongue of a snake and, in the same movement, grabbed my wrist tight inside her bony hand. Her strength amazed me and I could feel her nails digging in.

"Matthew wants us," she snarled, "and he is coming home. He's always chosen us. Don't you realise, you foolish little girl? You're insignificant and won't be bothering us for…"

Her words trailed off and she instantly let go of my hand. Remarkably, her face broke out into a smile, as though butter wouldn't melt in her mouth.

"Everything okay in here?"

I spun around sharply. I hadn't heard the nurse approach. How did Melissa know?

"Everything is fine," Matt's mother-in-law said cheerfully. "Lisa is just leaving, aren't you, dear?"

25

LISA

After dropping Hannah off, George and I returned to an empty house. Matt hadn't left a note, but I was pleased he wasn't around. Despite the drive home, and discussing matters over and over with Hannah, I still couldn't shake the image of Melissa or the foul things she'd said to me.

'...*If the child belongs to Matthew, then the child is a Reid. One day soon, you will give him up, back to whom he belongs.*'

At first, I thought I should go to the police, but as Hannah pointed out, Melissa would deny saying anything. Thinking things through, that wouldn't have been my smartest idea. And the way Melissa's entire manner changed as the nurse appeared told me all I needed to know about how she could manipulate a situation. They were evil, yet clever.

As I left, a nurse explained Melissa lost her sight a few months before and she was becoming frailer by the day. Enquiring how ill she actually was, I silently prayed the answer would be a matter of days, but the nurse couldn't clarify a time frame, instead saying Melissa was a fighter and who knew how long an inner strength could prevail. Not if I stab her right through the heart, I thought.

The key rattling in the front door made me rush through to the hallway before standing awkwardly as Matt stepped inside.

What am I doing?

Instantly, I smelt the alcohol. He grinned, pathetically trying to hide the fact that he'd been drinking.

"Hi, dear. Good day at the shops?"

He was making too much of an effort.

"Not really. But it looks as though you have."

Leaving him in the hallway, I returned to the kitchen and checked on George, erratically colouring a book with a green crayon. He didn't look up, instead, his tongue stuck out as he concentrated on the task at hand. Soon, Matt followed me in.

"Hi, mate," he said to George, ruffling his hair.

"Don't keep calling him that," I said, stepping forward and flattening George's fringe back down.

"What's up?" he asked, losing his initial spark and reverting to the awkward Matt I'd become accustomed to.

"Who have you been drinking with? Or have you taken to going to the pub on your own on a Tuesday lunchtime? What happened to the job hunting? Given up on that too, I presume?"

Finding it difficult to hide my anger, I fidgeted with a pile of letters in the rack. An hour before, his mother-in-law had threatened me whilst he was down the pub getting pissed.

"Give me a break, Lisa." Matt gave me a little stare of contempt before brushing past and filling the kettle. He grabbed himself a mug from the cupboard above. "I've only been out of work a couple of weeks. Am I not allowed to have a pint of beer during the occasional lunchtime? Besides, if you weren't always out with those weird busybodies, then perhaps we could go for a drink together sometime."

It wasn't his tone, his slurred voice or the words he used that irritated me. It was his sarcastic little laugh as soon as he finished.

"Do you want to know where I've been this morning?"

Suddenly, he appeared more interested. Was that even a glimpse of worry in his eyes?

"If it's with Hannah and Tom, I presume a visit around a police station or a tour of some prison cells?"

"What is it you've got against them? They're decent people, but you wouldn't recognise that in a million years. You just think about yourself."

He lost interest again, no longer concerned about where I'd been. Would I have told him if he asked?

Ever since we moved into the village, something kept me from talking to Matt, particularly personal subjects. Sure, we talked about money and George and other day-to-day issues, but anything to do with his private life was taboo. But I was just as guilty, as it suited me to keep certain things to myself too. Was it the less I knew, the better I could cope? But I knew things. I knew about Francis, and I now knew about Melissa. So what stopped me from blurting it all out? Hannah was a major influence since we arrived, like a mother to me and a grandmother to George. She was so level-headed and thought everything through before putting her opinions and suggestions forward. Realising how much of an effect she had on me, I was unsure if it was the medication or Hannah who kept me in check. Maybe a combination of both, but I don't believe I would have coped without her. Do all good things have to come to an end?

"Should I discuss it with Matt?" I asked her on the way home from Epsom. As usual, I allowed Hannah time to let the question sink in.

"I wouldn't," she replied, resting her hand on my arm. "Not yet, anyway. There's no chance of Melissa being able to get hold of George. She's just threatening you like an evil woman reaching the end of her time on this planet. She's jealous of you, Lisa. You've given Matthew something her daughter could never do."

"So why is Matt being so secretive about it all? Why hasn't he told me Melissa is out of prison?"

Again, a few moments' silence ensued.

"Could he be protecting you? Are we being too harsh on him? Believe me, I know he has his faults, but maybe he has *some* admirable qualities too."

Hannah smirked to herself whilst looking straight ahead. She didn't like Matt at all.

So, for the time being, I kept quiet. If he wanted to keep things from me, then I would continue to keep things from him.

MATT

"Do you want to know where I've been this morning?"

Thinking on my feet, I made a joke about Hannah and Tom, because deep down, I didn't want to know. Lisa gave the impression it was somewhere I wouldn't be comfortable with and I could therefore only think of one place. But how could she possibly know about Melissa or the care home? I made sure I deleted the texts from Melissa, or whoever sent them, the next morning. So, unless she somehow read them the night before, how could she have been to see her?

It's obvious we were keeping secrets from one another, which certainly suited me. What I couldn't understand, though, is why Lisa was hiding things from me. She spotted something on the day she did my laundry. And then the perfume. Had she smelt the same perfume as me? I was no longer convinced she would have said so.

However, I had other, far more pressing issues on my mind. I'd been putting off the inevitable all day. With Lisa and George at the shops, or wherever they were, I walked into the village and even contemplated going up to the copse. Nonetheless, the draw of the pub enticed me inside. A pint, a bite to eat, all an attempt to escape the present.

But after I settled in front of the open fire, the door opened and the pub fell into a moment of silence. Spinning around, I leant over the edge of the chair to see who it was. And that's when I saw somebody leaving the pub as fast as they had entered. The jet-black hair and the crimson coat. The same crimson coat I bought Amelia for her birthday. She loved it, and I loved her wearing it, especially when she accompanied it with my favourite matching lipstick.

But it couldn't be Amelia. It was impossible. Wasn't it?

Quickly, I gave chase, two guys at the bar now focusing their attention on me. Once outside, I stopped at the corner of the pub and scanned the park opposite. Nothing. Crossing the road, I strained my eyes, looking up and down the street. Deserted. Where the hell was she?

Grabbing my phone, I composed a text to one of the few remaining numbers stored.

> Who are these messages from? I know they are not from Melissa. You need to tell me who you are and how you got my number, otherwise, I will take it to the police.

Of course, I wouldn't take it to the police, and I fully expected the recipient to realise that too, but I still had to maintain a threat. It made little sense. Who could want me to visit Melissa, and why? Once she admitted she didn't own a phone, she never had, I'd been racking my brain to think who else it could be. Maybe Tracy from inside her prison cell? Are you allowed a mobile as an inmate? Perhaps now that they had *downgraded* her, they had given her further privileges?

My phone buzzed in my hand.

> I've been watching you. It's fun.

What the actual fuck does that mean?

> Who is this, and what do you want?

My fingers trembled as I hit reply. However, there was no instant reply. Instead, I didn't receive another message until I was almost home, and unlike before, this time, they withheld the number.

> You need to go to the house, Matthew. We have to meet.

The house? The family house? Why? Why would I

want to go anywhere near that place? And why have they withheld their number now? I couldn't even reply. Yet another thing which made little sense.

An idea entered my head as I fumbled with the front door key. If I go to the house, then I would also be very near the care home.

Maybe it was time to kill two birds with one stone?

Ooh, I've got goosebumps. Matthew has actually sent me a message from his phone, using those hands. I bet his fingers trembled as he sent it, even though he doesn't know who he's sending it to but he must have his thoughts. Surely he'll know it's one of the family, but he won't believe it when he finds out it's me and that I'm back, ready to carry on exactly where we left off.

With my patience wearing thin, I can't wait to see him, the look on his face, the smile which will inevitably spread from ear to ear. Yes, although I've been pissed off with him recently, I still can't shake these feelings that I've always held. They keep rising to the surface, like cream, and when it happens, I get all these butterflies flying around inside my tummy. They tickle me, making me all shivery, and I giggle like a schoolgirl. Oh, I wish I could hate him, wish I could put him to the back of my mind and try to move on with my life, but I know we are made for each other. It's why I'm back. And even though we set him up all those years with the new position at Opacy, I always knew how much he enjoyed working there. Because of me, not because of the job.

People will always wonder why Matthew was so vulnerable, so easily led, but they don't realise just how much we can get underneath people's skin. 'Why didn't he run?', or 'nobody would ever be that stupid', others will shout, but have they ever been in a similar situation? No, of course they haven't, so how could they ever understand? We are the Reid family, and the Reids always get their way.

Just a little longer now.
I'm nearly ready.
I can virtually smell you.
Hmm, Matthew, it's almost time.

26

MATT

THE PREVIOUS EVENING, after I realised I could no longer put off going back to that house, I involved Lisa, albeit hidden behind yet another lie. It had to appear genuine, plus I needed an excuse to use the car again, so I asked her to design and print off half a dozen curriculum vitae which I could hand out to estate agents hoping to find work. I wasn't convinced how credible Lisa thought my plan but at least she did a thoroughly professional job with the CVs.

"They would be a fool not to take you on with one of these in their hands," she joked. But it was a half-hearted attempt to lift the gloom which had descended between us. We were going through the motions, both treading on eggshells, with only George offering a genuine distraction. The only way forward was for me to meet my demons head-on, whatever the consequences. However, if it was who I thought it could be, then perhaps I carried a hint of excitement too. Probably best I didn't mention that bit to Lisa.

So, once again, I set off for Epsom, dressed in my finest suit to keep up the pretence.

"Knock 'em dead," Lisa said after I air-kissed her on the cheek before ruffling George's hair. Offering an unconvincing smile, Lisa said nothing. Her lack of words told me all I needed to know.

"I will. Wish me luck."

She stood on the doorstep, holding George in her arms as if she didn't believe I would leave our driveway unless she witnessed it with her own eyes. Again, I questioned what she might know. She came across so assured with her sarcastic remarks, teasing me, somehow daring me to cave in. As I reversed out of the drive, I considered if she could be receiving texts too. Had she heard from Melissa directly? And if Melissa did know something, had she told Lisa? None of it made sense. Why would Melissa involve Lisa separately? Surely she would target either me alone or both of us together? Lure us both into whatever trap she may attempt to set?

As I drove out of the village, I noticed the pub on the right, before passing the Wells' property a few houses along. I'm sure somebody was standing in the upstairs window. With a second glance, I made out the diminutive figure of Tom. He didn't wave or acknowledge me but moved his head slowly from left to right in conjunction with my moving vehicle.

Shaken, I checked the rear-view mirror and spotted something else. A person darting across the road. But as soon as I saw them, I turned a corner and lost sight of whoever it could be.

Calm down. You're delusional.

Attempting to divert my attention from such paranoid convictions, I pushed the radio button and music immediately filled the car. An eighties pop song blared through the speakers and I imagined George in the booster seat, smiling and clapping along. Giving it a few moments, I attempted to join in, desperately trying to shift my mind from its racing imagination. But it didn't work and soon my head was full of thoughts and images of my destination: that house. Why was I going? I had to keep convincing myself it was the right thing to do, realising I must keep my family safe as well as finally understanding why I was constantly being dragged into my past.

Once I arrives in town, I decides to leave the car in the station car park and walk the rest of the way. It was only a fifteen-minute stroll and I needed to clear my head. Quickly, already feeling overdressed, I changed into a sweatshirt, jeans and trainers and threw my suit onto the back seat. The prospect of meeting somebody like I was attending a funeral just didn't sit right. Fortunately, Lisa hadn't realised I sneaked into our bedroom and packed my holdall before I left.

The walk evoked so many memories of going back and forth to the station with Amelia as we commuted in and out of the city. Despite all that happened since we became a married couple, my feelings for her had barely wavered. They never did. I knew it was the real reason I was here. Deep down, I needed closure, an irrevocable goodbye maybe.

Turning the last corner, the property came into view, and I felt my legs momentarily buckle. As with Melissa, I wasn't expecting the transformation, and like my mother-in-law, the house had taken a significant turn for the worse.

The most evident alterations were the windows and doors with light brown chipboard replacing every opening, some with printed letters strewn diagonally across. It gave the place an air of abandonment, adding to the creepiness which always accompanied it. The turret to one side looked especially forbidding and it wouldn't have surprised me if a cauldron of bats suddenly flew from the windows.

The surroundings fared no better. The grass was ankle-high and several weeds grew taller still. Up to the left was Katrina's faded red swing, rusted and stationary despite the breeze which drifted from the woods.

Promising myself not to look in that direction, I desperately tried to keep my eyes forward and stick to the task at hand. The message said I needed to go to the house, not into the woods. If it had said the latter, I wouldn't have made the journey at all. But now there, I couldn't help myself from having a quick glance. The large blanket of evergreen firs were as uninviting as ever; dark, menacing, and holding secrets that I never wished to unearth again. And I caught myself staring, knowing what was in there and the part I played. The footpaths where I ran, the shack where Lisa was held against her will, and, of course, the graves. The proper graves and the make-believe graves. Both equally macabre and grotesque.

A sound distracted me, making me jump, but nothing was there. It was my imagination, threatening to send me into a chasm of despair, or was it the house, somehow communicating, expecting me, welcoming me home?

You're going fucking mad.

The wind whistled again, bending the tops of the trees, which in unison bowed in my direction; a curtsy to mock my return. Hunching up my collar, a strange habit I'd recently acquired, I dropped my head forward and marched purposefully towards the house. I had to get it over and done with, whatever *it* is.

Once I reached the beginning of the footpath, now almost not worthy of its description given the number of broken slabs and indiscriminate weeds growing between them, I noticed the postbox to my right. The postbox which Graham erected as far from the house as he could to stop me from talking to the postman. When we lived here, I would take my morning coffee outside and sit on a rusting bench. It was my ten minutes of serenity from the questions and the prying and the alto-gether oppressive atmosphere as the family gathered for breakfast. Inevitably, my few moments alone outdoors would coincide with Bob, the postman, arriving with the mail. After a while, we struck up conversation, politics and sport, to begin with, but after a few weeks, the subject of the family became the go-to topic. Bob told me of how strange the perception of the Reids was at the sorting office, and that they removed the previous postwoman from the round after Graham complained she tampered with their post. But the family didn't like me chatting with Bob, and they soon protested about opened letters and missing mail. In response to their notion, Graham erected a new postbox at the end of the footpath; as far away from the house as possible. They didn't want me to communicate with anyone in the outside world, particularly if it meant discussing them.

Out of habit, I opened the box. It stood at an angle, bent sideways by the weather, or so I convinced myself. It was empty, not a single letter, flyer, or takeaway menu in sight. Every address receives mail, especially junk, even if nobody lives there. So who was collecting it? With another look up at the house, I again bowed my head, and full of trepidation, traipsed forward the final few steps.

Once I reached the front door, my heart skipped several beats. Peering up towards the boarded windows, I noticed our bedroom, our marital room. Not only the room I spent my private time with Amelia but the place I used to escape, pretending to work or feign headaches. Anything for a few hours of isolation.

As with all the other doors and windows, the main entrance was boarded up too, although a rectangle had been neatly cut around the handle and lock. I still had my keys, the one thing they never asked me to hand in. I'm unsure why I held onto them, like some kind of memento.

You know the real reason, don't you?

With another glance over my shoulder, I attempted to insert the key. My fingers trembled so much; it forced me to concentrate fully on the simple task. The mechanism clicked open with ease — what was I expecting? — and my hand gripped the handle. It felt refreshingly cold against my sweaty palm.

There's no turning back now.

Into that house, the staircase, the landing, and the ghosts of a life gone by.

27

LISA

Unexpectedly, I actually enjoyed helping to configure his bloody curriculum vitae. I missed using a laptop for day-to-day tasks. When I worked at Opacy, several people would ask for my help to configure new Microsoft Word or Excel templates. Perhaps one day I could set up a small online business doing something similar, if things ever did return to normal. It would keep me busy and may bring in a little more money.

Talking of money and jobs, did he truly consider I believed him when he said he was going to cold call on estate agents looking for work? To begin with, he was far too neurotic. The way he continually paced the room and mumbled under his breath made it nigh on impossible to concentrate on the task he had set me. But more importantly, his heart wasn't in it. Searching for work was so far down on his to-do list, it may as well not exist. But we were walking on thin ice, half-scared to even talk in fear we might say the wrong thing. After a while, I told him to sit down or play with George, but he scowled and asked how long it would be before we printed off his precious CVs.

The following morning, I held George in my arms, air-kissing Matt goodbye before telling him to 'knock 'em dead'. He was so apprehensive, so highly strung, he couldn't even muster a reply. One good thing to transpire from his little charade was he finally shaved and actually did something with his hair. Matt had become so unkempt, a far cry from the man who used to pride himself on appearance, that I barely recognised him. He put on his best suit too, but I also caught him in the bedroom packing a sweatshirt, jeans and trainers in his holdall. He didn't know I spotted him, so I decided not to say anything.

We watched as he reversed out of the driveway. He glanced nervously through the passenger window and waved before driving off, through the village and towards the road which leads to Epsom.

"I bet he's going to see his hideous mother-in-law again," I said to George, carrying him through to the kitchen. "Why would he be going to see her again?"

I sat George down in his favourite chair at the back of the huge kitchen table. He could see everything from there and it allowed me to keep my eye on him. "Do you want to do some colouring?" I asked, going through the motions. "Perhaps they're going to discuss how to take you away from me?" Opening the colouring book, I soon found the first clean page. "But they don't know who they're dealing with, do they, my darling?" Kissing George on the forehead, I emptied a packet of crayons onto the table so he could select his colour. He looked at me; the strange woman talking to herself again. "Oh no, they don't know who they're dealing with."

Once satisfied he was settled, I filled the kettle and dropped a teabag into my favourite mug. And whilst I waited for the kettle to boil, I picked up my phone and quickly composed a message.

MATT

The front door didn't open as easily as the lock, but then again, it never did. With a slight nudge from my shoulder, it gave and I cautiously pushed it open. The smell of dampness was the first thing to hit me and I contemplated leaving the front door ajar to allow some fresh air in. But as I stepped inside, I realised how that may look to any passers-by. Not that anybody ever *passes by* that place.

As soon as the door clicked, it shut the light out too. Quickly, terrified of what might jump out on me, I flicked the closest switch, on-off-on — why do we always try it more than once? — but nothing. Unsurprisingly, the power must be disconnected, and my theory was soon confirmed when I tried another switch on the living room wall. Fumbling for my phone, the torch at least gave some brightness to work with. However, it also added to the creepiness of the old house, elongating the shadows and making the gloomy hidden corners even more unappealing. It didn't help that I knew what lay before me. The wide staircase and the landing beyond. What was it about the landing that scared the hell out of me so much? Is it where it lead, or is it the sheer dispirited expanse, never in full light, hiding secrets and macabre memories forever? I always imagined somebody watching me from above, lurking in the gloom, watching whilst knowing I could never see them in return. And then there were the rooms beyond the landing, where the house eventually wound itself to. The room they held me in, tied, drugged and most probably left to rot. The other rooms where I never ventured, past the turret. Where did it lead? Melissa's room was there somewhere, Tracy's and Katrina's before.

Starting downstairs, as a way of putting off the inevitable, I gingerly meandered from room to room, the smell of dampness accompanying me throughout. In the living room, I pressed my palm against the wall and could physically feel the moisture rising through the house. From somewhere deep underground.

I thought of the movies I'd seen of places being built on ancient burial grounds or some other long-lost cemetery which should remain undisturbed by the living.

The wind whistled from outside once more and I stood perfectly still as the familiar sound of Katrina's swing filtered through the cracks.

Squeak, squeak…

Yet again, I contemplated leaving, but I'd come this far and I had to figure out why I'd been summoned, and the part I was unsure I wanted to know, by whom.

Are they here now, waiting, watching?

Once I finished inspecting the ground floor, I was presented with the unavoidable. Standing at the foot of the stairs, I peered up into the dark void, the light on my phone suddenly very weak and unable to penetrate through the gloom.

Gripping the handrail with one hand, whilst attempting to keep my phone as steady as I could in the other, I began the ascent, one weary step at a time. I pricked my ears up like a cat, listening for the slightest of sounds, but the only noise I heard was the wind outside and the occasional squeak of the swing.

Squeak, squeak…

After what felt like a lifetime, I reached the top and found myself outside our bedroom door.

The memories.

Tentatively, I stepped inside, immediately convinced I could smell her; the faint scent of her favourite perfume or something else? But it was definitely there, the distinct aroma. Standing on her side of the bed, which appeared freshly made — clean sheets, pillowcases and duvet — my hand brushed across her pillow as I imagined her lying beside me, her eyes glancing up from her book and smiling towards me. I became lost in my own world, a fantasy invoked by the fragrance and the pain. Sitting down, I smiled back, caressing the cool sheets underneath the duvet.

"Oh, Amelia. Whatever happened to us?"

As my eyes welled, I did nothing to halt the emotions spilling out. Instead, I sat still, my hand gliding back and forth across the pillow like a pendulum on a clock.

Pull yourself together.

Standing once more, I took deep breaths, in and out, filling my lungs in an attempt to compose myself.

Checking the chest of drawers and wardrobes, I discovered they are all empty. So why was the bed made, and who prepared it? I had to check the remaining rooms.

With a click of our bedroom door, I crept along the landing to the next room: Katrina's. But it was stripped bare, no bed, no furniture. Melissa's the same, just the creaking of the boarded windows as the wind rattled them.

Hesitating outside the adjoining room, my hand gripped the handle, but I was unable to bring myself to turn it. The last time I was in there, I escaped through the window, Graham screaming after me. They tied me to the bed and Tracy kept me under her control with a cocktail of pills. But I somehow outmanoeuvred her, lodging the tablets into a gap between my back teeth. Once Tracy left, I spat out the offending articles and stayed awake on a far-reduced prescription. They made me sign paperwork in front of our solicitor, authorising half of my money to be transferred to Amelia's account. But it was never about the money for me. I didn't even know I had an aunt, let alone a rich one, and I would have willingly signed it all over if they only agreed to release me. But they would never allow that, especially Graham. He couldn't risk me leaving quietly and knew he had to dispose of me, just as he had Ryan Palmer, and, more recently, Lee Blackmore.

Counting down from ten, I forced myself to open the door, but once inside, I was confronted with more emptiness. No furniture, no clothes, only the boarded-up window.

And then I heard footsteps from behind, heavy and clonking against the stripped floorboards.

Clip-clop.

Slowly, they climbed the stairs with a slight hesitation at the top, before continuing along the landing.

Clip-clop.

One tortuous step after the other.

28

MATT

NOT ONCE DID the footsteps change pace. Scampering along the floorboards, I found myself propped upright against the farthest wall, as far away from the open doorway as possible. Waiting in trepidation, my nails clawed behind me, and ironically, the smell of dampness still overpowered my senses. Finally, she appeared.

Oh my...

Staring at her, I found it inconceivable to believe what I saw before me. My brain unable to register, and the ensuing dizziness threatened my very consciousness.

"Amelia?"

She smiled, her crimson lipstick stretching in sync with her lips. Her hair jet-black, shiny and shoulder length, just how I always loved it. And those eyes, the darkest, brownest eyes I'd ever seen. Suddenly, and I can't comprehend how, the room became flooded with light, the torch on my phone rendered unnecessary.

What is happening?

"It's me, Matthew. I've come back for you."

Is that a smile I could sense on my face?

"But how?" I stumbled, my voice uncertain and full of emotion. Slow-motion-like, I fell to my knees and bent forward until I buried my face in my lap. And I sobbed. Sobbed for my past, for the hurt, the suffering, the pain. And I sobbed for George, my beautiful baby boy. George!

"Matthew."

Raising my head, I forced myself upright. Darkness had once again descended and the stench of damp hit me hard. The outline of the person in the doorway became a blur and my vision failed me. Suddenly, with no prior warning, I bent forward and threw up the contents of my stomach.

I needed to get out and deal with whatever was happening in the cold light of day, away from that house. But as I stood, she was there again and Amelia straightened herself in the doorframe, somehow making herself larger than life. Her eyes hypnotised me, holding me in her trance. Months of heart-rendering pain threatened to submerge me.

"Oh, Matthew."

She stepped forward and I felt I should back away or attempt to dart past her. Run. This wasn't right.

So what's stopping you?

As Amelia placed her hand on my shoulder, it felt like a hundred electric shocks pulsating through me at once and I sensed myself re-energising. Slowly, I stood, until we were face to face, inches apart.

She took my hands in hers and amazingly, the only thing I could think of was I'd just thrown up. I tried to release her grasp, desperate to at least wipe my mouth, but she gripped tight and shook her head. The chemistry was unimaginable, sparks flying in all directions, and I was conscious she felt it too. Moving my lips to speak, Amelia quickly let go of my hand and pushed her finger to my lips before leaning forward and kissing me. Her hand slid to the back of my head and pulled me closer, and then we became lost, lost in each other. Within seconds, it felt as though the past year had been erased from memory, like one crazy dream which happened to somebody else far away during another lifetime.

We clung to each other as though life itself depended on it. I smelt her hair, her skin and, even though I couldn't hear a sound, I knew Amelia was silently crying into my shoulder.

We didn't talk much, like some unwritten pact not to ruin the hour together by daring to raise the past. We did little of anything, just held each other with an occasional kiss and a lot of tears.

Reluctantly, I finally let go. I had to leave, needed to return to Lisa and George. My emotions were out of control; the passion, the fear, and then the incredible guilt. Amelia sensed it too and she allowed her grip to ease.

She left via the back door, the same door she *escaped* from, but not before I begged for a few minutes to flee first. Even with my mind operating at an unprecedented rate, I still had the foresight to cover my tracks. But as I scooted past the leaning postbox at the end of the broken pathway, I realised I didn't have her number. Her message was 'Withheld', so how could I get in touch? Quickly, I ran around the side of the house, but Amelia was nowhere to be seen. Contemplating chasing her into the woods, the idea soon evaporated as I recognised she could be anywhere by then. So, once again, I found myself at her mercy and in the clutches of the family.

Hunching up my collar, I took a last look around and swiftly walked towards civilisation and reality. My heart was pounding, my mind was racing, and my entire body shook. It felt like a dream, an out-of-body experience. Did I really just meet my wife? She's supposed to have fled the country. She promised me.

'Go! Out the back. Get away. But never come back. Promise me you'll never come back.'

Amelia glanced out of the front window and then back to me.

'I love you, Matthew,' she mouthed. 'I promise with all my heart.'

So, if she gave me her word, she would never return, then why was she here?

She turned to go before hesitating at the door.

'And, Matt? Please look after our baby.'

LISA

His best suit was all scrunched up, leaving him looking as though someone had dragged him through a hedge back-wards. Surely he didn't visit potential employers dressed like that? Ha! Who am I kidding? He no more went exploring new opportunities than I spent the day sitting around a swimming pool drinking cocktails.

"Any luck?" I asked, taking his jacket from him before slinging it over the banister.

"Huh?" he replied, oblivious to me even standing there. His eyes were glazed over and his body shape was weird, kind of slumped forward, as if it was too much effort to drag himself upright. Despite all I knew and all he was going through, I felt sorry for Matthew. He wasn't a wicked man, just a deceitful one. And he could be a wonderful dad, the single reason I kept clinging onto the hope that something somewhere would click into place and everything would turn out to have been an awful nightmare. Nonetheless, I understood by then that normal would never be a phrase to describe our relationship.

And did he think of me as a good woman? After everything I'd been through too? The entire thing felt so one-sided. Looking at him trudging towards the kitchen, feeling all sorry for himself, I knew there wasn't one hint of concern for me or his son.

"I said, any luck?"

Raising my voice did the trick, and at least he had the decency to look at me.

"Who knows?" he replied with a shrug of his shoulders. "But don't raise your hopes, darling."

Don't worry, I never do.

"Yeah, I've had a good day, thanks," I sarcastically say, traipsing behind him into the kitchen. Why was I always following him? Like some lost sheep on the moors, as if he was my only hope of finding a safe route home. "And yes, thanks, George is fine, too. Perhaps you want to say hello to your child?"

He turned abruptly and for a split second, I wasn't sure if he would raise his hand. I'd said too much, and whatever he'd been doing that day, it somehow threatened to push him over the edge. But I was always confident Matt would never lay a hand on me. He might be a cheat and a liar, but he would never become violent. Well, at least I kept convincing myself of that. Finally, he responded.

"Have you, you know, seen or heard from anybody else lately, Lisa?"

His question threw me off-guard, so I pushed past him and busied myself with George at the table. Keeping my back to Matt, his silence, and the fact he stood perfectly still directly behind me, made me realise he wasn't going to let it go.

"What do you mean, have I seen or heard from anybody? Like who?"

"Shit, Lisa. It's a pretty straightforward question. Has anybody phoned you or messaged you? Somebody you wouldn't expect to hear from?"

The combination of panic and sheer angst in his voice gave me the strength to stand and face him. He was more scared than me, and that meant he couldn't know anything.

"No," I replied, feigning deep thought. "Apart from Hannah and Tom, I don't see anybody." Studying him, he digested my response, before walking over to the cupboard to retrieve his whisky. His silence made me angry, leaving me unsure whether he believed me or not. "Or did you have somebody else in mind?"

He shook his head. At least he had the decency to take two glass tumblers from the shelf.

"Want one?" he asked. He was in a world of his own,

lost and afraid, yet somehow invigorated. It was becoming a struggle to read his moods, like some kind of personality disorder, and I didn't know which one I would face. What the hell was happening to him, to us?

"Yes, please, with ice."

Matt tutted his disapproval before fetching the ice cube tray from the freezer. He believed it a waste to add anything to a decent single malt. In the past, when I was especially pissed off with him, I would pour a Diet Coke into mine too. He threatened to buy a cheap bottle of everyday Scotch if I continued to ruin such a sacred drink with fizzy pop. Matt could be such a pretentious idiot, but not that day.

29

LISA

It was Hannah's idea we went, so why did Matt keep looking at me as if I planned the whole damn thing, like some kind of punishment? And neither of us could blame Hannah, either. She was only trying to cheer us up, for crying out loud. I knew how angry he would be after I called her. It was within minutes of the police leaving our house and I needed someone to talk to. He sure as hell wasn't in the mood. He had barely spoken to me for two bloody days, ever since he arrived home in his crumpled suit. And, as soon as the officers left, he headed off to bed, feigning yet another migraine. Maybe he was telling the truth. He genuinely seemed unwell; pale, the sweats, his hands trembling whenever he took a drink, but I was finding it increasingly difficult to determine reality from fantasy. And if he wouldn't talk to me, then I had to find somebody else, and who better than my best friend?

Anyway, we were in the pub and we should at least try to enjoy ourselves and have a pleasant meal out. George looked content, playing with a beer mat, but after a while, even that annoyed Matt, as whenever he retrieved it from the floor, George purposefully dropped it again, accompanied by an exaggerated squeal of laughter.

Another thing I contemplated was how time appeared to be passing at such a ridiculous speed, and I often struggled to keep up with what day of the week it was, never mind how long it had been since Claudia West fell down the stairs and Francis Baker went missing. That's why it came as such a surprise when the same two police officers stood on our doorstep the night before, asking if they could come in for a few minutes and give us an update.

One thing I did know was that when Matt returned home from his make-believe job-hunting trip, he'd been a bag of nerves. And the way he kept looking at me. If he wanted to ask me something, why didn't he just bloody well ask? The only time he brought himself to speak was when he hinted he'd like to go out again, saying a job wasn't going to come to him. Possibly he wished to visit the same place he'd been before, but he either couldn't bring himself to ask or find a decent enough excuse to get past me. But something huge had happened, something so big his whole demeanour had altered again. If he had been to see Melissa, then could she have told him something, threatened him maybe? She certainly intimidated me. Deep down, I didn't particularly care if Matt went out again. I had my own task to complete, and I needed him well out of the way to do it.

. . .

"We thought we would drop by and ask if you've heard from your old neighbour, Miss Baker?"

The officer directed his question at Matt, who instantly glanced at me, as if I may have a suitable reply lined up.

"No. Why should I?" he replied, rather too abruptly. The little beads of sweat returned to his forehead, and, combined with his pasty complexion, two days of stubble and unkempt hair, he looked like some kind of ardent drug addict.

"No specific reason, Mr Walker. It's just that she hasn't returned to her apartment, and we have interviewed most of the other residents in the block, the majority of whom indicated that if anybody should know, it's you."

Matt appeared to go paler still, quickly followed by turning bright red. Again he looked to me for comfort, but I bowed my head, embarrassed on his behalf, as well as feeling like some kind of tramp in front of the officers.

"I told you before," he continued, his voice shaky, "that we were purely friends. We sometimes had a glass of wine or a cup of tea together. I'm not her best pal, you know."

He was on the brink of making a fool of himself and his rapid replies made him reek of culpability.

"Just calm down a little, sir. This is a routine call. Miss Baker has gone missing, and her only living relative is her mum. She's beside herself with worry. We've called by to check if you've heard anything."

"No. Nothing." Again, too quick, Matt.

The second officer produced a notepad from his pocket, flicked it over several pages, and spoke for the first time since they arrived.

"You said you were in Birmingham the day of Claudia West's accident?"

"Yes, yes. That's exactly where I was. Ask my boss, well, my old boss. He knows where I was."

Once I'd forced myself to raise my head, I couldn't take my eyes off Matt. His words were tumbling out at such speed they constantly tripped over one another. He stammered and stuttered and fidgeted from foot to foot. From my position, I could see his T-shirt clinging to the middle of his back and the rim of his collar visibly wet.

"We did, sir, and he corroborates—"

"There you go then. So why are you asking me the same damn questions?"

"Because, if you let me finish, sir, he also informed us you paid for the hotel yourself in Birmingham before claiming it back via expenses. Is that correct?"

Matt glanced at me before replying.

"Yes, yes. That's correct. Why?"

"Well, you don't mind us checking your bank statement, you know, just to clarify."

"Yeah, no problem," Matt said, some kind of confidence finally returning. "I should have thought of that myself. I'll need to print them off, though."

"Not an issue, sir," the first officer intervened. "Here's my card with direct access to my email address. If you could send me a copy within twenty-four hours, that would be great."

Matt's self-assurance appeared to knock the officers off their stride. Did they presume they were onto something, especially given Matt's inexplicable reaction? But his mood swing proved nothing to me. He could be up one minute and down the next, admittedly mostly down, for no apparent reason to an outsider looking in.

However, for the trained eye, Matt came across as mendacious.

"How's the job hunting going, Matt?" Tom asked as Matt bent down to collect the beer mat for the umpteenth time. He glanced at me as he straightened himself. Even George appeared to suddenly become disinterested in his little game and instead looked at his dad to see how he was going to get out of this one.

"Slowly, Tom. Slowly. Why do you ask?"

"He's only showing interest," I replied, before addressing our neighbour myself. "It's difficult, Tom. There isn't a lot of work around here in Matt's field, and he doesn't want to return to the city. Do you, dear?"

Matt stalled for a split second and I knew the answer was yes, even though he had to affirm the negative.

"No, no. I don't want to go back there. It's too far away."

What about a place like Epsom?" Hannah interrupted. I could have fucking killed her for mentioning that place. Knowing perfectly well why she suggested it, she still had no right to propose somewhere so connected with his past; our past.

"Why's that then, Hannah?" Matt asked, propping one elbow on the table and glaring directly into her eyes. This was supposed to be a fun night out, but it was rapidly going downhill.

"Oh, just you used to live there. I assumed you would know the area well. Isn't that important in your line of work?"

Matt glanced at me as I allowed an audible sigh of relief to escape. For one brief moment, I thought she would mention our conversation from two days before. I'd sent her a message after Matt left the house and she called me back within minutes. Half an hour later, Hannah and Tom were sitting around our kitchen table and we'd talked about Matt's past in more detail than ever before. Hannah and Tom, especially Tom, were always keen listeners. Tom suggested Matt may have returned to his old house, but when I asked why he would do that, Tom clammed up, claiming it was only an idea. At least Hannah's reasoning for job hunting around Epsom appeared to placate Matt.

"Yes. That might not be a bad idea, Hannah," he said, recovering just as quickly as he had when the police requested evidence of him staying in Birmingham.

A few moments of awkward silence ensued, and I dreaded what someone might say next. Fortunately, right on cue, the food arrived and we could at least be relatively quiet without the necessity of forced conversation. Not that it stopped Tom.

"I saw a police car outside your house last night whilst walking Charlie," he said, taking his plate of food from the waiter. "Hope everything is alright?"

Hannah glanced at me, both of us realising he was pushing Matt as far as he dare. Peeking at Matt out of the corner of my eye, I could see the whites of his knuckles as his hands gripped the cutlery. Shit, he looked as though he might stand up, reach across the table and stab Tom in the neck.

"Everything is fine," I interjected. "It's just routine enquiries after what happened to that poor woman living in Matt's old apartment block." Turning to Matt, I rested my hand on his. "Isn't it, darling?"

"Eh?" Matt looked at my hand, which at least had the

desired effect of stopping him from staring at Tom. His veins threatened to pop out of his temples. "Yeah, sure. Just routine," he confirmed awkwardly.

"That's alright then," Tom said, sticking his fork into a roast potato. "No doubt they'll keep me up to speed at our next meeting. You know, as community watchdog." Once again, I could feel Matt's hand tense beneath mine. Why was I still holding it?

"Enjoy knowing everybody else's business, do you, Tom?"

Oh shit, no. I wanted the ground to open up and swallow me whole.

Tom let out a sarcastic laugh.

"It's not like that," he replied. "It's just nice to know what's going on when you hold such an important role in the community."

Before Matt could respond, the pub door opened, allowing a gust of wind to rush indoors and whip up the flames on the fire. George laughed and the sight of his cheeky little face allowed me some respite from the unbearable tension around the table. Fortunately, everybody joined in with George's infectious giggle; everybody apart from Matt, that is. Instead, his attention fell upon the woman who'd just walked in.

Following his eyes, I tried to understand why she would hold his interest. She closed the door behind her and glanced nonchalantly around the pub, before making her way to the bar. I studied her as she ordered a drink, before turning and surveying the room once again. Finally, her eyes settled on Matt and she offered him a little wave of her hand. He nodded his head in return, but not before his cheeks began to burn.

"Friend of yours?" I asked casually.

But he didn't need to reply. He looked like a school-child caught with his hand in the sweet jar and it only confirmed what I already knew. Nothing would ever change with Matthew Walker.

30

MATT

WHEN SOPHIE WAVED to me across the pub, I instantly felt my face burn, even though I had nothing to hide. It was one brief meeting on the train, and that was weeks and weeks ago. Did I ask her to join me for a drink? It wasn't anything important, so why did I blush? Because of the way everybody glared at me, pre-judging without knowing the facts. Lisa didn't help the situation either.

"Friend of yours?" she asked, causing Tom to bow his head and stifle a laugh. What was he getting out of it? Struggling to quell the anger inside, my calm response amazed me, especially with everything else going on.

"Not particularly. Just seen her around the village a couple of times, that's all."

"Evidently, she seems to know you quite well," Lisa continued. "She's good-looking, isn't she, Hannah?"

Hannah momentarily peered up from her plate of food. It took a lot of effort not to lean over the table and push her face directly into the meat, potatoes, and gravy. She just nodded, probably unable to bring herself to admit the truth.

Instead, her grubby husband spoke on her behalf. "Yeah, I guess she is," he said, looking from Sophie and then back to Lisa. "Not as pretty as you, though. Don't you think so, Matt?"

The way he smiled at Lisa enraged me further. Nevertheless, it didn't help dissipate my embarrassment as everybody's attention returned to me. Even George looked. I've never been the type of person to blush easily, but it wasn't just a matter of self-consciousness, more of an unbridled desire to choke my neighbour with my bare hands.

"Erm, no, Tom." I hesitated, staring him in the eyes. Lisa shuffled uncomfortably next to me. "No, of course not. What a ridiculous question to ask."

Tom gave me a stare which I couldn't interpret before we finished our meals in silence. Although hungry, I only ate a fraction of my food assailed by an overwhelming sensation I might be sick ever since my encounter with Amelia. Once our plates were collected, Tom patted Charlie's head underneath the table.

"Come on, boy, let's take you outside."

As we watched Tom take an eternity to drag the dog from the floor, I drank the remainder of my pint of beer in one.

"You in a rush to get to the bar?"

Lisa nudged me and nodded at my empty glass before looking up at Sophie. It genuinely wasn't my intention, but when I followed Lisa's gaze, I noticed Sophie was waiting to be served another drink.

"You can fetch them?" I suggested.

Hannah and Lisa exchanged a look.

"Okay," Lisa replied. "You're kind of trapped in there. Besides, it's your turn to entertain George for a while. I could murder another gin and tonic."

She collected my empty glass and stood with a sarcastic grin etched across her face.

"Same for me, please," Hannah said, smiling broadly, pushing her glass forward. "And Tom will have his usual."

Watching Lisa as she purposefully strode to the bar, as if to conspire against me further, the only space was between a large gentleman and Sophie. With a quick grin over her shoulder, Lisa squeezed in next to her.

To save myself from talking to Hannah, I focused my attention on George instead, and attempted to make him laugh with silly noises. Not that I needed to bother. Hannah was far more interested in Lisa and Sophie at the bar.

Does she know her?

After a few extremely awkward minutes, my phone vibrated on the table. Hannah leant forward, but even if she saw the screen, she would only have read the same as me, 'Withheld Number'.

"Erm, can you see to George, please? I really must take this. It could be from the agent I dropped my CV into."

Without waiting for a reply, even though I realised Hannah would have seen straight through my lame excuse, I grabbed my phone and walked swiftly to the exit. Lisa and Sophie looked up as I passed. The moment I step into the pub car park, I hit the green button.

"Hello?" I ask, desperately. "Is that you?"

We spoke for less than a minute. I had so many questions which I'd stored in my memory bank since I'd last seen her, but as soon as I heard her voice, I couldn't recall a single one. Amelia did most of the talking and said she needed to speak to me urgently. The way she said it left all kinds of connotations cascading around my head. *Urgently*, as in she can't wait to see me, or as in she has some terrible news? Again, so many questions, yet I still couldn't form a cohesive sentence. We did agree to meet at the house before she abruptly hung up.

Allowing myself a few moments in the cool October air, the sight of Charlie trotting towards me caught me off-guard. Behind him, Tom ambled slowly across the car park.

"Come on, boy," he said to his faithful friend, clipping the lead onto his collar. "Let's get back inside to the girls."

Charlie offered me a low growl, but not once did Tom acknowledge me.

LISA

"Hi," the woman said as I approached the bar. I could feel at least two sets of eyes boring into the rear of my head.

"Hi," I replied, not being able to think of a single word to say.

"I'm Sophie." She introduced herself, turning her back to the pub as I squeezed in next to her. "Are you a friend of Matt's? I met him once on the train."

I glanced over my shoulder as if to remind myself who she was talking about.

"You could say that," I replied, kicking myself for being so sarcastic. It wasn't this woman's fault Matt flirted with everything in a skirt, but if they'd only spoken on a train once before, why the hell was I so worried? "I'm the mother of his child. My name is Lisa."

"Pleased to meet you," Sophie replied. She continued to talk whilst waving her credit card in the barman's direction. "I've seen you before. Always out with our *neighbourhood watch* friends."

She exaggerated their title in a derisory manner.

"What do you mean? Are you talking about Hannah and Tom?"

"Yeah, the village gossips. It wouldn't surprise me if they have a camera set up in every one of our homes."

Although facetious, her words still triggered something in the back of my mind. It was true. Hannah and Tom did know so much about everybody in the village, especially us. But it was also true they would show interest when in our company, and I realised I was never slow to discuss our secrets. I wondered if they were the same with everybody else.

"What makes you say that?" I asked, allowing myself a further glance over my shoulder. Matt was fidgeting uncomfortably as he addressed George whilst Hannah focused her attention on us. It didn't appear as though she was concentrating on me, but more on Sophie. As if she was trying to lip-read the conversation.

"I just don't trust them, that's all," Sophie continued. "And he gives me the creeps, the way he ogles women. Has he tried anything on with you yet? It's a wonder Matt allows him near his wife."

"Eh?" I'd become so mesmerised by Sophie describing Tom as some kind of lech that the word *wife* took me completely unawares. "His *wife*? I'm not his wife. How do you know his wife?"

Sophie looked at me as if I was having a mental breakdown.

"You're his wife, aren't you?" She nodded at our table and it finally dawned on me who she meant.

"Oh, me?" I giggled nervously, a mixture of her confusion and my relief. "We're not married, just partners. Partners with a child. Living together. That's all."

Sophie laughed at my agitated response.

"Okay. No need to explain to me."

She ordered a drink, whilst offering to buy me one too. Politely refusing, I nodded towards the three empty glasses on the bar. She took a sip of her wine and paid the barman with her card. As she did, I noticed Matt striding across the pub heading for the exit. He held his phone up and offered me a pathetic grin.

"Why do you keep meeting up with them, then?" Sophie asked. "I must admit, they don't seem your type."

She's not letting this go.

A space opened up on the far side of her, but she made no attempt to move away. Instead, her arm rested against mine and I felt relieved Matt had left the pub. I wanted to stay with Sophie. Something compelled me to get closer.

Does she feel the same?

"I like them. They've been good to me."

I'd been deliberately looking at the drink optics behind the bar, not having the nerve to face her. But when I allowed myself a glance to my right, I found Sophie staring directly into my eyes. Her face was only inches from mine, despite there being more than enough room for her to back away. My heartbeat increased and all kinds of thoughts entered my head. She was very attractive. What did she want and why was my heart beating like it never had before?

"Yes, madam?"

The barman's arrival snapped me out of my trance.

"Erm, let's see. What am I after? Yes. I know. Two gin and tonics, a pint of bitter and a single malt, please." The words rushed out, and I heard Sophie laugh beside me.

"I'll leave you to it," she said, brushing her hand over mine. "And if you ever need to talk, take this, so you know where to find me." She removed a business card from a case which I previously presumed only contained credit cards.

As I waited for the barman to fix my drinks, I took several deep breaths, Sophie's pretty face engrained in my mind.

"Someone looks pleased," Hannah said as I swapped places with her next to George. "What did she have to say for herself?"

Before I could reply, Tom and Charlie rejoined us.

"That's yours, Tom," I said, ignoring Hannah's remark whilst pushing the whisky glass towards him.

"Thanks, Lisa," he said, sounding somewhat breathless. "Matt will join us soon, once he gets off his not-so-secret phone call."

31

LISA

FOR TWO DAYS it had been on the tip of my tongue to ask Matt who he was on the phone to outside the pub, but I couldn't bring myself to face the consequences that would inevitably follow. Besides, the way he was being so bloody vacant, I doubt I would have got a straight answer from him anyway. His entire vocabulary had descended into a choice between, huh, yes, no and whatever. Attempting to get him to expand became far too much of a chore, so I let things go and we spent our time conversing with George instead.

On Saturday morning, he donned his now wrinkle-free suit and set off with a fresh batch of curriculum vitae in his hands. Tempted to ask if he would throw them in the same bin as the others, I again decided against confrontation. As soon as he left, I put George into his coat and Wellington boots and we strolled off into the village and in the direction of Hannah and Tom's. But I had another call to make on the way, an itch I'd needed to scratch since meeting her in the pub.

'…and if you ever need to talk, you know where to find me…'

After sending a quick text to the number on her business card to get the correct address, I could feel butterflies in my stomach as we walked towards her house. We were only inside Sophie's for thirty minutes or so, but again, I found her company fascinating and felt compelled to get to know her much better. She told me she was a video editor before divulging further information about Hannah and Tom, which didn't particularly shock me, especially since our original impromptu meeting had given me plenty of food for thought. But it was more the fact I couldn't take my eyes off her, which surprised me most. The way she spoke, the way she dressed and her entire demeanour captivated me. Perhaps it was just a different person to talk to. After all, I'd only really spoken to Matt, Hannah and Tom during the past year but we instantly bonded and I knew Sophie sensed a similar connection, too.

A while later, I found myself sitting at Hannah's table, armed with a pot of tea and a selection of cakes. But I didn't feel like eating. I just wanted to talk. Chat about everything, and as always, Hannah was the ideal listener. Fortunately, Tom left after the first drink. He appeared especially interested in Matt's recent behaviour. His attentiveness to detail amazed me, so much so, at one point, I thought he might start taking notes. Tom mentioned Matt's *secret* phone call but said he didn't say much, so he couldn't decipher who it might have been. However, just catching Matt on the phone appeared to have made Tom's day, and it somehow gave him a fresh spring in his step. Matt was right. He was obsessed with him.

And then Tom received a phone call, came back into the room and said he had a neighbourhood watch meeting to attend. Before he left, he kissed his wife and turned to kiss me too. I couldn't be sure, but it felt as though he left his lips on my cheek a few moments longer than he had Hannah's. It made me nauseous in her company, but she didn't appear to notice.

"What's that all about, rushing off like that?" I asked, noticing Hannah didn't appear to be the slightest bit surprised he'd upped and gone in the blink of an eye.

"He's late. He became so engrossed in your story that he's left himself short of time. Silly man. He was out most of yesterday too. These neighbourhood watch meetings are becoming very regular."

Hannah cleared the table, and I took it as my cue to get George ready for the walk home. Kissing Hannah on both cheeks, I said I'd be in touch.

"Make sure you are, Lisa. The slightest thing. Tom and I are anxious about what Matthew might be capable of."

Once I arrived home, I began some inane chores to keep my mind busy and try not to focus on where Matt was or dwell on what Hannah said. She didn't know him like I did, and I was convinced he wasn't capable of doing anybody any harm.

After stripping the beds and cleaning the bathroom, I entered the spare room; the room where Matt kept his laptop to do his infamous job hunting. But once I reached the desk, it wasn't his computer which grabbed my attention, instead, it was the bank statement which lay on top of it.

First, I checked the date. It covered the whole of August. Of course Lisa, the police asked him to provide proof of payment for the hotel in Birmingham before claiming it back on expenses. He must have scanned the document and sent a copy to prove his alibi.

Nothing to see here.

But then I turned the statement over. Page four.

Flicking it over, back and forth, I double and tripled checked the dates. Yes, he did check into the hotel at one o'clock on the Monday afternoon and he'd admitted being so bored at the exhibition he'd left early, but on the next page was another entry altogether.

At three minutes past three, Matt used his bank card again. And this time, he was nowhere near Birmingham.

MATT

At ten o'clock in the morning, I'd scarcely had any sleep since I received the call from Amelia two nights before. Not only did Amelia's words chill me, but I also couldn't shake the feeling of Tom eavesdropping. How long had he been there, what did he hear and, more importantly, had he relayed any of it to Lisa? But what could he have heard? I barely spoke. Did I even say her name?

'Hello. Is that you?'

Even Tom could decipher nothing from that.

If one good thing came out of our meeting up in the pub, it was Hannah's suggestion to try estate agents in Epsom. Without her realising, it gave me a viable excuse to go back out job hunting, leaving Lisa unable to argue as it was her best friend's idea. The night before, she reluctantly printed off ten more curriculum vitae for me to take. At one point, in the not-too-distant past, I'm convinced Lisa would have suggested she and George come along too, but she didn't mention any such thing. It felt as though she was giving up on me. The problem was, I couldn't shake the feeling that she knew something.

So, once more, I said my goodbyes and asked George to wish me luck. I'm sure Lisa stifled a laugh, but I wasn't in the mood for another argument, so I ruffled George's hair and hung my suit jacket in the back of the car before clambering into the front. At least Lisa had removed all the creases, again without question how I'd got it so crumpled in the first place.

The weather had completely broken, and the gloom of the previous few days finally turned to rain. A steady drizzle fell and I found myself mesmerised by the wiper blades as they swished back and forth. And in time with the wipers, everything I'd been through during the past three years flickered in and out of my mind, torturing me with every swipe.

With the combination of the weather and my haste to see Amelia, I decided to park near the house instead of at the station. Leaving my car along the road, I quickly changed from my suit into the sweatshirt and jeans I'd left in the boot from my previous *job-hunting* trip, before keeping my head low and passing the final few terraced houses. It intrigued me I didn't know any occupants in the row of six or seven identical properties, despite walking past them countless times before. I considered how much they knew about what happened at the end of the street in the boarded-up house.

Increasing my pace, I soon found myself at the end of

the lane, with only the shuttered house and the woods for company. And suddenly, as before, something felt very wrong.

Allowing myself a quick glance towards the trees, I convinced myself somebody was there; waiting, watching. The steady rain made it difficult to decipher the shadows from the gloom, so much so, the swaying branches could easily have been a myriad of dancing children. The very thought sent shivers down my spine.

Whilst scrambling around for the house key in my coat pocket, the door swung open and Amelia stood on the other side. I inadvertently smiled, and although she briefly reciprocated, she turned and walked to the living room instead. Quickly, feeling somewhat hurt by the lack of a warm greeting, I closed the front door behind me. Wait! Was somebody there? Dashing between the trees in the woods?

Oh shit. Should I be here?

Shutting the door with a bang, I leant against the frame to catch my breath. I realised how much warmer it felt than last time, and I heard the fire crackling from the room Amelia had disappeared into. As I stepped inside to join her, my heart faltered as she sat patiently in Graham's favourite chair, a glass of wine in her hand. Although pissed off she didn't initially embrace or kiss me, she nodded at the seat next to the fire and I noticed a generous glass of the same wine awaiting me.

The furniture? The room was bare only days before.

"We need to talk, Matthew," Amelia said calmly, raising her glass with a half-hearted smile. "Please, take a seat."

My initial perception that something was very wrong multiplied by the second. The two chairs and small table in the centre of the room made it appear like I was under some kind of interrogation, and everything already on her terms. Maybe it already had been, Amelia holding my phone number whilst not providing her own; just as it had always been.

"What's wrong?" I asked, perching myself on the edge of the seat, ready to run. The memories of a thousand hideous nights spent in this very room crowded into my mind.

"Nothing's *wrong*. Quite the opposite." Amelia sat forward, placing her glass on the small table between us. Interlocking her fingers, she stared me directly in the eye. "How's baby George?"

What?

"He's good. No, he's much more than that. He's great. Why do—"

"I'm just interested. That's all."

Wait, that's him! That's Matthew approaching the house. What the hell is he doing here? I haven't sent him a message since the other day when I teased him about watching him, so why would he be at the house?

I'm in the woods. Of course, I'm in the woods. It's my domain, my playground, my forever hiding place. And he's letting himself in the front door of our house like he's the lord and fucking master.

Hold on! Who's that? The door opens before he's even taken his key out. There's somebody inside.

Oh shit no!

It can't be. Surely not.

Is that actually her?

Please say no.

32

MATT

As I OPENED my heavy and weary eyes, Amelia's were the first thing I saw. Those lovely, wide, dark brown eyes. Yet they appeared vacant and glazed, and they stared directly through me. Attempting a smile, I soon discovered the smallest of movements sent a jolt of pain through my forehead before penetrating both temples, like blunt needles being slowly inserted.

What is this?

My mouth felt so dry I struggled to prise my lips apart, bonded by something which tasted uncannily like rusting nails.

"Amelia," I eventually managed, again sending a pulse of discomfort throughout my entire skull.

But Amelia didn't reply. Instead, she remained motionless, her eyes forever boring into mine. She didn't flinch, nothing stirred, not an ounce of life. Forcing myself to do something, anything, I shifted my pupils from side to side. To my left, I could see we were on the floor, hardwood panels directly beneath us. Looking up, the only thing I could make out was the white-painted ceiling and one light bulb suspended from its exposed wiring.

Where am I?

My eyes focused back on Amelia, but still, she didn't move. "Amelia. Are you okay?" Barely recognising my voice, the words escaped, scarcely more than a whisper, but certainly loud enough for her to hear. If she could.

The sight of my prostrate wife forced panic to rise inside me. This wasn't right.

Breathing! Is she breathing? Listening intently, I prayed for the slightest of sounds. Just the minutest shallow breath would give me all the satisfaction I required.

Tentatively, unsure if I had any internal injuries, I moved my arm forward. Although my head protested at the effort, my body didn't complain and I was able to stretch my fingers until they met with Amelia's. They were stone cold.

My breathing became more erratic and I knew something terrible had happened. But what, and where the hell were we?

Slowly, I propped myself up onto one elbow and realised the upper half of my body was injury free. Allowing my eyes to leave Amelia momentarily, I soon recognised where we are; the floor in the hallway, in the family house, and we were lying at the foot of the stairs. As soon as I looked back at my wife, I saw a huge dark pool of thick crimson fluid emanating from the rear of her skull. I followed it until it became no more than a trickle, eventually nestling at the skirting board on the far side of the room.

"Shit, no…" My voice groggy and my head throbbed so badly I thought it may explode. Forcing myself up further, I knelt at Amelia's side. Her eyes now staring into emptiness instead of into mine. Although I knew the answer, I felt for a pulse in her neck and immediately flinched at the temperature of her skin.

Standing groggily, my hand sliding against the wall for support, I peered up the stairwell towards the landing. That landing.

Had we fallen? Desperately, I racked my brain for answers. We met at the house, that much I recalled, and we drank wine in the living room.

Panic enveloped me and I knelt at Amelia's side, pleading for her to wake up, to show any sign of life. Thinking it probably best if I didn't touch her — *too late for that, Matt* — I instead paced around, constantly stepping over the pool of blood whilst pushing and pulling my fingers back and forth through my hair.

She can't be dead. My wife. My soulmate. Tears pricked at the rear of my eyes and my legs felt unexpectedly weak. "I'm so sorry," I said, barely audible against the deafening buzzing between my ears.

Pull yourself together. You need to think.

Lisa! How the hell could I tell her where I was? Checking my phone, I discovered it was almost nine o'clock in the morning, the day after I allegedly travelled to Epsom to drop off some stupid fucking CVs to disguise the real reason I was there. My phone also informed me I had seven missed calls and half a dozen texts, all from Lisa.

Quickly, I checked the house, not knowing what I was

actually looking for. Once I covered downstairs, I stepped over Amelia for the umpteenth time, barely able to set eyes on her, and took the stairs, two at a time. The pain was easing at last, but I knew it was down to adrenaline rather than whatever had caused it. I still couldn't believe I had no other aches or bruising, especially given my position on the hallway floor next to my wife. However, as soon as I entered our bedroom, the reason for my unbearable pain took shape.

We drank. A lot. In bed. Together.

Two empty wine bottles and a third almost drained on my side of the bed. An empty wine glass on each bedside table. The duvet tossed to one side and a pillow strewn on the floor.

What did we do?

It at least gave me brief relief that I didn't have to check the rest of the upstairs rooms. That corridor, the other bedrooms, *that* bedroom.

Returning to the landing, I leant over the banister, hopelessly trying to recall what happened and in some vain hope Amelia had stirred.

Dancing!

We'd been dancing, there, on the landing. Amelia plugged music through her portable speaker, and we danced and laughed and kissed as we smooched and twirled and embraced. Our figures a blur in my mind.

But how did it get so out of control? Three bottles of wine between us was plenty to drink, but not enough to forget most of the evening, and definitely not enough to trip and fall down a flight of stairs — both of us. I'd drunk much more in the past and my head never felt *that* bad the next morning. Did we take something? Did we argue or fight?

Yes, Matthew. You argued.

It began to return, piece by piece. Following the drinking, the dancing and the merriment, Amelia talked about George again. As soon as I arrived, she asked about him, but we moved on, drank wine and eventually ended up in bed. But Amelia wouldn't let it go. And then something else came flooding back. She told me the real reason we were here, in that house.

'*I want George back. He's my child.*'

Again, I gaped at the body below, panic now reaching a whole new level. I knew I had to do something about it. Calling the police was not a viable option. I'd met with a woman on the run, a person of interest to the authorities, and the very same person I allowed to escape all those months ago. And then there was telling Lisa? Both would lead to serious implications. The first could easily lead to imprisonment, whilst the second would be the last I ever saw of my son. Besides, either choice would inevitably lead to the other.

I spiked her drink! I remembered. Amelia had been out of control, a mixture of alcohol and conviction that George was her child.

'He's Lisa's,' I argued.

Isn't he?

Before we moved to Scotland, I was prescribed strong sleeping tablets. Although they never helped much, I still carried them wherever I went. *So what did I do?* I fetched a fresh bottle of wine, poured two glasses whilst I was in the kitchen and dropped a couple of pills into Amelia's drink. I needed her to calm down. But two? That wouldn't lead to her falling. *Then what?* Did I visit the toilet, look around the house for something? It was all so vague, yet I must have taken the drinks upstairs, as there were now two empty glasses on the bedside tables. Did I push her? Perhaps we fell together. Why else would I wake up next to her?

What the hell had I got myself into and why did I agree to meet her in the first place? I helped Amelia to escape over a year ago, along with her passport and phone; to go far away and make a fresh start, but with strict instructions never to contact me again. But she did, and I didn't hesitate in agreeing to meet her.

You've never stopped loving her, have you?

Ever since we met earlier that week, I felt a renewed urge deep inside. A genuine feeling of hopefulness. Even with a child to raise, something had been absent from my life. A spark. The spark which Amelia never failed to ignite. Despite all she put me through, I simply could not let go. People say they would have run a mile in my position, but what do they know? Have they ever been *that* deeply in love, so dependent upon somebody that it physically hurts if you don't see them? I'd had a rough life, flitting from place to place, job to job, partner to partner, until Amelia came along and changed things forever.

But now a cruel accident, I had to convince myself, was to part us eternally. A sign maybe. Some hideous manifestation to force me never to set eyes upon her again.

You've killed her.

Fighting back more tears, I was aware I had to dispose of her body. Nobody knew we are there and nobody could have possibly seen us. We purposefully arrived separately too. As far as the authorities were concerned, Amelia had fled the country, they said so themselves. She withdrew two thousand pounds from her bank account, had her passport, and no one had seen or heard from her since.

But could I really do it? Bury my wife along with our past forever? Standing over her whilst finally allowing the tears to flow, the answer was inevitable.

You have no other choice.

Barely believing it with my own eyes, I somehow carried Amelia to the woods alone. She wasn't heavy, more awkward. I took her to the spot where I knew the authorities recently dug the ground looking for evidence of any further buried bodies. It was where Ryan Palmer once lay. They found nothing else, but I hoped they made my life a little easier. The soil should be soft, easy to dig, easy to fill, and most unlikely to be disturbed again anytime in the future.

How the hell are you thinking so straight? You're as crazy as the rest of them.

As I ran back to the outbuilding to find a shovel, I couldn't believe I was so in control of the situation. Had I really killed somebody with my bare hands?

As I hoped, the ground was soft, and it took little effort to remove the first foot or so of soil. I was sweating profusely, my hangover a thing of the past, and pure adrenaline ran through every single vein.

Are you enjoying this?

Then the shovel strook something, something solid. Pushing it down firmly with my foot, the shovel hit the same spot, refusing to go any further. Spinning it around, I scraped the earth instead of trying to dig. To begin with, I made some progress, but it was short-lived and the blade hit the same thing again.

Dropping to my knees, I frantically scooped the soil away, throwing it to my left, my right, anything to reveal what the hell was there. And as soon as I cleared enough debris, I immediately recognised what was before me. The smell hit me too, the combination of both making me lean to my right and throw up bright yellow bile from the pit of my otherwise empty stomach.

Standing, my eyes didn't leave the object buried in the ground, and although I kept telling myself it couldn't be true, I knew damn well that it was Francis Baker's suitcase. And the rancid smell escaping from the small opening informed me it wasn't empty either.

33

LISA

HE DIDN'T COME HOME that night, and he didn't reply to my messages either, not until the following day, at least. But the thing which surprised me most? I wasn't all that bothered. Perhaps the time had long drifted by since I realised our relationship was over, or, in hindsight, could it have been something else altogether? I wanted total closure from that family and I understood I was using Matt as the only person who could lead me to them. Either way, when he did eventually call the next morning, I was already waiting for my lift to Epsom.

"Hey," he said, his voice croaky as though he hadn't slept in days. "I'm so sorry."

"Where are you?" I asked, not concerned with his latest sob story.

"I'm in a lay-by. Near Epsom. Yesterday, I had such a shit day, babe, so I stopped at an off-licence and bought a cheap bottle of Scotch. I parked up and necked over half of it. I must have passed out. Woke up feeling crap."

He attempted to laugh, but it came across as pathetic. The truth is, I could have believed his story. It was just the sort of thing he would have done by that stage. But I also knew Matthew very well, and he was lying through his back teeth.

"Okay. Why don't you make your way home and grab some rest? I'm going out with Hannah and Tom for the day. Get George out of the house for a while. I'll see you later, okay, babe?"

Satisfied to get my own 'babe' into the conversation, I hung up before he could reply. But despite my best efforts at not giving a shit, I still couldn't shake the question of where he'd been? The discovery of the petrol receipt on his bank statement proved that not only was he constantly lying to me, but could there also be something in what Hannah suggested?

'...*Tom and I are anxious about what Matthew might be capable of...*'

However, I needed to perk myself up and, with Matt out of the way, we could visit his crazy mother-in-law again. What felt like a lifetime ago, my last visit concluded with her threatening to take my boy away, and nobody ever does that. Tom and Hannah also encouraged me to face her head-on. "You can't let her walk all over you like that," Tom had said. "The more I hear about that family, the more I fear for both you and George." He didn't mention Matt because he believed Matt was part of the problem, and in no way, part of the solution.

. . .

Tom drove again, so I sat in the back of the car with George asleep in his seat next to me. Hannah and Tom made idle chatter, but I paid little attention and instead stared out of the window at the endless rows of hedges and trees rushing by. The Surrey countryside is quite exquisite, and I understood why so many rich commuters lived there rather than the manic streets of central London. Best of both worlds, Matt once described it, and he wasn't mistaken. I tried to picture where he was, where he had been, and who with. Somehow, I couldn't believe he was being unfaithful. His mind wasn't in the right place for fun and games, but then again, the way he blushed after seeing Sophie in the pub a few nights before, I guess he was capable of anything. Everything needed to conclude, one way or the other.

"You okay going in on your own, love?" Hannah enquired as we pulled into the care home car park. My eyes scanned the other vehicles, searching for any sign of our own. But there were only a handful, and it soon satisfied me Matt wasn't around. I asked Tom to park at the back, under the trees, just in case anybody was watching. It was farthest away from the conservatory too, so Melissa wouldn't see us arrive until I sprang my surprise visit.

"Yes, thanks. She won't do anything inside there. Besides, there are nurses and staff everywhere, so I can easily call for help if she gets nasty again."

Eventually, after he was content with his parking, Tom spun around. It took him bloody ages to manoeuvre his car, and I half expected him to take a measuring tape out to ensure he was an equal distance from both white lines. I wished it was just me and Hannah as before. Tom could be so domineering.

"Remember," he replied, his voice conveying an

authoritative tone, "the law is on your side. You know you can call me at any sign of trouble, and I'll be inside as quick as a flash."

Quick as a flash? You?

"Thanks, Tom, but as I say, I'm sure it won't come to that."

He reached over until his hand rested on my leg, a little too high for comfort.

"I'm here, dear," he said, beginning to pat his clammy palm up and down on my thigh. "I'm here."

It took considerable restraint not to brush it away and tell him to keep his grubby fingers to himself. But I didn't. I had to remain grateful to both of them for all their help.

"Thank you," I replied, before shifting my weight sideways until it forced his hand to leave my leg. However, he dragged his fingertips across the top of my thigh and I glared at him to let go. Fortunately, Tom turned back to the front before glancing in the rear-view mirror and smiling.

"Won't be long," I said, clambering out of the car as fast as I could, suddenly feeling extremely claustrophobic. Forgetting to kiss George, the idea of getting back inside didn't even register.

Forcing myself to concentrate on the real reason I was there, I walked towards the main entrance, before instinct told me to try around the back instead. Call it intuition, but I soon found out it was the best move I could have made.

MATT

Ironically, I *was* in a lay-by near Epsom, and I did have a bottle of cheap Scotch. I just hadn't spent the night there.

As soon as I discovered the suitcase, I quickly reburied it before digging a fresh hole adjacent. As before, the ground was soft and easy to dig, and I made relatively light work of completing my original task, however gruesome it may have been. The realisation I'd just buried my wife hadn't yet sunk in, or had I become immune to all that was happening to me? Death no longer concerned me and I shuddered to think what else I may be capable of.

Was it really Francis in her suitcase? Hidden in the same woods? But how? Desperately, I attempted to recall the day I returned home early from Birmingham.

…On closer inspection of her room, the only other thing missing is her suitcase…

Oh my God. I hadn't seen Francis since the Thursday night, the night she threatened to tell Lisa everything and forced me from her apartment.

'Now, get out of my apartment, Matthew Walker. And don't ever come back.'

Between that Thursday and the following Monday, someone must have visited and killed her, before burying her in her own bloody suitcase. But who? Somebody connected to the house, somebody connected to the family, somebody connected to me? Regardless, they found a way to get her to Epsom.

Claudia died the same day.

'… I was just wondering how many steps you would hit if I pushed you down the stairs…'.

I *wanted* her to die, imagined it, dreamt about it. But not Francis too. I thought she had left, gone somewhere new and started afresh. I'd told her it was all over.

'*Maybe it's time this Lisa woman found out what her precious partner gets up to during the week...*'

But I didn't kill either of them. And how could I know Francis was in the woods until I just bloody well dug her up?

A wave of nausea hit me again. What could I do? Francis, followed by Amelia. Both an integral part of my life.

Think. Think.

The clothes I wore were caked in mud and they were in a plastic bag in the boot of my car. I was back in my suit, once again crumpled, leaving me a complete mess. The stench of stale whisky added to my overall presentation. If I disposed of the bag of clothes, then nobody needed to know where I'd been; how could they? I had an alibi for Birmingham too; I even sent my bloody bank statement to the police.

My phone buzzed on the passenger seat, and I presumed it was Lisa again. Her manner on the call earlier surprised me, dismissing my whereabouts or safety without a second thought. Christ! I'd spent the whole night out. She didn't know where, who with or why, did she? However, as soon as I turned my phone over, I realised it isn't Lisa at all.

You shouldn't have been at the house.

Oh, shit, no. The other day, the text messages. I'd forgotten all about them. Did I ask who it was? Did they reply?

I've been watching you...

And whoever the fuck it is, they now knew I'd been

back to the house. Had they watched me bury Amelia too? Oh, no. No…

> **Who is this? What do you want?**

What about the pub, just before the messages arrived? Somebody darted out, jet-black hair and a crimson coat; Amelia's crimson coat. But it wasn't her. I asked the previous night. It was coming back to me. Amelia only returned to the country two days before, and she genuinely did not know where I lived. I interrogated her, over and over, before we drank too much; before it all went so badly wrong.

Ping! My phone.

> **Meet me at the house tomorrow. Three o'clock. I'll be waiting, Uncle Matthew.**

Uncle Matthew!

Katrina! Shit. I'd forgotten all about her. Didn't she begin a whole new life in the arms of experienced foster parents? Yes, the social care team called me, keeping their promise to inform me of her well-being, or was all that bullshit too? All the other messages. It's been Katrina all along, desperate to get me to see Melissa. But why?

You're family now.

And if she sent me all the messages, was it her in the copse, following me on the train, handing in my laptop at the station, running from the pub, the vomit in our garden, standing at our kitchen window? *Pretty lady.*

I've been watching you. It's been fun…

34

MATT

THE SIGHT of yet another police car parked outside our house made me want to puke. Surely they hadn't found something in the woods? So soon? Had Katrina told them? She wouldn't, not until she'd seen me. Katrina always liked me. No, she wanted something else altogether, although I dreaded to think what.

Were there any security cameras at the house? Shit. That would make sense with it being boarded up, desperate to keep trespassers out. The property was ripe for squatters, graffiti artists and amateur detectives obsessed with the story of the insane family who once lived there; so why had nobody defaced it in all the months it's lain empty? Racking my brain, I attempted to visualise the exterior of the house. Surely they would install cameras so prospective intruders could see them, an act of deterrent, rather than camouflage them from view?

As I slowed down, I recognised the same two officers who called round only days before. They were standing by their car, deep in conversation. Had they already been in to see Lisa or had they just arrived? Damn, the worst possible timing as one of them looked along the road and spotted me. He even had the audacity to wave his bloody hand, as if I was visiting for a cup of tea and a nice afternoon chat. Should I drive straight past? Pretend I hadn't seen them? Perhaps I should mow them down, add a hit and run to my list?

This is it, Matt. No more hiding.

Slowly, I pulled into my parking space, shoving the half-drunk bottle of Scotch into the glove compartment.

They didn't even give me an opportunity to close my car door before they approached. The two of them spread out, covering the width of the driveway. Were they expecting me to run?

"Hello, Mr Walker. Mind if we come inside?"

"Yeah, sure. Is something wrong?"

My voice was unsteady, and I could feel dampness under my arms. I was aware of my appearance and my breath must have reeked of stale booze. At least I'd remained out most of the day and allowed the alcohol to leave my system. Stupidly, I glanced at the boot of my car as I walked around to greet them. My filthy clothes were still in there. The officers looked at each other and for a split second, I became convinced one of them was going to ask if I mind opening it. Fortunately, they didn't appear interested and instead follow me to the house. As soon as I take the key from my pocket, the door opened and Lisa stood in the hallway, holding George in her arms. She looked as petrified as me. I'd been expecting a barrage of abuse for returning home so late, but with two officers standing behind me, I guess that could wait until later.

"Hi, love. The police are here again. They've asked if they could come inside?"

Lisa looked at me and then over my shoulder. She'd gone white, as drained of colour as I'd been myself the past few weeks. Her legs wobbled, and believing she might drop George, I quickly grabbed him from her arms. She didn't say a word, and instead ignored us all before turning and walking to the kitchen. Smiling pathetically towards the officers, I indicated with a slight movement of my head for them to follow.

The walk along the hallway felt like my last walk of freedom. And now they were there to arrest me. I momentarily forgot about Amelia and Francis. My biggest fear was how I would explain things to Lisa. That's why the police are there, wasn't it? My affair in London, which she knew nothing about, losing my job, which she didn't know the real reason for, and having to admit to burying my wife in the woods. I almost laughed out loud, such was the incredulous mess I had got myself into.

"Coffee? Tea?" Lisa asked, emotionless, as she filled the kettle without waiting for a reply.

"We're fine thanks, ma'am. Listen, do you mind sitting down, both of you? We've something to tell you."

Tell us? Don't you mean, *'sit down, ma'am, whilst we detain your partner, handcuff him and drag him away kicking and screaming?'*.

Lisa filled the kettle and took two mugs from the cupboard above, delaying the inevitable. Did she know why they were there? Finally, after what felt like an age, she joined me and George. I'd given him my phone, and he happily played a game. My heart panged for what I'd done.

"What is it?" I asked impatiently. Why don't they just apprehend me or at least ask me to move away from my child? The two officers looked at each other before one took a small step forward and addressed me directly.

"Melissa Reid is your mother-in-law, I believe, sir?"

Melissa?

Attempting to reply, the words got caught in my throat. Quickly fidgeting in my seat, I cleared it, realising how I must look. Lisa sat beside me and stared me in the eye, joining the officers in anticipation of what I might say next. She knew why they were there, didn't she?

"Sorry. Well, yes. Melissa is my mother-in-law. Well, technically at least. You see, I'm not divorced, well, not yet, you see——"

The same officer lifted his hand to inform me to shut the fuck up. Taking his cue, I readjusted myself in my chair and felt my arm rest against Lisa's. I detected her body shaking as if she might be the one losing control instead of me. Apart from asking if they wanted a drink, I recognised she hadn't spoken a single word since they arrived.

"Well," the officer continued, his voice undertaking an even more serious tone, "I'm afraid that Melissa Reid died earlier today."

Lisa gasped, prompting everybody to stop and look at her.

"You okay, ma'am?" the other officer asked, speaking for the first time.

Lisa ignored him, stood, and busied herself again, preparing the hot drinks. She lifted a mug towards the officers, who, once again, raised their hands in refusal of her offer.

What's wrong with her?

"Dead?" I asked, my eyes flicking between Lisa and the policemen. "Actually dead?"

The officers glanced at one another for the umpteenth time.

"You don't seem too surprised, sir? And, madam, anything you want to say?"

Lisa turned, a jar of coffee in her hand.

"I barely know the woman," she replied, lacking any emotion. "But I do know she is part of that family who tied me up in a shack and tried to abduct my baby. As far as I'm concerned, she's lived a year too long."

Neither I nor the officers had a clue how to react. But Lisa was one hundred per cent correct. Why should she care? However, it was the lack of sentiment or surprise which astonished me. The officer who was doing most talking addressed me once again.

"Yes, sir, actually dead. But the thing is, there is a further complication."

"Oh?" I replied pitifully. I may as well have just said, *'yeah, I know. There's been a queue of people waiting to kill her.'*

"Yes. Melissa Reid didn't die of natural causes."

My heart pumped harder still and I noticed Lisa grasp the work surface.

"Has she killed herself? Guilt finally caught up with her?" Lisa asked, eventually exhibiting a spark of interest.

"Her cocoa was spiked with something. Something poisonous. So, either she dropped it in herself, or somebody paid her a visit and dropped it in for her."

LISA

Did they expect me to give a toss about Melissa bloody Reid? As far as I'm concerned, it sounds as though it was all over far too quickly. Couldn't she have suffered for a while?

Anyway, the police finally left, albeit after a thousand damn questions about if and when either of us visited the care home. Of course, I said I hadn't been near the place, and I knew they couldn't prove otherwise. You see, once I got out of Tom's car and approached the main entrance, I went around the rear instead and looked through the conservatory windows. And Melissa was there. She sat with her back to me, completely motionless, oblivious to any outside interference. And then I noticed the door was slightly ajar. Great. There wouldn't be any record of my visit. With a glance over my shoulder, I shuffled along the damp grass to take Melissa by surprise.

Matt confessed to visiting Melissa once before. To begin with, he denied ever going, constantly looking at me whilst coming across as guilty as sin. He really thought I was as thick as pig shit, didn't he? However, when the officer produced an image of Matt's signature from the care home register, he had to fold. The date, two weeks earlier, coincided with the day he told me he needed to go back to London to empty his apartment. Smiling myself, I listened intently as he desperately tried to explain it to the police. But I wasn't interested in his alibi. I was much more interested in why he kept it from me.

"I was just trying to protect you," he protested, his eyes full of remorse. "Trying to protect you and George from that family. I knew if you realised Melissa was out of prison, it would freak you out. You believe me, don't you…"

His words trailed off, seemingly sounding as pathetic in his head as they did out loud. The policemen exchanged a look before continuing to ask Matt the purpose of his visit.

"I needed to know what she wanted. You see, she sent me a text telling me I *had* to go. What else could I do? I had to know if we were in danger."

"And why didn't you inform the police, sir?"

This I had to hear. He took his time before replying.

"Because I didn't think it was a police matter. It's personal, between me and a member of that family. And as I say, I was just trying to protect these two."

To be fair, Matt didn't break any law. Nobody expected or told him to inform the police either. It *was* a personal matter, and the officers weren't able to argue differently.

Before leaving, they asked if they could do a quick search of the house and the garden. Admitting to not having a warrant, they added they could soon acquire one. With nothing to hide, I nodded my head in agreement. All eyes fell on Matt, and he agreed too. We assumed they were looking for cyanide or some other poison, but unless Matt had a secret hiding place, I believed we were safe.

Sure enough, twenty minutes later, I watched from the kitchen as Matt saw the officers off our premises. He accompanied them around the house and also outside into the garden. At one point, they disappeared into our shed. Finally, Matt returned to the kitchen and appeared as sheepish as I'd ever seen him. But it wasn't just the news of Melissa. Something else had happened. Unable to look at him, I needed to know.

"Have you been back to the care home since, Matthew?" I asked, turning to the window. He fidgeted behind me.

"No, why would you ask that?" he replied, lacking any conviction. I turned to face him.

"The same reason I could ask why you never told me you went there at all, or where you've been all bloody night." He opened his mouth to reply. "And don't give me the same bullshit you just gave the police about trying to protect me or drowning your pitiful sorrows in some lay-by."

Matt stared at his hands, resting on the table. He annoyingly intertwined his fingers and thumbs. That's when I first noticed his fingernails full of dirt. Finally, he looked up at me and his next words caught me completely unprepared.

"Well, *I* haven't been to see Melissa today. You don't know of anybody who might have done, do you?"

35

LISA

COULD he possibly know I'd visited Melissa? Really? Desperate to press him, to find out what he knew, I couldn't think of the right words without giving my intentions away. Mind you, he didn't hang around long enough, anyway. He stood and we exchanged one or two words before he said needed a shower. After sitting next to each other, he wasn't lying. He stank of stale sweat and something else I couldn't put my finger on. At one point, our arms rested against each other and I realised he would have felt me shaking. My whole damn body shook. But who could blame me after what I'd been through earlier that day?

Once Matt disappeared upstairs, I watched George playing a game on my phone. Matt had snatched his away, leaving his son in tears until I intervened. Finishing making tea, something I hadn't quite achieved when the police were there, I joined George at the table.

Apart from the noises emanating from my phone, it was nice to finally have some peace and quiet. The shower spurted into life and I heard Matt clumsily close the door behind him. Sitting opposite George, I studied the concentration etched across his little face, and I worried about his future. Initially, I'd dreamt that once we bought our first house together, it would be the catalyst for an entirely new beginning. Maybe it was a mistake buying in the village, but I wanted to be there more than Matt, so I certainly couldn't hold him responsible for that. Then, the day he came home reeking of perfume, I traced it back to his apartment and that slut Francis, but again, I naively thought with her out of the way, that would be it. No women, no affairs, just the three of us. And then Hannah's brainwave to get Matt home during the week meant we would all be under the same roof, every single day. It was a few weeks since Matt lost his job at the agency, but at least John Brookes kept his word and never told him the true motive for letting him go.

You see, I called Matt's boss on the pretence of discussing his behaviour, but my real reason was Hannah's suggestion to get Matt the sack, so he came home to me and George. However, I didn't think it through and I made all kinds of accusations about Matt hating John, the way he operated the business and how he treated the female members of staff. My mind ran away with itself, and lie after lie tripped off my tongue. The real worrying thing, though, was how easy I found it, something I'd become quite the expert at over the past year. But once I finally finished babbling, John's response completely stunned me. He said he'd received a similar call earlier the same day, and the combination of both left him no option but to act. Hanging up, I wondered why Hannah would have called him too.

As I drank the rest of my tea, a sudden urge to get out threatened to overwhelm me; fresh air, just me and George.

"Want to go to the shops, darling?"

He looked up, non-committal.

"You can play on my phone on the way."

His face lit up. That's better.

Quickly, I grabbed his coat and put his shoes on for him, desperate to leave before Matt finished in the shower. Grabbing the car keys off the chest of drawers in the hallway, it came as a relief to be outdoors. The drizzle felt good against my skin, simultaneously cleansing and refreshing my mind.

However, my moment of feeling invigorated lasted only a few seconds. As soon as I opened the car door, the stench of Matt's stale sweat hit me once again.

But it wasn't the smell that bothered me, it was the amount of soil and dirt in the footwell of the driver's side that made my hairs stand on end.

MATT

As had been the obvious intention, the timing of my question caught her out just as much as the content. She obviously believed that she held all the cards, but I had seen Hannah and Tom exit the care home earlier. Lisa must have known they were going. It could only be her who put them onto it; why else would *they* be there? But how did she know Melissa was out of prison and how did she know what care home she was in? Simple. She already knew I'd been to see Melissa. The only thing I could possibly think of was the day I received the call from WPC Wright. I'd taken it in the living room, leaving Lisa to feed George. But did I leave the door ajar or raise my voice, allowing her to hear from the kitchen? Perhaps both. Either way, Lisa overheard the conversation. So why hadn't she mentioned it? The same reason we barely talked about anything. Was she protecting me or was I protecting her? But then why get Hannah and Tom involved? She was checking up on my every move, almost as if she didn't trust me. And our nosy fucking neighbours would jump at such an opportunity.

Francis! If she knew about Melissa, then did she know about Francis too? Realising I had no choice but to confront Lisa about everything, I first needed to know about Hannah and Tom and why they had been to the care home that day. Whatever their involvement, I had to find proof.

"No. Why, should I?"

With a burst of assurance surging through my veins, I stood so I was face-to-face with Lisa.

"No reason, love," I replied, and although I momentarily felt good about myself, I knew my world was crashing in around me. Leaving Lisa to stew on my words, I said I needed to take a shower. Maybe the only truthful thing either of us said since I'd arrived home.

As I scraped away at the dirt and grime in the shower, I contemplated what happened after I left the woods the previous dat. I was amazed I could push the memory of waking up next to my dead wife to the back of my mind with such ease. My brain had somehow triggered a coping mechanism. Either that or I was going mad.

Too late, Matt.

Once I returned to the car, I changed into my suit and put my dirty clothes into the bag and threw it in the boot. Drumming the steering wheel, I desperately thought about what to do next.

Is somebody watching me?

Although convinced someone was hiding, lurking somewhere in the car park, I tried to dismiss my overactive mind and instead thought of Katrina. I knew I had no option but to go back and see her the next day. She knew too much.

'Meet me at the house tomorrow… I'll be waiting for you, Uncle Matthew.'

Perhaps she was helping me, assisting me to move on? Could she have pushed Amelia down the stairs? Hell, no. She wouldn't, would she? But she was aware of where I'd been…

'You shouldn't have been at the house…'

So, if she'd seen me there, then maybe she would go to see Melissa the same day? Again, Hannah's suggestion to try finding work in Epsom played into my hands as the care home was only a couple of miles down the road and perhaps, as I originally intended, I could kill two birds with one stone.

Knowing I couldn't see my mother-in-law looking such a mess, I drove to a service station on the outskirts of town to clean myself up. Most of the soil came away with soap, but my fingernails remained caked in dirt. Next, in the attached café, I grabbed something to eat before calling into the shop and buying a ridiculously priced half bottle of Scotch. It made me smile, actually being bothered about a service station ripping me off.

It wasn't until I approached the care home that my plans were thrown into turmoil once more. Instantly, I recognised the vehicle pulling out of the car park. They were turning left, away from me, and I prayed they didn't spot me too. Fortunately, I was following a larger vehicle, an SUV, which slowed down to allow Tom to exit. Watching as he waved his hand in acknowledgement, he never looked beyond the black Audi; instead, he put all of his focus into the manoeuvre whilst keeping his hands steady on the steering wheel. He is such a cautious driver, and I almost laughed out loud at the concentration etched across his smarmy face.

But then Hannah looked over his shoulder from the passenger seat. Shit, did she see me? Ducking, I hoped I'd done enough.

As soon as the Audi pulled away, I quickly spun into the care home entrance and found a space at the far end of the car park, closest to the conservatory. Switching the ignition off, I leant forward on the wheel, breathing hard whilst trying to think. What on earth were Tom and Hannah doing here? They could only be here to see Melissa and surely only because of Lisa's know-how? She *had* overheard me. But even if she could easily find out which care home Melissa was in, how did she know I'd visited?

Could Tom have somehow followed me? He said he loved gadgets and regularly ordered items online. Surveillance equipment, he said, stuff to help with his neighbourhood watch duties. Had he attached something to my car or even tampered with my phone? Tracking somebody was easy nowadays if you knew what you're doing, and Tom definitely knew what he was doing.

And what about earlier, when I sat in the station car park, that overwhelming sensation of being watched?

Could it have been Katrina again? But if she was at the house, then how could she have beaten me to the station?

Although I dismissed it at the time — to be fair, my mind was operating on turbocharged — the more I thought about it, the more I knew somebody was there, in the shadows, lurking, watching.

36

MATT

MY HEAD THROBBED and my stomach grumbled as I dried myself. Had I had anything to eat or drink all day? It took a lot of effort to look at myself in the full-length mirror and I barely recognised what stared back. My unshaven face only held my attention for a split second and instead, I gawked at my scrawny and malnourished body.

Quickly, I got dressed, ran downstairs and helped myself to a pint of water and two chocolate bars. Next, I popped a couple of paracetamol, my headache getting worse, before realising I hadn't seen or heard Lisa or George since stepping out of the shower. Calling their names, I walked from room to room, munching on the snack without even tasting it, before going to the back door to check the garden.

"Lisa! George!"

Nothing, so I returned to the hallway before noticing their coats and shoes were missing. Hastily, I composed a text and Lisa responded only moments later. Something about needing some fresh air and they'll be home in an hour or so.

After traipsing around the house like a lost child, I realised I needed to keep my mind active and decided it the perfect opportunity to clean the car. Grabbing the keys and a roll of bin liners, I drove to the nearest refuge site, three miles out of the village.

Once I disposed of the rubbish, I called into the local garage, vacuumed the car inside and put it through the wash. It was the cleanest it had been for months, and once I returned home, I inspected it through the living room window. It had guilt written all over it. Contemplating whether to go outside and throw mud all over my now sparkling vehicle, my phone vibrated, and I assumed it was Lisa with an update on her whereabouts.

"Mr Walker. It's Officer Sutton. I called around earlier with my colleague."

Now what? Surely not?

"Yes, yes, I remember." Although my tone wasn't helping, I was past the point of caring about anybody in authority or what they thought of me.

"Everything alright, sir? You seem a bit snappy."

"All good here. Listen, what is it you've called about?"

Officer Sutton went quiet and I could picture him on the other end with his hand over the mouthpiece, talking to his colleague. "It's about Tracy Reid," he eventually said.

Tracy! If he hadn't gained my attention before, he sure as hell had now. Was it her, after all? Was she responsible for all of this?

"What about Tracy Reid? Where is she?"

"She's dead, sir. We thought you would like us to inform you of—"

"Dead! What do you mean, dead? Where? How?"

The officer cleared his throat, more in an attempt to shut me up than actually losing his voice.

"If you don't mind me saying so, Mr Walker, I think you should calm yourself down. I know your history and all that's gone on, but your behaviour is concerning me. Do you have anything to tell me?"

He was right. I needed to compose myself, especially in front of him.

"Yes, I'm sorry. It's just a lot to take in. Melissa and now her daughter. I keep thinking of my ex-wife too, and this brings everything crashing back."

"Okay. I understand." We both fell silent for a few moments. Knowing he wanted me to say more, I had nothing to add that wouldn't come across as possible implication. Finally, he cleared his throat again and continued. His voice sounded somehow different on the phone than face to face. "If you're sure you want to know the details…" He hesitated, before taking my silence as his cue to carry on. "Someone stabbed Tracy Reid whilst she worked in a garden. She was alone, away from the others, sometime yesterday."

Yesterday? When I was at the house?

"Where? I thought she was inside?"

"They have downgraded her. To an open prison. She was working in a garden at a community centre, near to where you used to live, actually."

Downgraded. Yes. WPC Wright told me on the phone.

"Do you have any more details?" I asked, unsure of my own words. "Who did it, or anything else?"

262

Again, the officer paused. He didn't appear as assured as before, as if he was also struggling to take everything on board.

"It's all a bit sketchy at the moment, and there is obviously a murder investigation going on. That's all I can say right now."

The phone call ended rather abruptly, but I was pleased it was over. I was on the brink of collapse.

A few minutes later, I found myself in our back garden having no recollection of actually stepping outdoors. I was dressed in a T-shirt and jeans, oblivious to the rain and chill. Trampling through the wet grass, I walked aimlessly in circles.

My phone pinged at the same time as I heard George shout my name somewhere in the distance. Suddenly, I became aware of where I was; soaked to the skin and standing outside dressed in just a bloody T-shirt.

Is this the next step to craziness?

Glancing at my phone, I had an email from Katrina, but it would have to wait until later.

"Daddy!"

Lisa was holding George's hand at the back door. She looked at me as though I was out of my mind. I glanced down at my attire, my shirt clinging to my body and my jeans threatening to fall to my knees, a combination of the heaviness and the fact I'd lost so much weight.

Sliding my phone into my pocket, I attempted a smile and trudged slowly towards the back door, unsure of what the hell I would say when I reached them.

LISA

With the amount of soil in the car — I didn't want to contemplate where it was from and I certainly didn't want George anywhere near it — the prospect of being in an invigorating drizzle enticed me to walk instead. George already had his coat and waterproof shoes on, so I popped the keys back on the chest of drawers and set off through the village. At first, George grumbled, but once I told him he could play 'splash-splash', his face lit up and he immediately searched for the nearest puddle. After a couple of 'jumps', we headed in the inevitable direction.

My phone buzzed in my pocket and Matt asked where we were. Responding with just a few words, I informed him we were out for some fresh air and would be back within the hour. I still needed to quiz him about where he'd been all night and what he knew about Melissa's death, but first I wanted to see a friendly face.

"Hi, Lisa, George," Hannah said, full of her usual exuberance. "What a lovely surprise." Tom appeared behind his wife, his face beaming, the same look in his eye. I recalled his hand resting on the top of my thigh.

"Come in, come in," Hannah said, noticing my hesitation. "You'll catch your death out here." Again, I looked at Tom, but thankfully, he turned away.

Once we were all settled around the table with tea and a plate of biscuits, I ensured George was okay before addressing Tom.

"Tom…" My focus appeared to unnerve him momentarily, and he lifted his backside from the chair before repositioning himself a little further forward. My voice faltered and I could have kicked myself for not preparing exactly what I wanted to ask. I tried again. "Erm, Tom. Today, when we went to the care home…"

Tom glanced at Hannah.

"What about it, Lisa?" His expression altered once more, amiable yet daring me to say too much.

Looking at Hannah, I attempted a smile, desperate to keep it friendly and non-confrontational.

"Well, the police were at our house earlier…" — more hesitation — "… and they said, how can I put it? They told us Melissa is dead." Neither of them flinched. "Did you hear? Melissa Reid is dead."

Hannah cleared her throat before replicating her husband's movement and hunched herself forward. She stretched her arms across the table, her hands only an inch or two from mine.

"Yes, dear. We know."

"You know?"

"Yes, dear," Tom echoed his wife. They were like a bloody double act. "Maybe I should have called around earlier, but I wanted to wait until I got you on your own." That goddamn smile again. He was making me retch with his provocative remarks and snide glances. Just as Sophie suggested. At least thinking of her allowed me a moment's respite.

Looking from one to the other, I searched for some kind of explanation. They were talking in riddles and I needed one of them to hurry the fuck up and tell me what they knew.

"What do you mean? Why didn't you just call me? When did you know, and what? Come on, Tom, spit it out."

Tom casually picked up his cup of tea and slurped the piping-hot liquid. I wanted to lean over and throw the scalding drink in his smug face. Is he going to admit he's a murderer and I'm in their house with two serial killers and my one-year-old son?

"This is exactly why I didn't say anything. You are so highly strung, and rightly so. We're just trying to protect you."

"Protect me from what?"

Hannah took over again.

"We're not sure, Lisa. We're endeavouring to find out if you're in some sort of danger."

"Danger? Who from?"

My mind was doing somersaults.

"From whoever killed Melissa Reid," Tom replied.

I stared at him incredulously. Did *he* think I was stupid too? Does everybody?

Tom leant further forward, pushing his chair back at the same time. His voice remained even, in total control, so much so that I found it difficult not to believe him.

"Lisa. I returned to the care home after I dropped you and Hannah off. Something was concerning me, concerning *us*, for your welfare."

"What do you mean?"

"Because we've been researching that family, the history of what happened in that house, and now they're all being allowed back into society, one by one, I wanted to check that Melissa Reid means you no harm."

The hairs on my arms stood on end and I stared at George instead, wondering if they knew everything. Tom continued.

"When I went inside the care home, via the conservatory, just as you did, Melissa was already dead. She was sitting in a wicker chair, totally motionless. I walked over, you know, to check her, and her head hung to one side.

There was saliva on her chin. From experience of seeing such cases before, I knew she had been poisoned."

"No, no," I said, standing up too quickly, making George laugh. "Why didn't you tell me all this earlier?"

"Why do you think, dear?" Hannah replied. I looked at her, shaking my head, until she answered her own question. "Because I saw Matthew pulling into the care home as we pulled out. I said nothing to either of you at the time. It wasn't until we dropped you off back at your house that I told Tom."

My head continued to shake from side to side. Were they saying what I thought they were saying? Tom confirmed it before I could ask.

"Matthew must have seen Melissa before I got back."

Backing away until I felt myself pressed against the work surface, George watched me, his face now nonplussed.

"No, no. He wouldn't. I know he wouldn't…"

"Lisa. Either you or Matthew were the last person to see Melissa Reid alive."

37

LISA

WE LEFT Hannah and Tom's house a few minutes after Tom's bombshell. Not only Melissa, but he told me about Tracy being murdered too. Apparently, his colleagues within the local community watch hub had informed him just before I arrived. My head was in such a spin. Did Matt go to see Melissa and could he really have killed her? Hannah suggested we stay at their place, at least until the police carried out their investigations, but I'd had enough of running. It was time to confront Matt face to face. No more hiding.

Once we approached our house, the first thing I noticed was the car. It stood gleaming against the dull facade of our property and the persistent drizzle and dark black clouds.

He had washed it. Why, on such a miserable day, would you wash a car? And, before we reached it, I knew what to expect from the interior. The soil and dirt in the driver's footwell had vanished. In fact, the entire car was vacuumed spotless. Hopefully, the stench of his stale sweat would have disappeared too. He couldn't make himself look more guilty if he tried. Maybe Hannah was right and I shouldn't go inside, but one thing I was certain of is that he would never hurt George and, therefore, surely he wouldn't hurt me?

If cleaning the car appeared strange, the sight of Matt standing drenched in our back garden made me want to laugh and cry in equal measure.

George screamed his name, but I was lost for words. His T-shirt stuck to his upper half, showing off his wiry frame beneath, and his jeans gave the impression they would drop to his knees at any moment. He looked pathetic, weak, malnourished, and afraid. What *had* he become?

"Hiya, mate," he said to George, his speech strained.

"Don't you think you had better get changed into some dry clothes?" I asked, looking him up and down. My voice was unsurprisingly shaky as he glared at me in response. Reluctantly, he nodded, pulling at his T-shirt so it no longer clung to his torso.

"Yeah, I guess so." He attempted a smile.

Watching as he dragged himself through the kitchen, it surprised me when he paused and turned.

"Where have you been?" he asked, genuine concern etched across his face.

"Hannah's. I wanted to get George out."

"Oh," Matt replied, flicking his head backwards. "I'll grab a shower."

"Matt," I called after him. "Once you're done, can we have a chat?"

He didn't reply, although I knew he heard. His footsteps stopped briefly on the staircase before mumbling something under his breath and continuing his journey.

With Matt's spiralling mental state and the prospect he could be capable of God knows what, I could no longer put off the inevitable, whatever the outcome.

Matt showered and changed into dry clothes, but when he came downstairs, he still resembled death warmed up. He stared out of the window and within minutes, I realised talking would be futile. So instead, we sat in relative silence for an hour before he inevitably made his excuses and went to bed for a ridiculously early night. He slept in the spare room and I could hear him moving around all night long. The following morning, he still looked like shit, but I couldn't put things off any longer. Making fresh coffee, I ensured he was seated next to George on the far side of the kitchen table. George concentrated hard on the crayons and colouring book in front of him. I became aware of how much I'd been neglecting our son and I should have been paying him a lot more attention, playing with him and reading to him, but compared to Matt, I was the most attentive parent on the planet.

"You know when you said you hadn't been to see Melissa yesterday and then asked me if I know of anybody else who might have done?" I pass him a drink, allowing him a few seconds for the question to sink in. He takes a while to comprehend what may have happened only the day before. Eventually, he nodded his head. "Well, I haven't been entirely truthful with you." His interest perked, and at last, he glanced up from his coffee. "The thing is, I know you went to see her yesterday. Just before they found her dead."

He didn't respond, just glared at me through vacant eyes. He really was on a different planet.

"Well?" I asked, my patience already wearing thin. "What happened when you went to see her?"

He looked at George and passed him a different colour crayon. George grabbed it with relish, dropping the green before scribbling away with the red one instead.

"I didn't go in," he eventually replied, his eyes fixed on the colouring book. "I only got as far as the conservatory."

"Matt." I wait until he looks at me. "We need to be honest with each other. The police are all over this now and it won't be long until they put two and two together."

The mere mention of the police appeared to arouse his enthusiasm. He knew as well as me that everything was reaching a climax.

"As I say, I didn't go in. Whatever happened is nothing to do with me."

His lies were beyond pathetic, so much so, he was no longer capable of convincing himself. For the first time, I doubted Matt recognised the difference between fiction and reality. I could hear the cogs turning in his head, trying to decipher what he knew and what he thought he knew. He looked broken, vulnerable, and extremely scared. The opportunity to twist the knife was too inviting, and I had to hear the truth from his own mouth.

"So, why were you there at all if you had no intention of going in?"

His eyes glazed over, and they flickered from me to George and back to me. Finally, they rested on his coffee. The levelness of his voice irritated me.

"I needed to speak to her, see what she knew, see what

she wanted from me." He looked up at me, the rims of his eyes red.

"And where did you get the cyanide, or whatever other poison you used?"

I was done with papering over the cracks. I required answers. Now. And my question had the desired effect. Without warning, he scraped his chair back and stood. His eyes glared into mine and then onto George, so much so, I became fearful of what he might do. I stood too, a parental instinct to protect my child kicking in.

"I didn't bloody well go in," he said, his voice raised for the first time. "She wasn't moving, so I left her there, came home, saw the police outside…"

His speech trailed off, and I realised he was once again unconvinced by his own words.

However, something clicked into place, and a hint of confidence returned to his voice. What he said next took me by surprise, but it was nothing compared to what he suggested a few minutes later.

MATT

"Why were Hannah and Tom pulling out of the car park when I drove in?" My question hit her like a hammer blow and her legs appeared to buckle. "You okay?" I asked, unsure if she was faking.

"Matt… help me…" she said, the whites of her eyes suddenly prominent.

"What? What is it?"

As I pulled a chair from underneath the table, she literally dropped into it. Quickly, I grabbed her arm and steadied her fall.

"Can I have a glass of water?"

"Sure, sure."

With my back to her, I filled a tumbler from the tap. I felt like shit. My hand were trembling and a cold sheen of sweat had formed across my forehead. Lisa's questions left me doubting my sanity, not that it needed her to achieve that. Desperately, I wanted to rewind the clock and write down what happened, day by day, like a teenager's diary.

Passing Lisa a glass of water, I sat next to her, aware I should already be somewhere else.

"I was in the back of the car, Matt."

"What?" I asked, again struggling to comprehend what she was saying. To clarify events, I more or less repeated the question I'd just asked. "What, when I saw Hannah and Tom pulling out of the car park yesterday when I arrived?"

My head throbbed even more ferociously as it struggled to compute all the muddled messages.

"Yes, Matt, yesterday," Lisa snapped. "Well, I guess so. I didn't see you, but Hannah did."

Is she lying?

"But what were you doing there? Did you go inside to see her? Did Hannah and Tom?"

She held out her arm and grabbed my hand. We were both trembling and it was hard to distinguish who was shaking the most.

"Just me. They only drove me there. I needed to find out what she wants with you, what she wants with us."

Lisa explained, albeit slowly, that it wasn't the first time she'd been to see Melissa. She told me of her threatening to take George back to the family where he belongs, and Melissa repeated the same threats the day before. Her shaking appeared to be worsening with every single word.

"Did you," I eventually asked, "you know, you didn't kill her, did you?"

Lisa suddenly snapped her hand away and sat upright in her chair. George giggled at her sudden movement.

"Of course I didn't bloody kill her. Did you?"

Her question made me falter, and a sensation of guilt enveloped me.

"No! No. Absolutely not," I replied. "Once I pulled into the car park, I realised I was making a huge mistake. I just walked to the conservatory and back."

She looked at me as if she didn't believe a single word I was saying.

"And what about Tracy? Did you murder her too?"

Shit. How does she know about Tracy?

It was my turn to shake, and I could see Lisa watching me. Licking my top lip, I felt a sheen of sweat had formed beneath my nose too. It tasted salty and vile.

"I didn't kill her. I don't even know what prison she was in, or what bloody garden she could be in…" I hesitated, but this time because I genuinely thought of something. However, before I could explain, Lisa stood and glared into my eyes.

"Wait there," she said, daring me to move. She was in the hallway and I heard a drawer open and close. A few moments later, she returned and dropped a sheet of paper on the table in front of me. Instantly, I recognised it.

"What's that?" I said.

"It's a bank statement, Matt," Lisa replied facetiously. "Your bank statement from the night you stayed in Birmingham. Remember your conference when John Brookes was pissed off because your performance was so damn bad?"

I was struggling to understand what she was alluding to, although my level of fear had increased another notch.

"Yes, yes," I said. "And there, at the bottom, is the entry for the hotel. I've already given this to the police."

I kept tapping the same line as if Lisa was too stupid to see it for herself.

"Turn it over," she interrupted.

Looking at her as if she was crazy, I gingerly turned the statement until the other side became face up. There was only one line on it and I instantly recognised the transaction.

"Fifty pounds," she said, now tapping the sheet herself to mimic my actions. "Fifty pounds spent on petrol. And what's the address of the service station, Matthew?"

Lisa was taking great pleasure in her detective work, ridiculing me.

"Hammersmith, London," I replied sheepishly, realising she wasn't going to let it drop.

"Yes, good, that's correct." She talked to me like a child. "And the date? Oh, let me tell you. It's the Monday afternoon, Matt. The same Monday afternoon when Claudia West fell down the stairs and the same Monday afternoon your tart Francis Baker went missing. Just like yesterday with Melissa, everything points at you. What was it you said when the police came around? You don't see a dead body every day of the week…"

It was difficult to read her expression. Was it satisfaction, was it pure glee, or was it something else altogether? Either way, I'd had enough of taking her hits. I was on the ropes, not just from Lisa but more so from the last twenty-four hours and my world spiralling out of control. However, I had one final punch left in me, what Amelia said, the one thing I'd never been able to shake from my mind.

I want my George back.

Pushing the bank statement towards her, I looked Lisa directly in the eye. I was more than aware of my appearance and realised I was faltering by the day, by the hour, but I *had* to ask.

"I want a DNA test, Lisa."

She gasped involuntarily, unable to suppress the rising panic.

"What, you and George?" She attempted a laugh, desperately hoping that's exactly what I meant.

"No, Lisa. Not *just* me and George. You as well."

The look on her face made me want to throw up.

38

HE'S late and I'm not happy. I've gone to so much trouble this morning, getting myself ready, ensuring I look just right. But I'm sure he will come. He has to come. I've seen too much, I know too much, he would not dare. Not only that, but we're also family, and Uncle Matthew is part of this family. And I can replace her, now I'm old enough, now I've matured into a woman and I'm no longer a child. In fact, after yesterday, I have replaced her.

Oh, my. It's happening.

He's going to be so pleasantly surprised. I'm even wearing her clothes again. This crimson coat and these black jeans are Matthew's favourites. I've even raided her make-up drawer and I'm wearing the lipstick that I know he adores.

I'm also blessed that I have her hair and eyes. I know he loved her dark brown eyes and her shiny black hair. Well, look at me, I've inherited her every gene and now I'm Aunty Amelia and no longer baby Katrina. It's why Melissa is, or was, my mother. I am Amelia Reid!

I've kept myself quiet ever since he came back, just watching and patiently waiting. The times in the copse, the pub and on the train. I even reported his stupid laptop to the man at the station. And making myself vomit in their garden, watching George through the kitchen window. Oh, I've been patient. Oh, so patient. Until the day I resembled her to a tee. Ready to take Matthew back. I even got him to see Mother, as I stupidly thought she would make him see me. But she was useless. Damn eyesight and worsening health. I'm glad somebody poisoned her.

And what about his girlfriend at Earl's Court? I followed Lisa and those neighbourhood watch people, sat outside that café and had to listen about Matthew screwing her and his bloody intimate relations. Well, I left them chatting and went back to see who this woman was. The door to her apartment opened when I knocked on it. Somebody must have unlocked it.

"Francis Baker?" I'd asked. "I'm a friend of Matthew Walker. Do you mind if I come in?"

It was weirdly quiet, and I did feel a little bit scared. And then I heard footsteps outside and thought about running, but I wanted to explore some more. You see, I've always had this gift where I know things will happen before they do. Uncle Matthew knows too. So, I crept around her apartment, very swish it was, and then I saw her dead body. The suitcase was lying next to her; the same suitcase Uncle Matthew dug up yesterday. Ha! She's in it, isn't she? That's why it smelt so bad.

However, the one thing that threatened to completely destroy my plan was when she turned up. That should never have happened. As soon as the front door opened, I saw her. Brazen as hell, as if she owns the house, owns Matthew. Well, she had that end coming, didn't she? Just what she deserved. But who was that who turned up late at night? You see, from the woods, it was difficult to tell. I watched as they parked their car along the street before slowly walking to the house. I thought about intervening, but instinct told *me they were there to cause trouble, trouble for one of them at least. And I had been furious, so I didn't care if he, she, or both of them, died. Once the person went inside, I gave up for the night and slept in the woods. My special place.*

Ha! Imagine my surprise the very next morning when Matthew was carrying his dead wife over his shoulder. What do they call it, a fireman's lift? Well, whatever it's called, Matthew was carrying Amelia and her arms were swaying from side to side with every step he took. It looked so funny. I had to hold my hand over my mouth so he didn't hear me giggle.

And then he ran back to the house, fetched a shovel and dug a grave, right next to where my father once lay. You can imagine, I wasn't thrilled, not thrilled at all. But then he hit something. Something hard. He got down on his hands and knees and started throwing mud everywhere. I wondered what it's like to be that crazy.

Hold on. There's a car coming now, and it's stopped along the road. This is it, this is him. I know, I'll wait on the swing. Uncle Matthew always looks here first, and I know why. It's because I'm his favourite; the real reason he comes to visit the family home. I'm shaking as I hear footsteps on the broken slabs.

Huh. Wait a minute. That doesn't look like Matthew. Oh, no. It isn't him. But it's too late. He's seen me.

"Hello, you must be Katrina."

He's friendly enough, but how does he know my name?

I nod my head even though my real name is Amelia. Suddenly I feel quite shy.

"Are you here alone?"

Why is he asking me that? Of course I'm here alone. Is he fucking stupid?

"Do you want me to push you on the swing?"

He's walking behind me. Oh, wait. What's that? He's got chocolate. Yippee!

"Would you like some?"

It tastes delicious. Milky, creamy, like velvet in my mouth.

"I can push you now. Do you like to go high?"

This man is friendly. I like him.

I nod my head again and I get goosebumps when his hands touch my back and push me forward. He's strong and I go quite high straight away. We talk a little and I tell him all about watching and waiting for Matthew. He's asking me a lot of questions, but because he has the most delicious chocolate, I don't really care. Then he pushes me again, harder still. Actually, it hurts my back a little. And again! "Ouch," I say, but he does it more and more, his fingers jabbing into me.

"I want to stop now."

"Oh, do you?" he asks. "Like this?"

Before I can react, he stops the swing and spins the chain around my neck. It goes tight quickly and hurts a lot. A lot more than his fingers jabbing into my back. I wish I hadn't complained about that now.

He's straining and pulling the chain tighter. Everything is going blurry and I can't breathe at all. I'm trying, honestly, but I can't get any air to go past my neck. The man says something else. It sounds nasty, but I'm falling asleep. My eyes close and there's a fuzzing noise in my ears.

Everything is getting quieter now, and the pain is stopping. That's better. All so quiet…

I taste the chocolate one last time and I think of Mother.

It makes me smile…

MATT

So, Lisa knew about Francis, our affair. She was also aware I went back to Earl's Court on that Monday afternoon. And the previous day Hannah saw me turning into the care home. But it all proved nothing, only my whereabouts, not my participation.

The day I left Birmingham early, after filling up with fuel in Hammersmith, I returned to the apartment. But there were police outside, blue and white tape crisscrossed over the front entrance. Panicking, I drove straight on, and eventually out of the city. Contemplating driving back to Birmingham — after all, I had a hotel room paid for — the prospect of covering the length of the M40 again made my heart sink. Instead, I travelled along the A3, towards Guildford. After finding a service station, I ate a meal deal and slept in the car. Nobody would know where I was. I even had the audacity to phone John and tell him how the day had gone before calling Lisa so I could speak to George. I'd covered my tracks and after spending the following day aimlessly driving around the countryside, I made my way back to the apartment before inevitably being met by a police officer still questioning everybody who entered.

"Everything okay?" I asked.

"Yes, sir. Do you live here?"

"Yes, why?"

"It's just that there was an incident here yesterday. A lady from your apartment block fell down the main stairwell. Quite a nasty fall."

"Oh, no. Who was it?"

"An elderly lady. She lived at number four-oh-one. Claudia West. Did you know her?"

So I called Lisa before running up the stairs, ready to confront Francis, but not before checking on my apartment first. That's when I realised somebody had been in; the open dishwasher, the bedroom door and the tampered-with packet of condoms. It was Lisa. She'd been inside. She must have had a copy of my key cut. But what about Claudia? Did Lisa push her too? And did she see Francis whilst in the apartment block?

Then there's Melissa. Lisa went to the care home. Her whereabouts at both crime scenes implicated her just as much as me. But I knew she wasn't responsible. Lisa simply could not kill somebody, not without huge implications upon her mental health. She could never cope with that amount of guilt wrapped around her neck. Jeez, she popped pills merely to keep herself sane. Imagine if she had the title *murderer* to contend with too. No, it wasn't Lisa, and it wasn't me. I'd told her the truth. I didn't go inside to see Melissa, only saw her through the conservatory window. Was she dead *then*? She didn't move, but I put it down to being asleep, or lost in her own world, literally staring blindly into emptiness.

But all the accusations paled into insignificance when I asked Lisa to do a DNA test. Following her initial reaction of total shock — I'd never seen anybody go so white, so quickly — she broke into a tirade of abuse, accusing me of being in cahoots with Amelia all along and never wanting to be with her. Was she right? She gave me no time to reply, instead grabbing George from his seat, sending his colouring book and crayons flying in all directions, and carrying him through to the hallway, kicking and screaming. Not moving, I just sat there staring into my barely touched and now cold mug of coffee. George was yelling as she put his coat on and I could imagine his legs flailing as she tried to get his Wellington boots on too. Eventually, the front door opened and slammed shut, reverberating through the entire house. With a glance at my watch, I busied myself, realising I was already two hours late for my agreed meeting with Katrina.

As soon as I turned the corner, I instinctively knew something was very wrong. My intuition had reached an entirely new level, ever since I first met Amelia Reid, but especially since I moved into that family house.

The house looked melancholy in the drizzle; drab and feeling sorry for itself. The boarded-up windows were soaked, the dark browns adding to the gloom. I noticed the turret had lost two or three more slates from its roof, holes now easily large enough for birds to nest inside. Maybe bats would take up residence? That's all the place needed, creatures with membranous wings flying around your head in the middle of the night.

But it wasn't the rain or the windows or the missing slates that informed me something was wrong, it was something much more sinister than that. Finding myself statue-still, I considered turning back, getting away and leaving whatever was there well alone. But I couldn't. Running was no longer an option and I began my ever-slowing walk down the broken footpath. Intuition told me to check the letter box, but of course, it was empty. Perhaps even the postman was too bloody scared to go that far along the street anymore.

It took all my effort to engage my brain to get my feet moving again, and it felt as though I had lead weights attached to the bottom of my shoes. My heart beat faster and I considered how much more it could cope with.

The drizzle patted lightly against the roof of the house, the sound hypnotic the closer I approached, but as I neared the front door, instinct told me to veer off to my left. The place where I *always* found Katrina.

As I climbed the small slope adjacent to the property, I rounded the corner until her swing came into view. And then I saw her.

The swing didn't squeak that day. Instead, it was completely motionless. But even if there were the strongest of winds blowing from the woods, the swing still wouldn't move. The weight of Katrina's body hanging from the chains rendered it useless, her feet dangling inches from the well-worn soil below.

However, amazingly, it wasn't the sight of another corpse which took my breath away, it was Katrina herself and who she had somehow metamorphosed into.

The crimson coat. And those tight black jeans. The lipstick, the shiny black hair and her wide-open dark brown eyes staring towards the woods.

Finding myself breaking into a run, I quickly released Katrina's neck from the chain, even though I knew I was far too late. Her skin felt frozen to the touch, and she was white, oh so white, translucent, and oh so cold.

Her head fell backwards with such force, I thought it might detach itself from the neck altogether.

How long has she been here?

Bending my knees to distribute the dead weight, I lay Katrina down, one hand on her back, the other supporting her head. Somehow, my emotions remained under control, as if it was a normal day-to-day chore. But something else altogether threatened to overwhelm me. A panic attack maybe. I felt myself shivering and the sensation of the rain running down the rear of my collar and under my shirt. What the hell should I do? Report it? But how? I'd have to explain why I was there, and that's if Katrina hadn't already told somebody. Of course she had. It's why she was dead. She gave me precise instructions to go back to the house. Therefore, someone knew I was going to meet her, intercepted our rendezvous and killed Katrina before I arrived. And like Francis, like Melissa, it all pointed to me. Katrina's phone records and my overnight stay with Amelia. Could they even find me guilty of killing Tracy too?

My mobile pinged and a message from Lisa lit up the screen.

> I'm at Hannah and Tom's house. Get here now!

39

LISA

A FUCKING DNA TEST? *All* three of us. Oh shit, what did he know? She was back, wasn't she? He met her. That's where he'd been. Disappearing for the night. He even got me to design his bloody curriculum vitae and watched me impatiently as I printed them off, just to get to Epsom, to meet her, to do God knows what with her. And then she put hideous ideas into his stupid head.

Unable to cope, I grabbed George and fought to put his coat and boots on whilst he screamed and kicked and punched me in return. But I needed to get away, to think, to plan. Hannah would know what to do. George complained all the way through the village as I dragged him through the rain and the puddles.

"He's totally unstable," Tom said as I explained what Matt had asked me. Tom had met me at the door. He looked flustered when I arrived and still had his coat on, spitting out some bullshit he'd only just got home himself. "You only have to look at him, his appearance, Lisa," he continued, sympathy oozing from every pore. "Have you ever seen him like this before? I'm sure he's not the man you fell for that night at the conference."

Tom's words were intentional, made to hurt, and it felt like a dagger through my heart, with an added twist for good measure. That night at the hotel in Cheshire, cuddled up around the log fire in the bar, drinking and laughing until almost midnight; and what followed after Matt walked me to my room. I thought we were perfect together, so much in common. Perhaps I'd always been a fool to believe Matt could ever feel the same way too, but why would he remain with me if he didn't possess *some* feelings?

"It's only because he's been through so much," I replied, desperate to cling onto something, even though I knew it was all over between us. Bloody DNA tests were the final straw. "We both have, and it's taking its toll. Just because he's not shaving regularly, or keeping his hair perfectly neat, doesn't mean he's off the rails."

"Come on, dear," Hannah intervened, "it's not only his appearance but also his all-round demeanour. He doesn't want to be near any of us, and we're only trying to help. He snaps at Tom; he snaps at everybody. And his lies, dear. Don't forget his lies. How can you ever trust him?"

Hannah was right, but she knew as well as me we all tell lies.

George grumbled again, and I stood to see to him. Hannah glanced at Tom, and he nodded in return.

"Why don't I take George to the park for a little while,

Lisa?" Hannah suggested. "Give you a break, a while to reflect. I'm sure Tom will leave you in peace, won't you, dear?"

Tom had been looking at me for a while, unnerving me, yet his smile remained sympathetic. Before I could reply, Hannah asked George if he wanted to play on the swings, and it at least succeeded in stopping his constant moaning.

"It's raining," I said, even though the prospect of a few moments' tranquillity felt like heaven.

"We don't mind, do we, darling?"

George grinned again, and I knew if I denied him that too, he would fly off the handle completely.

Once they left, along with fat Charlie, I finished my cup of tea and sat back in Tom's favourite high-backed chair, trying to regulate my breathing and think of my next plan of action. Tom rose from the sofa, catching me unawares, and stepped closer.

"Another tea?" he asked, his fingertips brushing my hand as he took the mug. The hairs on my arm stood on end as he leant over me.

"Mind if I just use your bathroom?" I asked.

Tom smiled, said I knew where it was and placed my mug on the table before sitting back down.

As I made my way along the hallway, pleased for a few moments' respite, I noticed the cellar door to my left. It brought back memories of the night we had dinner and Matt's mini-altercation with Tom about his infamous whisky collection. With a quick glance over my shoulder, I tried the handle, but it was locked, as expected. And then I remembered the key Tom put in the chest of drawers just down the corridor. Quickly, I stepped over to pull the drawer open. Feigning a cough to cover the noise, it opened effortlessly and there it was. The rusty key with a piece of brown string tied around it, but as soon as I went to retrieve it, I heard Tom shuffling from the living room.

"Everything okay out there?"

Shit.

As I put the key back, I noticed something else. With another glance back to the living room, I grabbed it and pushed it clumsily into my rear pocket before ensuring my sweatshirt covered my backside.

"Find the toilet alright, dear?" Tom asked. He stood in the open doorway at the beginning of their hall. The darkened space only allowed me to see his silhouette, and I could not make out his expression. Had he seen me rummaging around in his chest of drawers?

"Yes, thanks. Just on my way back."

"Oh good. I didn't hear the loo flush, that's all."

Tom stepped out of the shadows and as the light caught his face, I could see he was no longer smiling. My heart skipped a beat as he attempted to brush past me. Was he really going to check the toilet to see if I left anything in there?

"Oh, silly me. Didn't I flush it?"

Quickly, I turned, staying ahead of Tom in the chase for the loo. Amazingly, he hastened his own step in response. It felt so surreal, like playing a game of 'who can flush the toilet the fastest'.

Once I reached the tiny room next to their front door, I stepped inside and pressed the flush button without lifting the seat. I detected Tom directly behind me, his breathing heavy, his breath stale. Turning to leave, his bulky frame completely blocked the small doorway. And still, he didn't smile, just stared at the closed loo and listened as the water refilled the cistern.

What's wrong with him?

"Sorry, Tom. Slightly embarrassing for you to see what I left in there. I can't believe I forgot to flush it."

Tom's expression changed into something else altogether. He finally smiled, but not in his usual kind-hearted way. More creepy, hostile. And he was scowling, as if he might harm me. It began to freak me out, especially once I realised he was making no attempt to move.

"Can I get by, please? I need to see to George."

"Hannah is out with George. We've got some time alone."

What the actual fuck?

"For what?" I asked naively. "Come on, I haven't time for games. I need to get home. Speak to Matt about you know what."

The words were tumbling out of my mouth as panic rose inside. It certainly wasn't my idea of a game.

Unbelievably, Tom took another step forward. The closet was tiny with only enough space for the toilet and a minuscule basin to wash your hands. There was barely room inside for one, let alone a huge man encroaching upon me.

"Tom!" Purposefully, I raised my voice, hopefully hinting to him that I could shout much louder if required. He lifted his arm and pressed his finger to his lips. My heart threatened to leap from my chest.

As soon as he told me to be quiet, his arm extended further until his fingers brushed through my hair. By then, I was numb, unable to shout, scream or attempt to fight him off. Instead, I closed my eyes, thinking if I didn't look, it might not happen.

He moved his head closer still, his face next to mine. His hand brushed through my hair once more and then moved down my back. There was no space to move, and I felt overwhelmed with claustrophobia and fear. With my eyes squeezed tight, I sensed his mouth next to my ear, my cheek, my mouth. His lips almost touched mine and his hand slid effortlessly from my back and around to the front. I thought I might be sick as I closed my eyes tighter still.

"Let's take this to your bedroom," I said, louder than I expected, even now unable to comprehend where those words came from.

Tom left his hand where it was, but at least he backed his head far enough away so I could no longer taste his breath. The scowl from before was replaced by a huge smile. Perhaps it had been there for a while, but because I'd only just allowed myself to open my eyes to gauge his reaction, I'll never know when the look of delight spread across his face. Opening his mouth, I could see some kind of food residue stuck to his tooth. Saliva clung from his top lip to his tongue when he spoke, and I spotted tiny flakes of dandruff in his unshaven stubble.

Finally, he moved his hand and instead took mine in his. His palm was warm and sticky, and as he led me along the hallway, I noticed the hair on the back of his head was matted with sweat. Every single last molecule of him made me want to vomit.

Thirty minutes later, I closed the cellar door, grabbed my phone, and sent Matt a text.

40

MATT

Tom's car was parked outside, so I guessed they were all sitting there, waiting for me to arrive. I could only assume he was going to read me my last rites before placing me under citizen's arrest and taking great pleasure in frogmarching me to the local police station. Politely, I knocked on the door and stood back, as if calling round to borrow a cup of sugar. I'd just untied a dead teenager from a hanging swing, previously buried my wife in the adjacent woods, next to my ex-lover in her suitcase, and now I found myself standing whilst expecting the neighbourhood watch guy to let me into his property. What the fuck had happened to me?

"Quick, get inside." Lisa pulled me by the arm as soon as the door opened.

"What the…"

As she shut it, she turned to look at me and I was certain there were smatters of blood on one side of her face. She caught me staring and immediately wiped at it with the back of her hand.

"Where's George?" I asked, quickly leaving her and running along the hallway. Lisa called after me as I scoured the living room.

"He's out with Hannah. They're at the park." She noticed the panic on my face as I returned to join her. "Calm the fuck down, Matt. He's absolutely fine."

Calm the fuck down? Is she for real?

My eyes darted everywhere. From Lisa, along the hallway to the open toilet cubicle at the far end, and then behind me back to the living room and kitchen doors.

"What's happening?" I finally asked. "Why did you need me here so fast?"

Lisa leaned to her right, grabbed the door handle of the cellar, and slowly pushed it ajar.

"You need to see what's down there."

The entrance was dark and forbidding and my eyes flicked back to Lisa, looking for some kind of explanation. But she said nothing, instead taking a step backwards, allowing enough room for me to pass. She was acting so strange, so out of character, but also in control, both of her emotions and the situation, whatever that was.

"What's down there? Can't you just tell me?"

"You need to see for yourself. You've always wanted to know, and now here's your chance."

"Where's Tom?" I asked.

I'd forgotten all about him. The open cellar brought back memories of the night he wouldn't let me down there, but I knew from Lisa's expression she didn't want me to see a bloody whisky collection.

"Forget Tom. Just get down there and look for yourself, Matt. Hannah will be home soon, so you need to go now."

The way she spoke only added to how damn scary the cellar looked. Leaning forward, I pulled on the cord which hung from the ceiling. Click-click. But no light. Click-click.

Again, you've tried it twice, you fucking imbecile.

"Use your phone. The bulb is missing," Lisa said, repositioning herself until she was directly behind me. If I had a choice before, Lisa left me with one available route. Taking my phone from my jeans, I held down the torch button, and after a final glance at Lisa, I began the descent.

The wooden steps were silent beneath my feet, feeling kind of springy. Lisa waited on the top step, watching me.

"You're not going to lock me down here, are you?" I laughed pathetically.

"Just look, Matthew. Time is against us."

Time is against us? What the hell does that mean?

Once at the bottom, I swung the torch to my left, but I couldn't see anything of interest, just ancient furniture stacked against the wall. Again, one hesitant step after the other, I shuffled forward, but as before, I was met with what you might expect in a cellar; an old wooden desk and a few files piled on top. Some had writing along the spine, and as I shone my beam across them, they read 'Accounts Volume 1' and 'Accounts Volume 2' with months and years written below.

With a shake of my head, I moved to my right.

What's that?

Glancing up the steps, checking with Lisa if it is what I was supposed to be looking for, she was just a silhouette in the frame and I couldn't distinguish her face. However, she slowly nodded her head in approval.

There was some kind of elongated table, a collapsible trestle, bowed in the middle, with an array of papers strewn across it. But they didn't hold my attention for long, as my eyes were drawn to the wall directly behind.

Photographs. Lots of them. Arranged in a crude circle. And the one in the centre screams out the most. Me, a close-up picture. Stepping forward, a sudden chill wrapped itself around my body and I was unable to divert my eyes from what I was seeing. Photographs of Amelia, Tracy, Graham, Katrina, Julia. Holy shit. Photographs of the entire damn family, all encircling me. There was even one of my Auntie Edith, the woman I never met, but the very same person who left me a small fortune.

And there, to the right of the table, stood a whiteboard, perched at an angle like an artist's easel. All kinds of scrawls and circles and marks inscribed across it, but on closer examination, it also contained people's names. All of us again, some with red lines through them. The dead ones. The boldest ink, so I guessed the freshest, was struck through Katrina.

Stepping to the table, I shuffled through the papers. Police documents, newspaper clippings and an array of artefacts all connected to me, the family and, what I assumed are details of the case.

"What the…"

Without realising, I backed away. They had built up an entire collection of us, like memorabilia of your favourite screwed-up family. Were they mad, obsessed, or deluded? What could they want from us? My eyes kept returning to the names on the whiteboard, especially those crossed out. There was barely anybody left, leaving two standing out like neon lights. Matthew and Lisa.

My breathing had become irregular, my breaths shallow and rapid. I needed to get out and find my child. But as soon as I was halfway up the wooden steps, I heard a groan from somewhere behind and spun to where it emanated from.

Lisa started to descend, forcing me to turn and go down again.

With her hand in the centre of my back, she guided me to where the moaning was coming from and, as I manoeuvred my torch from side to side, I saw Tom, slumped against the wall. His face, his hair, his neck, all splattered in blood.

The blood on Lisa's cheek.

She was alongside me now, looking down at Tom, and I'm sure he flinched with whatever level of life was left within him.

"You?" I asked Lisa. "Did you do this?"

Again, she didn't speak and instead retrieved her phone from her pocket. She swiped it upwards before clicking on an app.

"Shh," she said, and pressed the play button.

"Find the restroom alright, dear?"

Tom murmured at the sound of his voice and Lisa kicked him in the side to shut him up. Glaring at Lisa, her face instructed me to be quiet and listen.

The conversation was sporadic, to begin with…

"Can I get by, please? I need to see to George…"

More mumbling, as if her phone was in her pocket, muffling the sound. Suddenly, her tone was more animated…

"Let's take this to your bedroom…"

Again, I glared at Lisa. Were they screwing each other? But as before, Lisa mouthed for me to remain silent.

A few footsteps followed, and then Lisa's voice again. The audio was more distinct now.

"Why don't we do it in the cellar?" she asked. Tom giggled, like a schoolchild about to lose his virginity.

More footsteps, stifled laughs and shuffling around. Eventually, more voices.

"What's this, Tom?"

Tom's speech was harder to discern. Lisa must have realised.

"Come closer and tell me," she said.

Standing immobile with a combination of horror and disbelief, I listened as Tom Wells explained the photographs, the whiteboard, the whole goddamn history of his obsession with me and the Reid family. When he finally finished, Lisa spoke again.

"Did you kill them, Tom?"

More shuffling. Was that the sound of a kiss?

"Do you remember the day when you first came to look at your house?" Tom eventually asked.

Silence.

"You know, and you stopped by the pub for sandwiches?"

"Uh-huh? What about it?"

"I recognised Matthew immediately. His story, the family story from a house in Epsom already fascinated me. It followed my meetings with the neighbourhood watch. You see, I have many contacts in the police force, I'm kind of their go-to man..." he laughed, a pathetic one-upmanship sort of laugh, *"... so I couldn't believe it when Matthew Walker sat at the far end of my local pub."*

I recollected the very day. They *did* recognise us.

"A couple of new faces, Hannah. Mind if we join you?"

"So, I naturally dug further," Tom continued, now on a roll, relishing his story with the promise of what lay ahead. *"The regional group in Epsom has been a tremendous help, and I was able to reconstruct Matthew's arriving, his marriage with Amelia, Ryan Palmer, Lee Blackmore, every damn body."*

He really was enjoying it. I looked at him, his eyes widen in return. Was that a smile?

"And then you came along, didn't you, Lisa? Oh, you knew him at work. You even used to sneak off to the café together. Little rendezvous away from his wife. All leading up to your time in Cheshire."

"I didn't want—"

"Shh, now, Lisa. Shh. I've looked out for you. You know, made everything safe for you."

"What? What do you mean you've made everything safe for me?" Lisa continued to prompt.

Tom went on to explain about the day in Earl's Court when Hannah and Lisa returned to the car before heading off to Costa to meet Claudia. After they left him, Tom went to the apartment block and saw Francis. She admitted having an affair with me, and following a brief struggle, he killed her there and then.

"I left her on the bed," he chuckled. *"Went back later that night and I had to cut off her arms to fit her in the suitcase. Of course, I took some of her clothes too to make it look like she'd done a runner. I carried it out the back and drove her home before burying it the next day."*

That night he was talking about! I'd driven straight on. Slept in a car park on the bloody A3. I stared at Tom lying prostrate on the cellar floor, anger building inside me on his every word, but knowing I had to remain as calm as I could. Not that he was capable of doing much harm given his state.

"When I left the first time, that Claudia woman returned and started asking who I was and why I was in the apartment block. Her neck went with such a loud snap on the bottom step. After I whacked her on the back of the head, of course."

Tom was in full swing. Enjoying every last word dripping off his tongue. I couldn't move; dare not move. He was fucking crazy.

"That night, I had to go in via the rear entrance to avoid the police tape and stuff. But I had all the keys, didn't I, Lisa?"

"And Melissa?" Lisa asked, ignoring his boast.

"Well, yeah, Melissa. She threatened you, my sweetheart. You know. Threatened to take our George away. We couldn't have that, could we? So, after I left you and Hannah, I went back to the care home and added a little something to her cocoa. Ha! Lisa. You would have loved it. She started frothing at the fucking mouth." A pause. *"Come on, Lisa. Let's do it…"*

The recording appeared to cut out and then began again.

"Who else, Tom?" Lisa prompted further.

"His ex fucking wife, of course. And her manipulating sister, who you hated."

Lisa grabbed my arm to stop me from beating what little life he had left in him.

"Tell me about Amelia first, Tom."

"You know, Lisa, tracking Matt's mobile…"

The recording stopped after I'm sure I heard Lisa sigh. I tried to get her attention, but she pressed play again.

"Oh, yeah," Tom continued. *"My friend from Aylesbury neighbourhood watch taught me how. It's an app. Oh, so simple."*

"So you've been following Matt?"

"Only for you, dear. For us."

Us? He's absolutely insane.

"You know he spent the night with Amelia on Saturday, don't you?" It was Tom's turn to push Lisa. *"The time he didn't come home and told you he slept in a lay-by? Well, one of them left the front door unlocked, such was their haste to get their grubby little hands on each other. I hid downstairs, and I'm sorry to tell you this, my darling, but they went to bed together."*

Lisa looked at me, her face barely illuminated by the phone torch. But incredibly, she smiled. Was that an 'I've known all along' kind of smile?

"There, there," Tom whispered as the recording appeared to restart again. Had Lisa been upset? *"It's alright. She's gone—"*

"Gone? Gone where, Tom?"

"Dead, darling. Fucking dead. You know, Matt came downstairs to get more wine, and he popped a couple of pills in her drink. The idiot then went to the toilet, so I dropped three or four in his and put the remainder in hers. When they were both out for the count, I carried Amelia to the top of the landing and threw her over the balustrade. Just like Claudia, her head actually cracked when it hit the ground. All I had to do was lay Matthew next to her, and the next morning he woke up and thought he'd done it."

Silence again.

"Are you not pleased, Lisa? I've done all of this for you. Amelia's sister, Tracy. You hated her. Haven't you always told me that? You despised her at work and you still despise her today. And what about her daughter? I went back to the house yesterday and hung that crazy fucking bitch Katrina by her neck on her swing. But not before plying her with chocolate first. Remember when you mentioned to me how much she enjoys that stuff? What more do you want me to do? What more?"

Tom sounded desperate now, pleading with his

mistress. The recording shut off again before restarting only seconds later.

"Come on. I've told you everything you wanted. Done everything you've asked of me. Let's do what we really came down here for."

The velocity of Lisa's voice made the recording vibrate.

"You absolute bastard! Get your hands off me!"

"You had better do what I tell you, Lisa, or else you'll be the next red cross on my board. Where are you going? Where did you get—"

Bang!

The deafening sound made me jump. My eyes finally left the phone and I looked at Lisa. Yet again, she silently told me to shut up.

The recording continued. Scuffling interspersed with profanities from both parties.

"What the hell are you doing with—"

Bang!

Flinching, I stood mesmerised, before noticing what Lisa was now holding in her other hand. Is that a gun? She clicked the off button on her phone.

"You shouldn't leave things lying around in your chest of drawers, should you, Tom?"

Tom flinched again as she raised it to his head, and with a sickening blow, she swiped the magazine of the gun downwards until it met the top of his skull. It was the most hideous cracking sound I'd ever witnessed.

41

LISA

THE BIGGEST SURPRISE was how much hatred I could carry inside me, but Tom's lecherous intent finally pushed me over the edge. Don't get me wrong, his revelations regarding the killing of lovers and wives and crazy, screwed-up members of that dysfunctional family did make me smile inside. And it was Matt's wife who produced the icing on top of the cake. It wasn't that they met up and spent another night together, which bothered me. It was her suggesting George is her child.

"What now?" Matt asked petrified, as I casually wiped the blood from the gun with a piece of rag I found in Tom's cellar. Finally, everything was on *my* terms, and Matt would be subservient to me. I'd been to hell and back. Did he never consider what being tied up for months in a shack in the middle of the woods could do to a human being? Shit, I'm surprised I held it together for so long.

"I sent Hannah a text from Tom's phone just before you arrived. They'll be here soon." My even tone astonished me.

Matt looked like he might be sick. Was it pure shock? Whatever, he stared at me as if I were a total stranger.

"And then what?"

"Wait in the cellar until Hannah and George return home."

"What? Me? Down here? Why, Lisa? You've gathered your evidence now. Tom's admitted to it. You just plead your innocence, suggest he went for you and you acted in self-defence. We're free, Lisa. Free to—"

"I'm not taking the shit for you and your lovers and that crazy batshit family you got yourself involved with. This is on my terms now; else I'll destroy the recording and tell the police you did it all. Your fingerprints are everywhere, Matt. Even I was convinced it was you. CCTV will pick you up at every location they have found a body. The soil in the woods has been tampered with by you, and your fresh fingerprints are all over the house. You went to see Melissa. In fact, yours is the only name in the visitors' book. The chain on Katrina's swing will contain your prints too. Even darling Amelia died because of your prescription sleeping pills. You're screwed, Matthew Walker, unless you do exactly as I say."

He looked at me, opened his mouth to reply, and closed it again once he realised words were useless. I expected some kind of comeback, and if he had, I'm not sure what I would have done next. But even though the recording sounded authentic, especially with a little editing, I was certain it hadn't convinced Matt. As I ascended the cellar steps to wait for Hannah and my son to return, Matt called after me, confirming my suspicions.

"Did you make Tom say all of that?"

Pausing, all I could think to do was laugh before continuing for the door.

"So, you want me to kill Hannah and we're equal?"

As I reached the last step, I turned to face him.

"Just sit down here quietly whilst I wait upstairs. I'll see how much she believes."

With a final smile, I closed the cellar door and locked it behind me.

MATT

I was plunged into semi-darkness once more, the torch from my phone offering scant respite from the damp and gloom. The thought of a dead body lying in the corner only added to my rising nausea.

To kill time, or more accurately an attempt to slow my racing mind, I found myself at the long trestle table and began to aimlessly flick through some papers and returned to the endless photographs which were strewn in front of me as well as on the wall. As I did, I thought about the voice memo Lisa just played me.

Something didn't fit. I turned and shone my light on Tom. His face was blanketed in streaks of dark crimson liquid from the fresh wound on his head. It amazed me as it contoured around his nose and followed the outline of his lips before eventually dripping from his chin. But it was his mouth that grabbed my attention. Not the physical aspect, but his voice on the recording. He *had* sounded different. It wasn't his natural voice. Monotone, lacking any intonation or expressiveness. Tom *never* spoke like that. The entire thing seemed forced, as though rehearsed or planned. Lisa continually prompted him; guided the exchange.

"*Did you kill them, Tom?*"

"*And Melissa?*"

"*Who else, Tom?*"

"*So you've been following Matt?*"

And with every question she asked, Tom replied with the answer she craved. It didn't come across as a natural conversation, especially given the situation they were both in. And then the recording would stop, before restarting at the same point of the discussion. Had Tom screwed up and said something he shouldn't? Gone off-script?

Hmm. Something else. The way he kept saying 'you know'. Not Tom's usual, incredibly annoying mock cockney accent, 'you know', but more as a statement. You. Know. In the literal sense.

You. Know.

Lisa *did* know. That's what he meant. All Tom did was say what she wanted to hear. But why? What was he getting out of it?

"*Come on. I've said everything you want. Let's do what we really came down here for.*"

That's when Lisa finally snapped. The sound of the gunshot, twice. By then, Lisa had a full admission, so Tom whimpered and begged. It was obvious what Tom expected as a reward, but by then, did he also realise she had set him up?

I scampered over to Tom and sat by his side. Pulling his head back, I noticed a tiny glimmer of life in his eyes.

"Tom. Tom. It's me, Matt. I can get you out of here."

His eyes moved ever-so-slightly to the right, trying to focus on me.

Shit. He's almost dead.

"Tom. Did you kill Francis, Melissa, Amelia and the others? I have to know."

Nothing.

"Tom. Think, please, think. Did you kill them?"

His words escaped as a gargle, but not before a mouthful of blood spilled out first.

"For her…"

Shit.

"You killed them for Lisa? But did she just make you confess? What do you get in exchange, Tom? Please think. Please."

More blood dribbled down his chin. He smiled, his teeth crimson. And without warning, his head slumped forward and Tom Wells breathed his final breath.

Leaving him, I returned to the table and flicked through the papers much faster, unsure of what I was looking for but hoping for some kind of clue to piece it together. It was obvious from all the paperwork he was obsessed with me, the family and the original case, but Tom Wells had not murdered at least four or five people for the sake of it, even if instinct was already telling me why.

There. A large envelope with 'Private' written crudely across it. My hands trembled as I opened the flap and tipped the contents onto the table. And there was my answer, right before my eyes. Half a dozen photographs of Lisa, all scantily dressed. Nothing over the top, just teasing pictures of her underwear or holding a seductive pose. I turned back to Tom. He was not only obsessed with the Reid family but he'd become infatuated with Lisa, too. And she obviously led him on. Used him to do the deeds which she would never have the nerve to carry out herself. But she'd endlessly sought revenge. Revenge for what they did to her, and maybe for what they did to me. My affair with Francis, meeting with Amelia after all this time, even going to see Melissa again. She knew what I always wanted. And just like DCI Small all those months ago, she must have realised I let Amelia escape that night. She just couldn't prove it.

Fuck.

When did the recording stop and restart?

"You know, Lisa, tracking Matt's mobile…"

You. Know. Lisa.

She knew he tracked my bloody phone. How long for? Since Earl's Court? Before? The perfume on my shirt. Following that?

It doesn't matter when. Tom had always known where I planned to go as soon as I did. The text messages to see Melissa, Katrina and Amelia. Had he simply passed that information onto Lisa, and in return she sent him a photograph for what he could expect if he bumped off another one of her targets?

The red crosses through the names on the white-board. I didn't even know if it was Tom's or Lisa's bloody writing. They'd been in cahoots all along. Ever since that initial night in the pub in the village.

'A couple of new faces, Hannah,' Tom said. *'Mind if we join you?'*

'Of course not,' beamed Lisa. *'I take it you're local? I'd love to pick your brains.'*

The way he looked at her that day. He was infatuated from the very first time we met.

The sound of the front door opening brought me back to the present.

"Mummy!"

George's tiny footsteps ran across the bare floorboards above and Lisa squealed with delight. My heart melted, but I had to remain patient. Lisa was out of control, finally tipped over the edge and capable of anything.

Slowly, I climbed the cellar stairs until I was next to the door and pressed my ear against it. They were on the other side and Hannah asked Lisa why she was looking so strange, what had happened and what the blood was on her cheek. "Where's my husband, Lisa?" She was becoming more animated by the second and Charlie started to bark too.

"Go and put the TV on, darling," Lisa said. Her voice remarkably calm, especially in contrast to Hannah, who was threatening to lose control.

"Where. Is. Tom?" she demanded, before mumbling something else to silence the dog. But Charlie barks and barks, louder and louder.

"Can't you shut that fucking thing up?" Lisa shouted above the din.

"Don't you use that language in here! Just tell me where Tom is and you can get off my premises."

Charlie still barked, mimicking his owner's displeasure towards her now unwanted guest.

And then the loudest bang I'd ever heard. A low whimper ensued, then scratching sounds on the wooden floor, and finally, the dog was quiet.

A moment's silence followed by a high-pitched scream. Hannah began to wail, and I'm sure she dropped to her knees.

"Mummy! Mummy!"

Oh shit. George was back.

Frantically I wobbled the door handle, calling George's name.

"Daddy!"

"Go and watch television. Now!"

George's cries became muffled.

"Get up, woman," Lisa demanded.

Hannah was scrambling to her feet.

"Stand there."

A second later, the key rattled in the cellar door, and it swung open. Hannah came flying through backwards, taking me with her, until we landed in a heap at the bottom. Hannah screamed out loud. Another high-pitched, piercing scream and as I adjusted myself to inspect my injuries, I soon saw why. Her leg was sticking out at a right angle just above the knee. It looked surreal, so much so, I thought I might be sick.

A sound from above caught my attention as Lisa pushed the dog inside with her feet. Incredibly, she got George to help her and he giggled uncontrollably as Charlie dropped three or four steps down into the caller. Before I could say anything, the door slammed shut and the key turned in the lock.

"Come on, George. We're leaving."

Another door closed with a bang and we were left in silence; apart from Hannah's sobs and wildly erratic breathing. Gingerly, I pulled myself free from underneath her and slowly climbed the steps, pushing the overweight dead dog to the bottom. I had no time for Hannah or Charlie or Tom Wells. Their hatred towards me only added to their love for Lisa and their hideous plans and crimes.

I ached badly, yet it was just bruising. Rattling the door against its frame, I soon realised it was impossible to open. It may be old, but it was made well; strong and firm.

And then the most incredible scream came from behind, and as I turned, I saw Hannah had found Tom. She'd somehow crawled to his side, and she hugged him tight, sobbing, wailing, brushing his hair from his forehead. It was pitiful, but I still couldn't help but feel a tiny bit of delight.

"He killed my fucking wife!" I shouted at the top of my voice.

We sat in relative silence for another twenty minutes or so, Hannah cradling Tom, between grunts of physical pain, and me on the other side of the cellar, as far away from those two as I could get. I do not know what I was waiting for, but that's all I could do, wait. Lisa couldn't just leave us here, could she?

Right on cue, the front door opened and I crawled towards the stairs again. But as soon as I reached the bottom step, I smelt it. Hannah did too, and she attempted to shuffle herself upright beside her deceased husband. Her eyes caught mine and I was unsure who held the most fear.

"Is that…?" Hannah's words trailed off.

I nodded. And, as if to prove us both right, a gurgling sound was immediately followed by liquid flowing underneath the cellar door, slowly meandering down the steps before forming a steady trickle across the floor.

Opening my mouth to scream, the scratch of a match against the side of its box halted me. A blue flame flickered beneath the doorframe and the petrol ignited in seconds. Hannah screamed again, a more elongated wail, and I crawled backwards on my hands and feet until I reached the far wall. I looked at the door. Would it give? But it was too late. The flames were already blazing in the tiny room and smoke filled the air.

It's all over, Matt.

"Lisa!" I screamed. "George!" But I knew they'd already left.

What was it that Melissa said to me when I first visited her in the care home?

"Something bad is going to happen… I can sense it."

Lying flat, I crawled towards the stairs again, but the heat was far too intense and I realised I was only hastening my death.

Hannah screamed from the other side of the room, and through the flames and smoke I could see she and Tom were now alight. Although I realised it was only a matter of seconds until the same happened to me, it still felt surreal to witness somebody burning alive.

Remaining motionless, I awaited the inevitable and closed my eyes, desperate to force Hannah's wails to the back of my mind. I didn't want that to be the last thing I heard.

George.

Drifting in and out of consciousness, my throat burned as I inhaled more and more smoke.

Squeezing my eyes tighter still, I saw George running, chasing, giggling. Then he asked me to push him higher on the swing before he kicked his football past me as I dived in slow motion the wrong way.

This heat. This pain.

And who's that behind him? Up in the copse?

Flames flickering at my feet.

Melissa, Tracy, and who else? Graham. He's laughing. Mocking me.

Hannah was silent now.

Back in the family home, I visualised Amelia's jet-black hair and deepest brown eyes. She beckoned me forward and I felt myself float upwards, gently, leaving my body before gravitating towards her.

The heat. This intense heat.

And when I was finally by her side, she took me in her arms, held me tight and whispered softly in my ear.

"Thank you for looking after our son."

42

SIX MONTHS LATER

LISA

Dɪᴅ I mean for Matthew to die? Maybe. But he knew. I could see it in his eyes as I played the recording back. There were mistakes or more to the point, Tom fucked up his lines, but either way, Matthew knew. So what choice did I have? Besides, that wasn't the main reason Matt had to perish.

Fortunately, the police *did* believe the recording. It helped that my new best friend, Sophie, cleaned it up that night. I dropped George off before returning to their house with a jerrycan full of petrol, and afterwards, I explained everything to her and she was delighted to help me. I knew she would since my previous visit. She hated Tom with a vengeance. She also happened to like me. 'Anything to pin all the blame on that lech Tom Wells', she said. So, in her capacity as a video and voice editor, she removed all my prompts and stop-starts and ensured the entire recording came across as one smooth confession from Tom. He even sounded as though he was bragging about his foray into the Reid family. And there were no mentions of my flirting, my promises, just Tom and Hannah on a mission to dispose of everybody connected with Matthew and that family.

The police considered it suicide. You see, once the fire took hold, I had the foresight to throw the jerrycan, the matches and the gun down into the cellar. The melted can and warped gun next to Tom's body played right into my hands. It was, of course, registered in his name, and given his confessions on the recording, the authorities soon ascertained he had taken Matt and Hannah, not forgetting his ever-faithful Charlie, into the basement and set the place ablaze, before turning the gun on himself. He was deluded, infatuated and obsessed, and once I told the officers I'd said I wasn't interested, I explained he totally lost the plot and even threatened to kill George too. "We ran for our lives, leaving Tom Wells to go on his merciless killing spree."

It helped that a couple of the policemen appeared to take some kind of delight in Tom being behind it. They said he was the bane of their lives at neighbourhood watch meetings and was forever calling with information about crimes he considered his right to interfere with. One officer, in particular, told me of Tom's unnatural interest in the Reid family history. He had shown an unusual fascination as soon as the case came into the public domain, but his preoccupation turned into obsession within weeks of us buying the house in the village. Of course, I knew already. The questions he asked me, over and over. What was Graham like? Was Melissa possessive? How did you cope with working with Amelia and Tracy? Relentless fucking interrogation about a family I wanted to forget.

However, as soon as I discerned Matt was having an affair, the lipstick on his shirt and the perfume on his collar, I knew I could use Hannah, and particularly Tom, to my advantage. Whenever they visited, which was practically every bloody day, much to Matt's annoyance, I teased Tom, especially on the afternoons when Hannah volunteered at the local library. I'd take George round and purposefully flirt with him, making brief comments such as 'you don't need sugar in your tea, you're already sweet enough.' Tom would blush, but I knew he loved it and even thrived upon it. And after a while, once I realised things would never work out between me and Matt, coupled with Tom's fascination with both the case and me, I took things to another level. I allowed my kisses on his cheek to linger longer than necessary and brushed my fingers against his leg underneath our ridiculously sized table. He was like putty in my hand.

The day at Earl's Court, after I returned to the car and before meeting Claudia at the café, I sat in the passenger seat next to him whilst Hannah looked after George outside. I was livid at Claudia's revelation. Despite suspecting something was awry, hearing the truth hit me like a hammer. I always wanted to believe that the lipstick and perfume were innocent, a product of client meetings or business deals. But deep down, I perpetually knew what Matt was capable of.

So, I told Tom that Matt was having an affair and the woman we met in the apartment block was aware of all that was going on.

"I'm scared, Tom," I said. "Will you hold me?"

His little face lit up and almost made me puke, but I knew I had to go through with it. He held me tight, and I whispered in his ear. What I asked was rhetorical. I guess *testing the water* to gauge exactly how far Tom would venture in pursuit of us, of me.

"I want her dead, Tom. I want her out of the way. And that crazy nosy bitch alongside her. She knows too much."

Tom lifted his head until our faces were only inches apart. I could see his nose hair and a tiny nick on his cheek where he'd cut himself shaving that morning. What he said next made me realise that not only had Tom Wells fallen for me, but he would also do absolutely anything to prove it.

"And what would be in it for me?" His eyes glazed over and spittle formed in the corner of his mouth. Squeezing my eyes together, I leant forward and kissed him. Clenching my lips firmer than my eyelids, I felt his tongue trying to prise my mouth open. Fearing I could genuinely vomit all over him, I pulled myself away and forced the most fraudulent of smiles across my face.

"There's a lot more where that came from," I said, alarmed I could actually go through with it. His grin resembled a child who had been promised a trip to Disneyland, and he instructed me to head to the café while he sorted things out. "Be quick, Tom. And make sure nobody sees you."

Tom grinned again. "Who, me? Tom Wells, the greatest detective and undercover assassin ever to walk this planet?"

Twat.

He never did tell me what he did, or more to the point, how. It was like a secret pact between us, an unwritten rule. The night Matt called me from outside the apartment and relayed the story about his nosy neighbour taking a fall, I immediately knew Tom had done it.

"You'll never guess what's happened."

Bet I can.

"Go on."

"A woman fell down the stairwell in our apartment block yesterday afternoon. Killed instantly, apparently."

"Really?"

"Yeah. And it's someone I know."

I'm sure it is.

"Who?"

"It's that nosey bitch from across the landing."

But nobody mentioned Francis, and it wasn't until the police called round two weeks later and informed us she was missing that I realised Tom had disposed of her too. His confession in the cellar about cutting her up and putting her in her own fucking suitcase made me finally realise what he'd done.

It was around the same time I began to send him photographs. Nothing too revealing to begin with, just enough to keep him interested and the promise of what was to come. The gullible fool fell for it without even questioning me.

Melissa was easy. She threatened to take George away, for heaven's sake. Tom adored George and knew if he had a future with me, it would involve my son too. On the way back from the care home I told him and Hannah that she'd warned me again and said the baby was a Reid.

It was like a red rag to a bull for Tom. He dropped Hannah and me at home and immediately returned to Epsom, via his own house, of course, to pick up the poison to spike her drink.

After Francis and Claudia, he began to trace Matt's movements, with the help of his text messages and not-so-private phone calls. That was my biggest gamble. Matt was tech savvy, so I got him to hide the app amongst a group of others that I knew he never touched. Compass, Measuring Tape, Voice Memos, and the like.

So, the day he set off armed with a dozen curriculum vitae, I got Tom to follow. He parked only a few spaces from Matt at the train station. Matt's attention must have been so fully focused on meeting his favourite woman, the love of his life, that he wouldn't have spotted Tom if he jumped out in front of him. And two days later, we didn't even need the app. Tom overheard his conversation outside the pub. Matt said little, but he said enough, and after Tom told me, I realised I just needed to remain patient and await the next rendezvous. Fortunately, Hannah played into his hands when she suggested Epsom for his job-hunting exploits. Matt's face lit up like a lighthouse beacon; the perfect excuse to see his tart for a second time; the *ultimate* time.

Tom was good, sneaking in late at night and popping Matt's sleeping pills into their drinks. It was flawless. That's when I sent Tom a photograph of me in my underwear. A special reward for the prize killing.

Not long now.

Matt hitting the suitcase whilst burying Amelia wasn't part of the plan though. Tom watched from the trees, it was when he spotted Katrina watching too, and he admitted a massive panic attack almost ensued. But Matt didn't follow it up, just reburied the suitcase before digging a fresh grave adjacent to it. He must have had the same idea as Tom. The ground would be soft and the likelihood of the police returning so soon after excavating that area would be most unusual.

Great minds think alike, I'd suggested to Tom, although he never liked to be compared to his nemesis.

Next on his hit list was Tracy. Oh, I did despise her, I always had. Even at Opacy, she would boss me around, ensure she kept all the excellent accounts, and pull me down with her snide remarks whenever the opportunity arose. And this was where Tom's contacts came in most handy.

He knew Tracy had been released, well, kind of released. One of those more *open* prisons, or whatever they're called. Matt got a phone call from Officer Sutton the day after she died, but I already knew Tom had been to see her. One of his more regular 'meet-ups' with other neighbourhood watch groups, Hannah called them. But she was naïve, and by that stage, I realised he was capable of anything. Instead of gathering with like-minded, nosy bastards, as gullible Hannah believed, Tom instead drove to a community centre in the Surrey countryside. Someone had tipped him off that Tracy was gardening there, part of her release back into a society-type scheme. He told me on the recording, another section which no longer exists, he had to remain patient and study the small group of ex-cons as they pottered around doing various jobs. And he was in luck. Tracy separated from the main gang and began to cut a large expanse of lawn on one of those ride-on mower things. It took her to the periphery of the gardens, and that's when Tom struck. As she turned a corner at the far end, he jumped from behind a hedge, pulled her backwards off the mower, and slit her throat in one clean movement. The noise of the motor concealed everything and allowed him ample time to make his escape. The perfect murder Tom called it, laughing.

And Katrina was as easy as Melissa. Her texts were childlike, and it amazed me Matt never saw through them. But Matt was so desperate for it to be Amelia, he would have convinced himself it was his wife, even if Katrina signed them in her own name. Tom intercepted the messages, so he knew where to be and when. Katrina sat innocently on her swing, so Tom approached her with a giant bar of chocolate to gain her immediate trust. I never did like her and would have loved to witness her choking on the rusty chain of her rusty swing.

"Thank you," I say as Sophie passes me a glass of red. George is on the carpet, glued to the TV yet again. I know he shouldn't watch it so often, but a little treat now and then doesn't hurt anybody, does it? Besides, seven o'clock at night is treat time for Sophie and me too. A glass or two of wine helps us both relax. It's strange because, until the evening in the pub when I experienced electricity fizzing through me, I would never have considered I could be attracted to another woman. She experienced it too, she's told me since, and even though she has been in same-sex relationships, she always tells me she's never felt quite this way. Having somebody to finally trust is a tremendous relief, so much so, I'm often confused by what my feelings truly mean.

I've sold our house and moved in with her now. We're still in the village where I yearned to live, and George will still go to the same school which I enquired about all those months ago. But for now, we are taking our time, adjusting to life after Matthew, as well as our neighbour-hood watch team.

Talking of whom, the day I left Matt in the cellar with Hannah, dead Tom and equally dead Charlie, Sophie told me to do what I had to do. Although she had no perception of my plan, or indeed what I'd already carried out, she agreed to look after George whilst I 'sorted out unfinished business' at their house. She never asked what I did or what part I played in the fire, but she also showed no remorse or concern for the demise of the 'weirdos at number 264'. She's also told me since about the day she met Matt on the train. I asked if she had considered going for that drink with him, and I have to admit, she did hesitate slightly before replying with a somewhat reluctant 'no'.

Bloody Matthew Walker.

Anyway, a year before we arrived in the village, Tom inappropriately *touched* her as they queued at the pub bar. It wasn't the first time either. Sophie told me he occasion-ally followed her to the supermarket in the next town, as well as standing outside her house with Charlie and peering up at her bedroom window. When she threatened to report him, he said he knew more police officers than she'd had hot dinners. Perhaps, in hindsight, the police would have believed her and taken great delight in arresting the pervert, but she wasn't to know, and Tom could be so convincing with his role in the community. I recalled Hannah's animosity towards Sophie in the pub the night we met for a meal.

"What did she have to say for herself?"

. . .

"You're welcome," Sophie replies, pecking me on the lips before sitting on the sofa next to me.

George giggles, which makes us giggle too.

"Mummy!" he shouts, and we look at one another before breaking out into fits of laughter.

Yes, George has two mummies now. Two perfect parents to raise him in this fragile world.

And Sophie has never doubted I'm the actual mother. She's never asked for a stupid DNA test. As far as she's concerned, there's nothing to prove.

But Matt thought otherwise. His bloody wife planting all kinds of conspiracies into his already overactive mind. And he would never have let it lie. I realised as soon as he suggested we all take a test. He believed Amelia. He always did.

So, the day I poured petrol into the cellar, I knew Matt had to die too. Forget the recording and the look of doubt in his eyes. That wasn't important. What is important is my role to bring George up safely in this fragile world. It's my duty. Why couldn't Matthew just accept it?

And now, I watch George from the sofa and smile to myself. His features are taking on a remarkable resemblance to his father. His cheekbones, his mouth, his small dainty ears.

Oh, and those eyes. The largest, deepest, brownest eyes I've ever seen.

HE IS HERE
OUT NOW!
The Brand New Psychological Thriller
by
Jack Stainton

FROM THE AUTHOR

Thank you for reading 'Last One To Lie' - I hope you enjoyed reading it as much as I enjoyed writing the entire 'Family' trilogy.

The feedback for all three books has been astounding, beyond my wildest dreams, and it makes me so happy to hear from readers all around the globe who give me such positive feedback.

Thank you once more and look out for my next stand-alone later in 2023! To find out more about me and my books, please sign up to my FREE newsletter below…

www.jackstainton.com/newsletter

 facebook.com/jackstaintonbooks

 x.com/jack_stainton

 instagram.com/jackstaintonbooks

REVIEWS

Enjoy this book? You can make a big difference

Honest reviews of my books help bring them to the attention of other readers.

If you've enjoyed this novel I would be very grateful if you could spend just a few minutes leaving a review (it can be as short as you like).

Thank you very much.

A GUEST TO DIE FOR

Jack Stainton's debut Psychological Thriller

Available online in both eBook and Print Versions

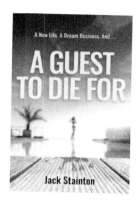

…I bought the book and read it in two sittings. Very good, lots of twists and red herrings.

This does exactly what a thriller should; it keeps you guessing until the end…

Excellent book full of twists and turns. The characters are brilliant… The ending was totally unexpected…

Sucking you in with a dreamy hope of a better start, the fear of what might happen next will keep you turning the pages!

A fantastic, gripping debut!

Printed in Great Britain
by Amazon

34247215R00192